Was she up for this?

Flynn's gaze was intent on her face as he closed the distance between them. He stopped a scant few inches away. Mel could feel his body heat. His beard was starting to grow through and shadowed his chin.

Her gaze slid to his mouth, tracing the sensuous curve of his lower lip. She'd been too scared to allow herself to even think about kissing him before, but now she let herself go there, wondering how it would feel to press her mouth to his, to feel his tongue inside her mouth, to taste him.

The thought alone made her knees weak. Hot desire unfurled inside her, foreign and familiar at the same time.

He cupped her face, his thumb brushing along her cheekbone, his fingers cradling her jaw. She swallowed, awash with nerves and lust and anticipation and fear.

"I don't know," she said. "I don't know if this is a good idea."

"I do. I think it's the best idea I've had for a long time."

Dear Reader,

I'm not going to lie to you—this was a tough book to write. I'm not sure exactly why, but it took me a while to work out what Mel and Flynn both needed in life and from each other—but I'd like to think I got there in the end. By the time I'd finished writing, these people had become very real to me, and I hope that you feel the same after you finish reading.

I did a lot of research into Alzheimer's disease for this book and read some incredibly heartwarming and moving stories written by both sufferers and their caregivers. I'd like to acknowledge the people who have shared their time and stories, and if this is something that is or has affected you or your loved ones, my best wishes go out to you—it's a sad, tough road to travel.

The Summerlea Estate as imagined in this book does not exist in Mount Eliza, although there are a number of homes on the Mornington Peninsula that open their gardens to the public as part of the open garden's scheme. I have been to one of them and could only marvel at the owners' dedication to their six acres of beautifully landscaped and maintained gardens, complete with bridges, lily ponds and topiary. Edna Walling was a real person, and her gardens are still celebrated in Australia. As described in the book, her style was very "English," with rustic stone fences and rambly pathways and lovely vistas.

I love hearing from readers, so drop me a line via my website, www.sarahmayberry.com.

Until next time, happy reading,

Sarah Mayberry

All They Need
Sarah Mayberry

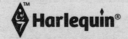

TORONTO NEW YORK LONDON
AMSTERDAM PARIS SYDNEY HAMBURG
STOCKHOLM ATHENS TOKYO MILAN MADRID
PRAGUE WARSAW BUDAPEST AUCKLAND

Recycling programs
for this product may
not exist in your area.

ISBN-13: 978-0-373-78487-5

ALL THEY NEED

Copyright © 2011 by Small Cow Productions Pty Ltd.

www.Harlequin.com

Printed in U.S.A.

ABOUT THE AUTHOR

Sarah Mayberry lives in Melbourne with her husband in a house with a large garden by the sea. She loves to cook, read, go to the movies, shop for shoes and spend time with her friends and loved ones. She's starting to love gardening, which is just as well, and she's hoping to begin a major renovation on her house in the near future. Exciting times!

Books by Sarah Mayberry

HARLEQUIN SUPERROMANCE

1551—A NATURAL FATHER
1599—HOME FOR THE HOLIDAYS
1626—HER BEST FRIEND
1669—THE BEST LAID PLANS
1686—THE LAST GOODBYE
1724—ONE GOOD REASON

HARLEQUIN BLAZE

380—BURNING UP
404—BELOW THE BELT
425—AMOROUS LIAISONS
464—SHE'S GOT IT BAD
517—HER SECRET FLING
566—HOT ISLAND NIGHTS

This one is for Wanda and Chris, the two best hand-holders in the business. Thank you for the long phone calls, the patience, the humor, the meals, the tissue-passing and for your faith in me.

There were times when I was ready to sink rather than swim, but you two were my lifeline. Bless your little cotton socks!

Special mention also to Lisa for brainstorming over the fence and listening to my rambling monologues.

Go the steam press!

PROLOGUE

FLYNN RANDALL SWALLOWED a mouthful of champagne as he stepped through the French doors onto the terrace.

It was February and even though it was nearly ten o'clock at night, it was still warm. Sweat prickled beneath his arms and he tugged at the collar of his shirt as he surveyed the sea of people. Like him, the men were all in formal black and white, the perfect foil for the women in their colorful gowns. There must have been close to two hundred people congregating on the wide, long terrace and the sound of their laughter and chatter drowned out the jazz band playing on the lawn below.

He searched in vain for a familiar face but everyone looked the same in their penguin suits. He shrugged. The perils of arriving late.

He was about to start down the stairs to the lawn when someone called his name. He glanced over his shoulder. A tall redheaded man was waving at him.

"Tony. Good to see you," Flynn said as he joined his friend.

"Bit late, aren't you?" Tony said, tapping his watch.

"I'm a popular guy," Flynn said, deadpan. "Gotta spread the love around."

"I bet."

Flynn kissed Tony's wife, Gloria, before turning his attention to the tall, blond man standing next to her.

"This is a bit of a coincidence," Owen Hunter said as Flynn shook his hand. "I've been trying to get an appointment to see your old man all week."

It was said with a grin, but Flynn could see the glint in the other man's eyes. What was that Shakespeare line his mother was always quoting? *Cassius has a lean and hungry look.*

In Flynn's experience, Owen always looked hungry, despite the fact that there was nothing lean about him. He was as tall as Flynn and built like a football player. Flynn guessed women probably found him attractive, with his square jaw and very white teeth.

"Well, you know, my father's a busy man." Flynn raised his glass to his mouth.

"Don't I know it," the other man said ruefully.

Flynn smiled but didn't pursue the subject, well aware that Hunter was waiting for Flynn to offer to set up an appointment. Owen Hunter had political ambitions; no doubt he planned to ask Flynn's father for a donation.

Maybe Flynn was getting cranky in his old age, but he couldn't help thinking that Hunter could have waited a few minutes before hitting him up for a favor. A little civility never hurt anyone.

A cry rose over the general hubbub, drawing people to the balustrade. Flynn drifted over with the rest of his group, idly curious. The lawn was six feet below, a lush green carpet dotted with yet more people. A large marble fountain sat in the center, decorated with cavorting cherubs and nymphs, many of whom spouted plumes into the wide, deep basin. The thing had to be well over ten feet tall, easily dominating the formal garden. Flynn winced, wondering where his hosts had found the monstrosity, before he shifted his attention to the source of the scream.

A couple he recognized as Andrea and Hamish Greggs were standing at the edge of the fountain, Andrea gripping the edge with both hands as she peered into the bubbling water. In their fifties, they were old friends of his parents and regulars on the social circuit. Towering over them both was Melanie Hunter, wearing a blush-colored gown, her hair in a sophisticated updo.

Her face was creased with concern as she talked to the older couple.

She was easily the tallest woman at the party—at least six feet tall—with broad shoulders that would put a lot of men to shame. Her breasts were full and round, her hips curved. As much as Flynn was wary of Owen's naked ambition, he'd always liked the other man's wife. There was something about Mel Hunter that always made him want to smile. Maybe because she was often smiling herself.

"I wonder what happened?" Gloria murmured.

"Looks like someone's lost something in the fountain," Tony said.

"Isn't that your wife, Owen?" Gloria asked.

"Yes, that's Melanie," Owen said. He was frowning, his gaze intent on the trio by the fountain.

"Shit," Owen said, so quietly Flynn almost didn't hear him.

He glanced at the other man briefly before returning his gaze to the lawn. He soon realized what had made Owen swear—his wife had stepped out of her shoes and was hitching up the skirt of her long dress. A crowd had started to gather, drawn by the promise of a spectacle.

Still talking to the older couple, Mel put a knee onto the waist-high rim of the fountain and boosted herself up so that she was balanced on both knees. She held out a hand and Hamish grasped it. Mel laughed, the sound floating up from the suddenly silent lawn—this was gripping stuff, much more interesting than any gossip that was being exchanged.

"Oh, dear. This has the potential to end badly," Tony said with a smirk.

Flynn didn't take his eyes off Mel as she leaned out over the water, while the older man used his weight as a counterbalance.

The crowd held its collective breath as she dipped her hand into the water and leaned farther and farther away from the rim, straining for all she was worth.

"Almost got it… There!" She pulled her arm from the water and the floodlights threw sparks off what looked like a diamond bracelet.

The crowd started to applaud—then Mel gave a startled yelp and fell into the fountain with a mighty splash. There was a communal gasp, followed by a wave of titters as she broke the surface. Her elegant updo had dissolved in the water and her dark hair hung in a tangled mess down her back. Mascara ran down her face as she pushed herself to her feet. Another round of titters washed through the crowd. The water had turned her blush gown translucent, leaving very little to the imagination. The dark outlines of her nipples were clearly visible, as was her underwear—which appeared to be bright pink with white stripes.

She should have looked ridiculous, standing there wet and bedraggled in her silly underwear, but she looked magnificent. Like some kind of mythical goddess rising from the mists of time.

Statuesque, utterly feminine. Breathtaking.

Flynn couldn't take his eyes off her and only remembered to blink when she threw back her head and laughed. The sound—loud and boisterous and incredibly sexy—echoed across the lawn. She wasn't alone in her amusement— Flynn couldn't keep the smile from his own face and everyone around him was either smiling or laughing.

Except Owen Hunter.

Without saying a word, he pushed his way through the crowd and headed toward the stairs to the lawn. Flynn barely registered his departure—he was too busy watching Mel fling a long, athletic leg over the edge of the fountain and extend both hands forward in an unspoken request for assistance. Two men rushed forward, and within seconds she was standing on dry land, dripping from head to toe and thanking her rescuers.

She presented the bracelet to Andrea Greggs with a little bow, which earned her more laughter, then turned and held up her hands as though accepting a standing ovation.

"Thank you, you've been wonderful. I'll be here all week," she said.

Her audience was still laughing and applauding this show of chutzpah when her husband pushed his way to her side. Shrugging out of his coat, Owen flung it over her shoulders and leaned close to say something in her ear. The smile fell from her lips and she nodded, then ducked her head. The crowd cleared a path for them as he led her away from the fountain.

"Someone's in trouble," Gloria said with a quick, expressive lift of her eyebrows.

"It was hardly her fault. Hamish shouldn't have let her go," Flynn said.

"Or she could have let the Hollands take care of it," Gloria said, referring to their hosts. "Like a normal person. They could have easily arranged to have the bracelet retrieved tomorrow morning."

Flynn drank the last of his champagne instead of continuing the discussion. Melbourne society was notoriously stuffy for a supposedly egalitarian culture. Old Money only very grudgingly accepted New Money, and No Money didn't stand a chance in hell. There was an unspoken social hierarchy and a set of rules that were only bent for the right people—and Melanie Hunter was not one of them. Personally, he thought she was bloody gutsy, the way she'd waded in to do her bit while everyone else stood around watching. And he definitely wasn't going to object to the view he'd enjoyed when she'd stepped out of the fountain—he had a pulse, after all, as well as a healthy appreciation for the female form.

He glanced at his glass. "I'm hitting the bar. Anyone else want a refill?"

A series of head shakes meant he was on his own as he made his way into the house. The bartender was working at full pitch to serve a slew of people and Flynn stood to one side, waiting for the crush to subside. He nodded to various acquaintances and friends and lifted a hand to acknowledge an ex-girlfriend, but didn't go out of his way to connect with anyone.

He was tired. He probably should have gone home instead of come to the party. As a rule, however, he liked to honor his commitments and he'd said he'd attend.

His thoughts drifted to the conversation he'd had with his mother earlier in the week. She'd asked him to meet her for lunch and then surprised the hell out of him by asking if he'd noticed anything "different" about his father, Adam, lately. She'd cited several instances of finding things in odd places around the house— the kettle in the fridge, shoes in the washing machine—as well as a number of memory or attention lapses on his father's part. At the time, Flynn had been quick to assign his father's slips to stress. His father's property development business was closing a deal to build several apartment towers on government land in a former industrial suburb and his father had been working around the clock. Still, Flynn couldn't get his mother's concerns out of his head. She knew his father better than anyone, after all.

But his father was only fifty-eight. Way too early to be hitting the panic button over a few memory lapses.

Flynn stared into his empty champagne flute, brooding. He made a snap decision. He'd put in an appearance, done his duty. Now he was going home. Life was too short to waste time at parties talking to the same people about the same things, over and over. And he had a garden to view tomorrow with an eye to developing a design. If he was successful, it would be yet another win for Verdant Design, the landscaping firm he'd founded nearly three years ago.

He set his glass on the nearest flat surface and wove through the crowd. It took him five minutes to find his hosts to say goodbye, then he made his way to the foyer and out through the open double doors into the portico. He was about to start down the drive when he noticed a movement out of the corner of his eye.

It was Mel, standing in the shadows beneath the carefully manicured hedge that bordered the driveway. She was facing the street, her husband's tuxedo jacket draped over her shoulders. Gravel crunched beneath his shoe and her head swung toward him. They locked gazes across twelve feet of driveway.

There was no mistaking the unadulterated misery in the depths of her gray eyes. After a few short seconds she looked away.

He opened his mouth to say something—what, he had no idea—as his phone rang. He pulled it from his jacket pocket and saw that it was his father. He glanced at Melanie again. Her focus was once more on the driveway. Waiting for her husband to bring the car around, he guessed.

He hit the button to take the call. He kept his gaze on her tall, straight back as he spoke. "Hey, Dad, what's up?"

"Flynn. Thank God. You have to help me. I've tried to get home but none of it makes sense. The roads have all changed...."

Flynn's grip tightened on the phone as he heard the panic in his father's voice. "Sorry, Dad. I don't understand. Where are you?"

"I don't know, I don't know. I was driving

home. But the roads are all changed. Nothing's the way it's supposed to be."

Dread thudded low in his gut. This man did not sound like the assured, confident father he knew. This man sounded scared and confused and utterly lost.

But he was only fifty-eight.

Flynn pushed his own panic from his mind. There would be time for that later.

"Okay, Dad. Listen to me. We're going to work this out, okay?" Flynn said, keeping his voice calm and clear.

"Why can't I recognize anything? Why has it all changed?"

"We'll sort this out, I promise. I want you to look around. Are you on a highway or in a residential area? Are there houses around you?"

"Yes. Lots of houses."

"Good. I want you to pull the car over. Turn off the engine, and walk to the nearest corner to find the street sign and tell me what it says."

He could hear his father's panicked breathing. He dug in his pocket for his car keys and started down the long driveway at a jog.

"I'll be with you every step of the way, Dad. We'll do it together, and I will be with you as soon as I can. No matter what happens, I will find you. So take a deep breath, pull over and *find me that street sign.*"

CHAPTER ONE

Eighteen months later

MEL PORTER GLANCED UP as she exited her house. A smile spread across her face as she took in the clear blue sky.

Despite the fact that it was barely June, Melbourne had been in the grip of winter for over a month—including overcast skies, rain, bitterly cold wind, overnight frosts—and it had been particularly bad here on the Mornington Peninsula, where her turn-of-the-century farmhouse was located. Today, however, the weather gods had granted the huddled masses a reprieve. The winter-bare liquid-amber tree in Mel's front yard stretched its branches toward the sky as though worshipping the unexpected warmth. She wondered what the neighbors would say if she did the same.

She settled for turning her face to the sun and closing her eyes.

She'd never been a winter person. Summer was what it was all about as far as she was concerned. Long days at the beach, barbecues, zinc on noses and the smell of coconut-scented sunscreen… She couldn't wait for the warmer weather.

Rubbing her hands together, she walked down the porch steps and across the driveway to the letterbox to collect the morning's mail. She pulled out a number of smaller envelopes with transparent windows—bills, hip hip hooray—and one larger, thicker envelope. Curious, she turned it over.

Everything in her went still when she read the words typed across the top left corner. *Wallingsworth and Kent, Lawyers.*

She stared at the envelope for a long beat. Then she started walking to the house.

Strange, after waiting and waiting for this moment, it had snuck up on her.

She waited until she was standing at the battered wood counter in the kitchen before she tore open the envelope and pulled out its contents.

There was a short covering letter, but she didn't bother reading it, simply flipped to the next page. *Divorce Order,* the heading said in crisp black font, accompanied by an official looking seal from the Federal Magistrates Court of Australia.

Mel's breath rushed out in a woosh.

There it is. It's over. Finally.

Her knees felt a little weak and she rounded the counter and sank into one of the oak chairs she'd inherited from her grandmother.

Six years of marriage, gone. At thirty-one, she was single again. Free.

She blinked rapidly and tried to swallow past the lump in her throat. This was a good thing. She'd had a lucky escape. There could have been kids involved, it could have been so much messier and uglier. No way was she going to cry.

This was a good thing.

The urge to call her mother or her sister gripped her, but she resisted. She'd leaned on her family and friends enough in the past few months. They'd comforted her, held her hand while she negotiated to buy the old farmhouse and holiday cottages that now constituted her combined home and livelihood, pitched in whenever she needed help…

It was time to start standing on her own two feet.

Her gaze found the clock on the kitchen wall and she gave a little start. She needed to get moving—she had guests arriving before lunch and she needed to clean Red Coat Cottage in preparation for their arrival.

She grabbed the keys on her way out the door and took the scenic route via the garden path to the first of the four cottages on her four-acre plot of land. The property had once been part of a vast orchard that had stretched along Port Phillip Bay from Mount Eliza to Mornington. The land had been broken up and sold off years ago for residential development, and Mel's plot included the old manager's residence as well as four of the compact workers cottages that had once housed the pickers and other laborers. The former owner had reconfigured the latter to appeal to vacationers, and when Mel bought the property six months ago she'd revamped all four cottages, updating the decor, kitchens and bathrooms so that they would appeal to a more affluent market.

At the time, her parents had said she was crazy, wasting money on antiques and fancy bathroom fixtures when the cottages had been attracting perfectly good business for many years as they were. But if there was one thing Mel knew about, it was people with money. She might never have been fully accepted by them, but she understood what they liked. She knew that if she wanted to increase the income from her business by attracting a wealthier client base, she needed shiny, imported things that screamed of luxury and exclusivity.

Once she'd renovated the cottages to a higher spec, her good friend Georgia—the only one of her so-called "friends" to maintain their relationship postseparation—had used her network of contacts to spread the news. Between word of mouth and the ads she'd been running in various publications, Mel was hoping she was in for a busy year.

She pondered today's guests as she cleaned the bathroom. She'd met Flynn Randall a handful of times during her six years as Mrs. Owen Hunter. He'd always struck her as being halfway decent for someone who had been born with not just a silver spoon, but a whole cutlery service in his mouth. Owen had done his damnedest to turn their casual acquaintance into a friendship, but Flynn had perfected the knack of being friendly while somehow keeping people at a distance. A necessary evil, Mel imagined, when your family was amongst the richest in Australia.

Georgia had secured the Randall booking for her—she and Flynn were old friends—and Mel had already sent her flowers as a thank-you. Next time she made the trek into Melbourne she planned to take her friend out to lunch as well.

She gave the bathtub a final swipe with the sponge before stepping back and giving the room a last inspection. Everything looked good, so she moved into the kitchen. Once she'd finished there, she laid out fluffy white towels and made the bed with high-thread count Egyptian cotton sheets. She arranged luxury-brand soaps and toiletries in the bathroom and hung matching robes on the back of the bedroom door. She fluffed the king-size quilt and arranged the down pillows, then spent ten minutes in the garden gathering a bouquet of flowers to go on the tallboy.

There was champagne in the fridge, along with Belgian chocolates and a selection of gourmet teas and coffees. The living room boasted the latest magazines—cars and business for male guests, home decoration and fashion for the women—and there was kindling and wood for anyone who wanted an open fire.

Mel did a last check to ensure everything was in place before locking the cottage and heading to the main house. It occurred to her that Owen would be horrified if he knew what she'd done with her divorce settlement. The thought made her smile grimly. The notion that his ex-wife routinely got down on her hands and knees to scrub away other people's dirt would make his eyes roll back in his head.

Mel made a rude noise and offered a two-fingered "up yours" gesture to her absent ex as she crossed the rear lawn. She didn't care what he thought anymore. It was one of the many blessings of being a divorced woman—along with having the whole bed to herself, never having to argue over whether the toilet seat belonged up or down and the luxury of reading into the small hours if the mood took her without having to worry about keeping her husband awake.

Oh, yeah. Divorced life is one big party.

Mel paused. She didn't like the bitter note to her own thoughts. She'd fought hard to claw back her confidence and her sense of herself in recent months; she hated the thought that she might still be grieving the loss of her marriage in some secret part of her heart, that she might miss Owen in any shape or form.

Her marriage had been unhappy for a long time and very ugly toward the end. Her husband's constant criticism had shaped her days and her nights. She'd bent over backward trying to please him—but it had never been enough. In hindsight, she'd come to understand that it never would have been.

Her chin came up as she entered the kitchen. She regretted the failure of her marriage, but she knew she'd done her damnedest to save it and she wouldn't go back if her life depended on it.

So, no, she didn't miss her ex. A fairly important realization to acknowledge on this, of all days. A realization that surely called for a celebration.

She walked to the fridge and opened the freezer door. A box of her favorite Drumstick sundae cones was on top and she grabbed one and tore off the wrapper.

If she were still married, Owen would have warned her that she risked getting fat if she ate ice cream full stop, let alone for breakfast. She took a big, defiant bite.

After all, she only had to please herself now. And what a glorious thing that was.

ROSINA ANSWERED THE DOOR, her face a mask of worry.

"Any change?" Flynn asked as he entered his parents' house.

The housekeeper shook her head. "Nothing."

Flynn nodded tightly and strode down the hallway. His father's study was at the rear of the house, at the end of a short hall. The door was almost always open because, even when his father was hard at work, he always made time to talk. Today it was closed and his mother, Patricia, sat in a chair beside it, her usually stylish salt-and-pepper hair a disheveled mess, her face streaked with tears.

She stood the moment she saw him and walked into his open arms. "I'm so sorry for calling you over," she said, her voice muffled by his shirt.

"We talked about this. We're all in it together."

"I didn't know what else to do. I've begged,

I've bullied, but he won't unlock the door. I keep talking to him, making him answer because I'm so scared he's going to do something...."

He kissed her temple. "I'll break the door down if I have to, don't worry. But Dad wouldn't do anything to hurt himself."

"You don't know that. He's never locked himself in his study before, either. My God, this disease... If it was a person, I would hunt it down and kill it with my bare hands."

Flynn could feel the grief and anger and fear coursing through her and he pressed another kiss to her temple. "We'll sort this out."

She nodded, then stepped back from his embrace. He watched her visibly pack away her emotions as she pulled a scrunched-up tissue from the cuff of her turtleneck sweater and blew her nose. By the time she'd finished she was once again in control.

That was the really great thing about Alzheimer's disease—it affected entire families, not just individuals. It killed slowly, over years, and it wore loved ones down with its relentless attack. In the twelve months since his father had been formally diagnosed with early-stage Alzheimer's, Flynn had watched his parents grapple to come to terms with what the future would hold. He'd seen them both rise to the occasion with humbling dignity, even while

Flynn had quietly freaked out in private over the imminent loss of the man who was such an integral part of his life.

Somehow, they'd all hung in there. It wasn't as though any of them had a choice, after all. Least of all his father.

Giving his mother a reassuring squeeze on the shoulder, Flynn rapped lightly on the study door. "Dad, it's me. Can I come in?"

There was a short pause. "No."

"Can I ask why?"

"No."

"Mom's worried about you. We all are. Talk to us, Dad."

Silence. His mother shook her head helplessly.

"Dad, if you don't let me in, I'm going to have to break the door down."

More silence. Flynn eyed the frame. The house was over a hundred years old, the door-jambs solid. It was going to take some effort, but it was doable.

"For God's sake, just leave me alone." There was so much despair and anguish in his father's words.

Flynn exchanged glances with his mother. "Stand back from the door, Dad."

His mother pressed her fingers to her mouth. Flynn stepped away far enough to give himself a run-up. He'd never kicked a door in before, but he figured that if he aimed his foot at the latch, something would have to give. Eventually.

He tensed his muscles, ready to power forward.

"Wait." His father's voice was resigned. Weary.

The key turned in the lock and the door opened an inch or two. Only a strip of his father's face was visible through the opening.

"Just Flynn."

Flynn's mother swallowed audibly and Flynn squeezed her shoulder again. She gave him a watery half smile.

"You got him to open the door. That's the important bit," she said quietly. She sank onto her chair as Flynn entered the study.

"Shut the door," his father barked the moment Flynn crossed the threshold.

Flynn complied and turned to regard his father. The older man stood behind his desk chair, both hands gripping the high leather backrest. His steel-gray hair was rumpled, his face pale with fatigue and anxiety. His blue eyes watched Flynn almost resentfully.

"What's going on, Dad?"

"Nothing. I want to be left alone. Is that too much to ask? Aren't I entitled to privacy anymore? Do I have to lose that, too, as well as everything else?"

The gruff anger in his father's voice was alien to Flynn. Adam Randall had always had high standards and he didn't suffer fools gladly, but he'd never been a bully and he'd certainly never been a man who let his emotions rule him.

"No one wants to take anything away from you, Dad. We love you. We were worried about you. Can you understand that?"

"I'm not an imbecile!"

"I'm sorry. I wasn't trying to be patronizing. I want you to understand our point of view."

His father stared at him, his eyes filling with tears. His chin wobbled and he took a quick, agitated breath.

"What's going on, Dad?"

His father continued to stare at him for a long moment. Then he stepped out from behind the chair. The crotch of his navy trousers was dark with moisture.

Bone-deep empathy washed through Flynn as he lifted his gaze to his father's anguished face.

"I was checking my email. I needed to go, but I wanted to check on something first. Then I just…lost track of things."

Flynn could hear the shame in his father's voice, but he didn't know what to say. He knew how unmanly this must be, how terrified his father must feel to have lost control of his own body. He closed the distance between them and wrapped his arms around his father.

"It doesn't matter, Dad."

His father hugged him so fiercely his body trembled with the effort. It was a moment before he spoke. "I don't want your mother to see me like this. Not yet." His voice was low and determined.

"She won't care."

"*I* care."

After a long beat, Flynn released his father, stepping away to give him breathing room.

"I'll get you a fresh pair of pants. Okay?"

His father nodded, dashing his knuckles across his eyes. Flynn exited the study. His mother rose to her feet.

"He's okay," he reassured her.

Her eyes were full of questions.

"He needs a clean pair of pants," Flynn explained quietly.

Comprehension dawned. For a moment her face seemed to sag. Then her chin came up and she nodded. "I'll take care of it."

She strode down the hallway, head high. Flynn rubbed the back of his neck and stared blankly at the framed Picasso sketch on the wall.

There were going to be many, many moments like this in the future. Too many to count. Bit by bit his father's dignity would be chipped away. It was as inevitable as the sun rising every morning, and as unstoppable.

Flynn returned to the study. He found his father slumped in his office chair, his eyes closed.

"Won't be a minute," Flynn said.

His father nodded. Flynn's chest hurt, watching him. Seeing how hard this was for him. There was a knock on the door. He opened it to find his mother armed with a towel, a fresh pair of boxer shorts and a pair of trousers.

"Thanks." He shut the door again and handed the towel and clothes over to his father.

"I'll be outside," Flynn said.

His father nodded, his gaze fixed on the pile of clothes in his lap as Flynn left the room.

Five minutes later, his father emerged. His mother stood and the two of them simply stared at each other for a long moment. Flynn could see how much effort it took for his father to hold her gaze, but he didn't look away. Not for a second. His mother closed the distance between them and took her husband's face in both her hands.

"I love you, Adam Randall," she said, her voice strong and clear. "No matter what. Okay?"

His father blinked rapidly. "I'm sorry."

His mother shook her head. "You don't need to apologize. Not to me."

She stood on her tiptoes and pressed a kiss to his mouth. His father's arms closed around her.

Flynn turned away, using the excuse of checking his phone for messages to give them privacy.

"Come on, let's have a cup of tea," his mother said.

Flynn glanced surreptitiously as his watch. He and Hayley had been on the verge of leaving for their weekend away on the Mornington Peninsula when he'd received the panicked phone call from his mother. They had planned a leisurely drive along the bay before their appointment at midday to view the old Summerlea estate in Mount Eliza, but at this stage he was going to be lucky to make it at all.

He shrugged off the concern. His parents were more important than the opportunity to tour a piece of real estate, even if that piece of real estate was one of a kind. It was just a house and a garden at the end of the day.

He followed his parents into the conservatory and sank into one of the wicker chairs around the rustic table. Rosina appeared almost immediately, a tray of tea and banana bread in hand.

"I swear, you're psychic, Rosie," his mother said.

Out of the corner of his eye, Flynn watched his father fiddling with the newspapers, aligning the stack of supplements into a neat pile. Flynn guessed that he was feeling self-conscious now that the crisis had passed, and very aware that

Rosina must be privy to at least some of what had occurred.

"How is the Aurora development coming along?" his mother asked as she slid a brimming cup of tea toward Flynn.

It has been a little over a year now since Flynn had stepped in as CEO of the family business. He was still feeling his way, learning the ropes, but somehow he was managing to keep his head above water.

"It's getting there. We've had to renegotiate a few contracts with suppliers thanks to the high Australian dollar, but we should be starting the groundwork on schedule."

His father's gaze was sharp as he eyed Flynn from across the table. "How has it affected the margins?"

They launched into a business discussion as his mother handed around slices of banana bread. His father was asking after the latest news from the sales department when his mother straightened in her chair.

"I just remembered—weren't you and Hayley going away for the weekend?"

Flynn shrugged easily. "There's no rush."

"But you're looking through Summerlea, aren't you? I'm sure you told me you had an appointment with the real estate agent," she said.

"It's fine. I'll reschedule."

"What time is the appointment?" his father asked, looking at his watch.

"Don't worry about it."

"I don't want you missing out because of my stupidity," his father said.

Flynn frowned. "I'm not missing out, and you're not stupid, Dad."

"What time is your appointment?" his mother asked.

Flynn sighed. "Midday. But it's really not a big deal. I was only taking a look at the old place out of curiosity."

"Rubbish. You wouldn't be going down there if you weren't serious," she said.

Flynn opened his mouth to protest but his mother fixed him with a knowing look. He lifted a shoulder.

"I'll admit I was excited when I first heard the estate was on the market. But the agent said the house needs a ton of work, which probably means it's a money pit."

"If there is one thing we have plenty of, it's money," his father said dryly. He pointed toward the door. "Go."

Flynn gave him an amused look. "I take it that's an order?"

"It is. Don't make me give it twice."

Flynn pushed his chair back. "A guy could get a complex over this sort of rejection."

"Call me and let me know if the garden is as magnificent as always," his mother said. "And before you ask, that's an order, too."

"A joint dictatorship. Lovely."

He kissed them both goodbye and ducked his head into the kitchen to say goodbye to Rosina before heading for the door. He phoned Hayley the moment he was in the car, aware she'd be wanting an update.

"Flynn. Is everything okay?" she asked immediately.

"All good. Dad was upset about something."

"Thank God we hadn't left already."

"Yeah."

"Speaking of which, I called the real estate agent and pushed our viewing back an hour."

Flynn smiled as he negotiated a left-hand turn. "Have I told you lately that I don't know what I'd do without you?"

"Hold that thought."

"What's that supposed to mean?"

"Can't tell. It's a secret."

"Oh, well, in that case…"

"When do you think you'll be home?"

"Five minutes."

"Then I'll see you soon."

She was waiting on the doorstep for him, her long auburn hair pulled into a ponytail. She was wearing a pair of skinny jeans, which she'd paired with a snowy white turtleneck and the tailored brown leather jacket he'd bought for her birthday, and she looked effortlessly elegant, as always. His overnight bag rested on the step beside her, as well as her own Louis Vuitton duffel.

"You packed for me," he said as he got out of his car.

"Didn't want to waste time," she said with a smile and a shrug.

He ducked his head to kiss her. "Thanks."

She rested a hand on his shoulder and smiled into his face, her brown eyes steady. He kissed her again, comforted as always by her no-nonsense calm. They'd known each other since they were children and had always been friends. Only in the past year had their relationship become something more, much to their respective parents' delight.

"So. Are we going to go buy a house or not?" Hayley asked.

"Why does everyone keep talking as though it's a done deal?"

"If you could see your face when you talk about Summerlea, you'd understand."

Flynn gave her a skeptical look.

"I know you hate the idea of having a bad poker face, Flynn, but it's true."

"I haven't seen Summerlea for at least ten

years. The house is probably falling down. I'm going with no expectations at all."

"Please. As if you care about the house. It's all about the garden, admit it."

He shrugged a little sheepishly. Summerlea *was* all about the garden for him, but that didn't change the facts of the situation.

"It's not practical. It's too far out of town, too far from Mom and Dad," he said, voicing the objection he hadn't been able to raise with his parents earlier.

"You have been in love with this place since you were a kid. I've listened to you rave about how it's Edna Walling's last great garden design so many times I've lost count. Getting your hands on that garden would be a dream come true for you. If you want it, we'll work it out. It's that simple."

He bent and grabbed both the bags. "We'll see."

Like his father, he had learned not to plan too far ahead these days.

As for dreams... Flynn had traded them in for responsibility a long time ago.

Mel was weeding the border of the rose garden in the backyard when she heard the sound of a car engine. She glanced over her shoulder, trowel in hand.

A vintage sports car cruised slowly up her driveway, its glossy black paint and chrome highlights glinting in the afternoon sun. The car disappeared around the bend in the drive and she stood, tugging off her gardening gloves.

She walked over to greet her guests, arriving at the parking bay as the driver's door opened. Flynn Randall stepped out, his back to her. He seemed taller and his shoulders broader than she remembered—or maybe it was simply that he was wearing faded jeans and a sweater instead of a tuxedo or a suit. Men always seemed sleeker and neater in suits.

"Mr. Randall. Welcome," she said in her cheeriest tone.

He turned to face her and she blinked in surprise as she gazed into his bright blue eyes. Again, she hadn't remembered them being quite so…*startling* was the only word she could come up with. Although maybe *piercing* was more appropriate. Especially in contrast to his almost-black hair. She'd always been aware that he was attractive but now that she was standing only a few feet away from him for the first time in over a year, she was hit with the realization that he was a very, very handsome man. He was studying her as intently and it occurred to her that he probably didn't remember her—they'd met only a handful of times and their exchanges had mostly consisted of polite small talk about nothing special. Hardly memorable stuff. She offered him her hand.

"Sorry. I'm Mel Porter. You probably don't remember me, but I used to be married to Owen Hunter. We met a few times…."

His hand, warm and large, slid into hers. "I remember you. How are things?" he asked, a smile curving his mouth.

She was a little thrown by how sincere his greeting was, as though he was genuinely glad to see her.

"I'm well, thanks. How about you?"

"Good, thanks. And it's Flynn, by the way."

He was still smiling and suddenly it hit her that he'd been at the Hollands' midsummer party the night she'd fallen into the fountain. She glanced away, unable to maintain eye contact.

Owen had pointed out to her in no uncertain terms exactly how see-through her dress had become after her dunking. Flynn was probably remembering her hot pink panties and whatever else she'd had on display, as well as the raft of jokes that had circulated in the weeks after the party.

The passenger-side door opened and a slim, auburn-haired woman exited the car. Mel recognized her immediately. It was hard not to, since

Hayley Stanhope had been one of the women her ex-husband had constantly encouraged Mel to befriend in the hope that it would further his political ambitions. The Stanhopes had been in banking for generations and no one had more pull in the upper crust of Melbourne society— except, perhaps, the Randalls.

"Sorry. My mother called as we turned into the driveway," the other woman said apologetically. She smiled at Mel, her brown eyes warm as she offered her hand. "I'm Hayley Stanhope."

"Mel Porter. Pleased to meet you."

The other woman's gaze flicked up and down Mel's body in a lightning-quick assessment. Mel knew what the other woman was seeing—no labels, no jewelry worth mentioning, uncontrollable hair, faded cargos, a raggedy long-sleeved T-shirt. The old self-consciousness stole over her.

"I hope you'll enjoy your stay here," she said, tugging on the hem of her T-shirt.

"I'm sure we will," Hayley replied.

"I've put you in Red Coat Cottage," Mel said, gesturing toward the cottage peeking through the screening shrubs she'd planted. "I'll give you a quick tour then leave you to settle in. I live in the main house, so if you need anything, knock on the back door or give me a buzz on the phone."

She was talking too fast and her palms were damp with sweat. She took a deep, calming breath as Flynn opened the trunk and pulled out two overnight bags, one an exclusive Louis Vuitton duffel, the other a well-worn leather number that looked as though it had seen an adventure or two.

She didn't know what was wrong with her. She'd had wealthy guests before. So why was she feeling so edgy all of a sudden?

She took refuge in action, leading the way toward the cottage, unlocking the door and stepping to one side to allow Flynn and Hayley to precede her.

Flynn was too busy examining the big terracotta pot of roses positioned to the left of the door to pick up on her unspoken cue.

"Red Coat roses." His gaze met hers, bright with interest. "You named the cottage after the rose, right?"

Mel stared at him, surprised he even knew the name of a David Austin rose, let alone that he could recognize one by appearance.

"That's right. All the cottages are named after David Austin roses," she said slowly. "Windrush, Pegasus, Tea Clipper."

"Clever idea," he said.

Hayley looked amused. "Trust Flynn to find

something green to fixate on the moment he arrives."

Mel smiled politely. Clearly, this was a private joke between the two of them. "The bedroom is the first door on the left." She stepped a little closer to the wall as Flynn brushed past her, followed by his girlfriend. They both disappeared into the bedroom.

Mel waited in the hallway. Ten seconds later, Flynn returned.

"Lead on, MacDuff."

She gathered by the other woman's absence that Hayley would not be joining them. She led Flynn into the living room, explained how to adjust the flue on the chimney should they wish to use the fireplace, then showed him the kitchen and bathroom.

"All pretty self-explanatory. The instructions for the appliances are in the top drawer in the kitchen if you need them," she said as they returned to the porch.

"Nice spec. Did you renovate this place yourself or was it done when you bought it?"

"I did it. It was a little tired and worn around the edges when I took possession."

"You've done a great job." His warm gaze traveled over her face, and for some inexplicable reason she could feel heat stealing into her cheeks.

"Thanks. That's a pretty big compliment coming from a Randall."

She hated the nervous note in her voice, hated the on-edge, eager-to-impress feeling in her chest. She didn't need to impress this man. He might have more money and more social pull than God, but he wasn't her friend, and he definitely wasn't her husband.

She needed nothing from him. He was her guest. Nothing more, nothing less.

Flynn's gaze ran over the front of the cottage. "I'm simply stating the obvious. You have good taste."

She was so surprised she let out a crack of incredulous laughter. "Can I have that in writing? My ex in-laws would be stunned."

The moment the words were out of her mouth she regretted them—way too much information, and way too revealing of the bitterness she was still trying to move past. All of which was made worse by the fact that he actually knew Owen. Hell, he probably knew Owen's parents, too.

She took a step away and jammed her hands into the pockets of her cargo pants. "I'll leave you to it. No doubt you have heaps of things you want to do and see."

She flashed him a tight smile before turning, putting her head down and walking briskly toward the main house. She didn't slow her pace until she was around the bend and out of view of the cottage. Then she let her breath out on a sigh.

Stupid, but for some reason Flynn Randall and his girlfriend had really rattled her cage. She didn't quite understand why. Maybe it was simply that they reminded her of a time when she'd been miserable and full of self-doubt and constantly aware of all her shortcomings. Or maybe she was like Pavlov's dog, forever programmed to respond with quivering servility when in the company of her social betters.

Now that's a depressing thought.

She shrugged off her disquiet. They were staying one night, and then they'd be gone. Depending on their movements, she probably wouldn't even see them again until they checked out.

Right now, that felt like a very good thing.

CHAPTER TWO

FLYNN WATCHED MEL stride away, her long, muscular legs eating up the ground.

She wasn't conventionally beautiful—her facial features were too unbalanced and she was built on too grand a scale for that—but she was incredibly appealing. He'd forgotten that about her.

He wasn't sure what it was that he found so compelling. Her gray eyes were clear and direct but otherwise perfectly ordinary, her nose was a little on the large side, her mouth slightly too wide. And yet the whole time he'd been talking to her he hadn't been able to take his eyes off her.

She, however, had seemed nervous. Not at all the way he remembered her.

Hayley joined him on the porch, sliding an arm around his waist.

"I like it here already. The air smells cleaner." She rested her head on his shoulder.

"That's because it is," he said dryly.

She followed his gaze up the driveway. "She was married to Owen Hunter, wasn't she?"

"That's right."

"I can remember seeing her around. She's pretty hard to miss. She always used to remind me of Xena, Warrior Princess. Or Wonder Woman."

"She's tall, but she's not that tall."

"She's taller than me. Were you there the night she fell into the Hollands' fountain?"

"Yes."

"Was it as bad as they say?"

"In what way?"

"In every way. I heard her dress was transparent, and that her husband marched her off and then spent the next month apologizing for her to anyone who is anyone."

Flynn frowned. "She was trying to help. It's not like she leaped into the fountain for kicks."

Hayley held up a hand. "Whoa there. I didn't mean to step on any toes. I didn't realize you two were friends."

Her gaze was searching, questioning, and he realized he'd spoken a little too heatedly.

"We're not. I hardly know her. But that fountain thing was blown way out of proportion. Gabrielle Holland needs to get a life."

"That's true. She dined out on that story for a *very* long time." She sounded amused, but she'd always been far more tolerant of the social piranhas amongst their circle than he had.

He checked his watch. "We should get going."

"Let me grab my bag."

She was back in a minute with her sunglasses and handbag. He backed his vintage Aston Martin out and cruised up the driveway. They were nearing the main house when Mel appeared around the corner, lugging a tall ladder. She leaned it against the back of the house beneath one of the sash windows before looking over her shoulder toward them. She gave a small acknowledging smile then turned to her task.

He hit the brakes and wound down the window.

"Hey. It's been a few years since I've been down on the peninsula and old Gertie here doesn't have GPS." He patted the Aston Martin's dash. "Do I turn left or right onto the Nepean Highway if I want to go to Summerlea estate?"

Mel approached the car, bending so she could see in the window. "You take a left. Then it's the first street on your left, and the estate is at the end of the road."

Her T-shirt sagged as she leaned down. It took more willpower than he cared to admit to stop himself from taking a good long look at what he suspected was a pretty spectacular view.

He was only human, after all, and she was built on very generous lines.

"Great, thanks."

"I guess it's true then, huh? It's up for sale? I heard a rumor but I didn't believe it."

"The owners have gone into a retirement home, according to the estate agent."

"Really? That's so sad. They both loved that place so much. It must be hell to have to give it over to someone else."

"You know them?"

"Oh, no. Not personally." She tucked a long, dark curl behind her ear. "I used to go to Summerlea when it was part of the Open Garden tour, and Brian and Grace were always there, talking to everyone. It's been years since they last let the public in, but I can still remember how beautiful the gardens were. I've never seen flame azaleas like theirs anywhere else. And the roses… Mind-blowing."

She had a far-off look in her eyes. Then she seemed to recall herself. "Sorry. I'm holding you up." She straightened and stepped back from the car, waving a hand to indicate he should go.

"Thanks for the directions."

She gave an awkward little shrug. He drove out into the street.

"If you're feeling guilty about looking, don't," Hayley said after a few seconds. "I looked. Couldn't help myself. She has amazing breasts." She sounded wistful.

Flynn glanced at her briefly before concentrating on the road. "I didn't look."

"Flynn. Come on. This is me. A blind man would have looked."

"I didn't look," he repeated. He glanced at her again as he signaled to pull onto the highway.

She looked bemused. "Why on earth not?"

"Because I'm with you," he said simply.

A slow smile curled Hayley's mouth. "Sometimes I think you're too good to be true, you know that?"

"If you believe that, I've got some swamp land to sell you."

"I think I just might buy some swamp land if you were selling it."

The real estate agent was already waiting for them when they parked in front of Summerlea's familiar white fence. He scrambled out of his Mercedes as Flynn cut the engine.

"Flynn Randall? Spencer Knox. Pleased to meet you." His eyes were assessing as they exchanged greetings.

One problem with being a Randall—everyone knew your net worth before you walked through the door.

"We really appreciate you moving the viewing time for us," Flynn said.

"Not a problem, and it's great to meet you both." Spencer paused a moment before offering Flynn a shrewd smile. "We can talk about the weather a little if you like, but you're a busy man and I suspect you're keen to cut to the main event. So shall we?" He gestured toward the gate.

"Absolutely," Flynn said, appreciating the other man's bluntness.

Spencer walked ahead of them to the pedestrian entrance, situated to the right of the main gate. The paint was peeling off the wood and streaks of rust ran down from the lock. The main gate wasn't in much better shape and Flynn took a step back to assess the fence line itself.

"As I mentioned on the phone, the old place has been a bit neglected in recent years," Spencer said. "A combination of old age and money issues, I gather. So things might not be quite as you remember them."

"Sure."

The other man struggled with the latch for a moment before the gate swung open with a painful screech.

Hayley gave a nervous laugh. "That sounds a little ominous, doesn't it?"

Flynn murmured something noncommittal, his focus on what he was about to discover on the other side of the gate. Adrenaline had his heart racing as he stepped into the grounds.

In many ways, Summerlea was where he'd

first discovered his love of gardening. He could still remember dragging his feet as his mother led him into the grounds as an eight-year-old, past the crowds of tourists milling about the entrance. He'd been bitching and moaning all the way from the city, sure that he was missing out on doing something cool with his friends. The moment he'd gotten his first look at the garden his complaints had blown away like dust.

Rolling lawns, archways heavy with roses, whimsical benches made out of gnarled local tea-tree branches, copses of birch trees, their trunks silver-white in the sun... He'd been roped into helping his mother in the garden often enough by then to understand that he was looking at something special. A living treasure.

Twenty-six years later, he looked at the same view and saw that the rose arbor was rotted and falling down, the lawns patchy and overgrown, and the benches absent, no doubt having fallen prey to the weather or insects long ago. And still his heart soared, because he knew that not only could he fix all of the above, but he could also make it better. His fingers literally itched for pen and paper so he could start sketching and jotting down ideas and he had to stop himself from stooping to pull the nearest weed from where it sprouted between two paving stones.

He glanced at Hayley, keen to see her reaction, but she'd put on her sunglasses and most of her expression was hidden behind the lenses.

"What do you think?" he said quietly as they walked up the pathway toward the house.

"I imagine it was once very beautiful," she said diplomatically.

He looked out across the garden once more, and again he felt the pull of possibilities. This place was special. It would be an intoxicating challenge to restore it to its former brilliance. He'd have to pare things back, rebuild. The lawn was a mess, the garden beds overcrowded and full of weeds. With water restrictions in place, the whole space would probably benefit from a modern reticulation system—

Aren't you forgetting something?

Flynn tore his gaze from the garden and fixed it on Hayley's slim back as she walked ahead of him. He didn't have time to indulge this dream. He was responsible for Randall Developments now, and things would only become more intense with his father.

This was too much for him to take on right now. No matter how much a part of him wanted to.

And yet the thought of walking away from this opportunity made him want to grind his teeth. He'd already walked away from Verdant Design and the career of his choice. He needed something of his own. Some way of keeping a small part of his dream alive.

Hands thrust deeply into his jacket pockets, Flynn climbed the steps to the house. For better or worse, the next twenty minutes had the power to change his life.

THEY WERE BOTH QUIET on the way back to the cottage. Flynn was lost in his own thoughts, shuffling things around in his mental diary, formulating scenarios for himself and his parents that would allow him to have his cake and eat it, too.

Not that any of that was going to change the outcome of today's inspection. At a certain point in the tour he'd given in to the inevitable and admitted to himself that he was going to put in an offer for the estate. It was too rare and precious an opportunity for him to pass up. He had no idea how he was going to make it fit with everything else, but he would work it out.

Somehow.

He turned off the engine when they returned to their accommodation but made no attempt to get out of the car. Instead, he looked at Hayley, who was staring pensively out the windshield.

"What do you think?"

"I think that it's terrifying, frankly. That

house needs new everything. And the garden…
I wouldn't even know where to begin."

"I would." He could hear the relish in his own
voice.

She looked at him, a small, curious smile on
her face. "Which is why you're going to buy it,
of course."

She knew him so well.

"Yes. I am." Anticipation spiked through him
as he finally said it out loud.

She opened the car door. "Come on, then.
There's a bottle of French bubbly in the fridge
thanks to our efficient hostess. I think this calls
for a celebration."

He followed her into the cottage. She opened
kitchen cupboards until she found long-stemmed
flutes and he tore the foil and the wire cage off
the top of the champagne bottle. The pop of the
cork sounded loud in the small space and Hayley laughed and pulled a comic face when the
sparkling wine foamed up over the neck.

"Don't waste it!"

He poured them both a glass and Hayley
raised hers in a toast.

"To finally getting something you've always
wanted," she said.

They clinked glasses and drank, and Flynn
kissed her. She surprised him by deepening
the kiss, one hand sliding behind his neck.

She wasn't usually aggressive sexually but she pressed herself against him and kissed him deeply, her fingers digging into the muscles of his shoulder. When she finally broke the kiss she looked at him for a long moment, her gaze very intent and serious.

Then she took his hand and tugged on it. "Come into the living room. There's something I want to say to you."

Flynn smiled. "This is all very mysterious."

"It won't be for long, trust me."

She led him to one of the cream couches and pushed him onto the cushion. Then she sat beside him and took his hand in hers. She looked into his eyes, then she squeezed her own shut for a long beat.

"Wow. This is harder than I thought it would be." Her hand was trembling.

Flynn frowned. "Is everything okay?"

"Yes. At least, I hope it is." Hayley opened her eyes and gave him a small, nervous smile. "Remember what you said this morning about not knowing what you'd do without me and how I told you to hold that thought?"

"Yes."

"I've been thinking a lot lately, about us. And the future. I've been thinking about what I want, how I'd like things to be."

Flynn tensed. He had a feeling he knew where

this was going. "Look, Hales, I know that things haven't been great lately. I know that I've been working all hours and the situation with Mom and Dad has been chewing up my spare time, but—"

Hayley smiled and pressed her fingers to his lips. "Relax, Flynn. I'm not breaking up with you."

Flynn's shoulders dropped a notch. "Good."

"I'm asking you to marry me." She slipped onto one knee on the floor and opened her hand, palm up, in front of him. A simple gold wedding band rested against her pale skin. "So, will you, Flynn? Will you marry me?"

It literally took Flynn a full ten seconds to comprehend what she was saying. She knelt before him, her brown eyes fixed intently on his face, a faint, hopeful smile on her lips, and his brain simply refused to work.

Probably because this was the last thing he'd been expecting. They'd been seeing each other a little under a year, living together for six months. Things were good between them. Comfortable. But he simply hadn't gotten around to thinking about marriage. He simply…hadn't.

The silence stretched. He needed to say something. Now.

"I'm sorry," he said. "I'm a little blindsided here. I wasn't expecting anything like this."

"I can tell. You look like I hit you up for a loan." Her smile wobbled a little and she curled her hand into a fist around the ring. "I was kind of hoping we were on the same page with this. But I guess I was wrong." She was still kneeling and Flynn reached out to guide her onto the couch.

"I need a minute to get my head around this, that's all."

She nodded but didn't say anything. Flynn took a deep breath, trying to get his thoughts in order, trying to find the one right thing to say that would take away the hurt dawning in her eyes.

"I think you're great, Hales. You know that. I've always thought you were great. We get on well, we understand each other."

"I know, and I'll admit I was kind of hoping you would beat me to this. Then I remembered that this is the twenty-first century. Women are supposed to go for what they want, right? And I want you, Flynn. I always have."

For the second time in as many minutes, he was without words. He'd given Hayley a black eye with his soccer ball when he was six. He'd danced with her at her debutante ball when she was seventeen. He'd laughed with her at any number of parties and theater shows and functions over the years, caught up with her for lunch every now and then—with or without other friends in the mix. He'd always thought of her as a good friend, and only recently had he considered her as anything more than that.

"I didn't realize," he said, then immediately kicked himself. Could he sound like more of an idiot? He wasn't an inarticulate teenager. He was thirty-four years old. He'd had his fair share of lovers and relationships. Yet he was handling this with all the sophistication and finesse of a pro wrestler.

"I guess that means I'm a better actor than I thought. Mom has known for years."

She was watching him intently. Flynn realized he hadn't answered her question yet.

It should have been a no-brainer. She was beautiful. Their parents were friends. They had everything in common, from their acquaintances to their educations to their tastes in wine and food and art. She was elegant, clever and kind.

She was perfect and she would make the perfect wife.

So why couldn't he look her in the eye and say yes? Why was he feeling trapped and uncomfortable and deeply guilty all of a sudden?

An image flashed across his mind's eye—his mother capturing his father's face in her hands this morning and telling him clearly and unequivocally that she loved him, no matter what. The love and devotion in her expression had been undeniable, as had the love and devotion in his father's eyes. They were crazy about each other, always had been. They preferred each other's company to anyone else's, finished each other's sentences, tickled each other's funny bones.... They were a matched set. Soul mates. Inseparable.

They were the best example of marriage a man could have, and Flynn had taken the lessons he'd learned from watching them to heart. When he married, he planned for it to stick. He wanted to grow old with the love of his life, to mellow with her, to store away memories and take on challenges and evolve with her. He wanted a forever kind of love, the kind that only increased and grew richer and deeper and broader with time. A love that was strong enough to withstand the slings and arrows of outrageous fortune and then some.

He looked into Hayley's eyes and tried to imagine the two of them twenty years from now. He tried to imagine their children. He tried to imagine the two of them dealing with the tectonic shift that his parents were experiencing.

And it just wasn't there. He couldn't see it. Hayley was his dear, dear friend. But she was not the woman he wanted to marry.

His chest was suddenly tight. He was about to hurt her—the last thing he'd ever wanted to do.

He looked at her hand in his, her skin very pale in comparison to his, trying to find the words. "Hayley, I care for you a great deal. You're one of my best friends. The past year has been great. Really great. But marriage is a big step. And I don't feel even close to ready to take it with you."

She was very still for a moment. "One of your best friends." He could see the disappointment and hurt in her face.

Flynn stared at her helplessly. If it was in his power, he'd flip a switch and love her with the same fervor that she apparently felt for him. But it wasn't, and he didn't.

"I'm sorry. There's been so much going on.... I never meant to create expectations." His words sounded lame, even to himself. He'd fallen into a relationship with her, allowed her to move in, shared his days and his nights with her, but he'd never once thought about where they were going, or wondered what she thought their relationship was about. He'd been too busy flailing around in his own crap after his father's diagnosis—winding down his own company, stepping up to take over the reins of the business, trying to support his mother, trying to do anything and everything to ease his father's distress.

"You didn't create expectations. I did." Her voice was heavy with tears but she was doing her best to hold them in.

"God, Hales, I'm so sorry." He pulled her into his arms, guilt a physical burn in his chest.

She might be prepared to let him off the hook, but he wasn't. He'd been selfish, taking comfort where he could find it. Not thinking about the consequences. Not thinking about tomorrow at all.

She rested her head on his shoulder but didn't try to return his embrace. After a moment he let her go. Her eyes were filled with tears and she brushed them away with her fingertips.

"I'm sorry," she said, not quite meeting his gaze. Then she stood and rushed from the room.

Flynn heard the bedroom door click shut. He mouthed a four-letter word, angry with himself, angry with the situation. He fell back against the cushions and raked his fingers through his hair.

He had no doubt that right now, Hayley was howling her eyes out on the bed they were supposed to share tonight. He swore again. He was a bastard. A stupid, selfish, thoughtless bastard.

The urge to get up and go gripped him, to walk away from the cottage and the scene that had played out, but he didn't move. The least he could do was be here if Hayley needed him. The very least.

MEL SPENT THE first half of the afternoon repairing the rotten windowsill. Her thoughts drifted from topic to topic as she chipped away the damaged wood with a hammer and chisel, but she kept coming back to Flynn and his girlfriend.

They were an attractive couple, with his dark good looks and her pale skin and fiery hair. They were socially well-matched, too, both bringing equal clout to the table. No one would look down their noses when they arrived at functions or events. No one would whisper behind their backs or laugh and speculate about how long their relationship would last and what, exactly, Hayley had done to land her man.

The chisel slipped and Mel's breath hissed out as the sharp metal sliced into the fleshy part of her thumb. She sucked on it for a second before inspecting the wound. Blood welled, but it was a shallow cut. She'd live.

She went inside for a bandage and returned to finish the repair, replacing the excised wood with builder's filler. Afterward, she made the ten-minute drive to her parents' place to help her mother finalize the invitations for their upcoming thirty-fifth wedding anniversary. She stayed for an early dinner, then drove home.

She was in the bedroom, ready to pull on her pajamas for a cozy night in front of the TV, when a knock echoed through the house. It came from the back door, and she quickly pulled her cargo pants on. She fastened the stud as she made her way to the kitchen and the door.

It was Flynn, his face shuttered, his body half turned away. "Sorry to disturb you. I need to give you this." He handed over the key to the cottage.

Mel stared at it for a second before lifting her gaze to his. "You're leaving?"

"Yes."

"Is something wrong with the accommodation? If there's a problem, I can offer you one of the other cottages."

"It's nothing to do with the cottage. Everything's been great. Something has come up."

She tried to gather her thoughts. She'd had last-minute cancellations, and she'd had no-shows, but she'd never had guests walk out halfway through their stay.

"Okay. Well. I hope you enjoyed your time here. What there was of it, anyway."

"We did, thanks." He gave her a small, tight smile before turning and walking down the steps.

She watched him for a minute, frowning. Maybe it was her imagination, but he looked tired. Defeated.

She caught her own thoughts and made a rude noise. Flynn Randall was filthy rich, better-looking than any man had a right to be and in the prime of his life. He probably didn't know how to spell defeat, let alone how to experience it.

She, on the other hand, was an expert.

On that cheery note, she went to get ready for bed.

CHAPTER THREE

THREE WEEKS LATER, Mel stooped to wrap her arms around the hessian-covered root ball of the orange tree she'd excavated from her front yard. She'd pruned the branches and dug the roots out in stages, giving the tree time to adjust to the brutal surgery she was practicing. But now it was time to haul it to its new home. She felt a little like the horticultural equivalent of Atilla the Hun in uprooting the tree from its old home, but this was a necessary evil—it had been badly sited by the previous owners and would never thrive or even bear fruit in its current position.

Once she was confident she had a reliable grip, Mel flexed her legs and attempted to lift the tree onto the waiting wheelbarrow. As she'd half expected, the tree barely budged, despite giving it her all. Between the weight of the tree and the amount of dirt and clay contained in the root ball, it was bloody heavy. She might have rugby league shoulders, but she wasn't a miracle worker.

She sat back on her heels and looked up at

the shiny green foliage towering over her. She was tempted to call her father or brother to ask them to lend a hand, but she didn't want them to feel as though she only called when she needed something.

Which meant it was time to move on to Plan B. Not that she was a hundred-percent certain it would work, either. But what the hey.

She headed to the house—the canvas drop sheet she was looking for was in the spare room. After she'd grabbed it and was on her way outside, she glanced into the living room. The clock on the mantel told her it was ten, which meant she had an hour until Flynn Randall was due to check in. Plenty of time to do what needed to be done.

She still couldn't quite believe he was coming to stay with her again. He'd called on Wednesday and she'd been so surprised to hear his voice it had taken her an embarrassingly long time to respond to his greeting. After his last stay—or, more accurately, his nonstay—she'd thought she would never hear from him again. Even though he'd said the accommodation had been fine and she'd been inclined to believe him, his visit couldn't exactly have been called successful.

Yet he'd made another booking, and she'd been feeling nervous and on edge ever since she'd marked the reservation in her diary. Which was genuinely pathetic given that she'd long since sifted through her reaction to his last visit and come to the depressing conclusion the reason he put her on edge was because of who he was—a Randall.

Old habits died hard, apparently.

She was determined to get over the anxiety this time around. He was a man, he put his pants on one leg at a time, and she would respond to him as she would any other man. If it killed her. The same went for his girlfriend. They were people, and they were guests, and that was it. They weren't any more special than anyone else she played host to.

The drop sheet snapped open as she spread it across the lawn. As she'd hoped, the orange tree was a few inches shorter than the length of the tarp. She positioned it at the most advantageous point, then braced her legs and rocked the root ball from side to side, "walking" it onto the canvas. As gently as possible she tipped the tree onto its side. She gathered up the corners closest to the root ball and bunched them together into a big wad. Then she took a step backward, using her body weight and her grip on the drop sheet to drag the tree across the lawn behind her.

By the time she got to the driveway her arms and thighs were burning. She put her chin down and kept hauling, making her slow way along the side of the house and onto the rear lawn. She stopped to peel off her sweater, wiped her hands down the sides of her jeans, then picked up the corners and put her back into round two, trying not to think of how much farther she had to go before she reached the new site she'd prepared.

"Are you all right there? You look like you could use a hand."

Her head snapped around. Surprised, her grip on the drop sheet loosened as she hauled backward and she fell onto her ass with a painful thud—all while staring straight into the very blue eyes of Flynn Randall.

Her pride urged her to immediately scramble to her feet but her tailbone was vibrating with pain and it was all she could do not to groan out loud.

"Are you okay?" He strode to her side and held out his hand to help her up.

"Fortunately, the ground broke my fall."

He smiled faintly at her attempt at bravado. She could feel embarrassed heat flooding into her face and she reached up to grab his hand, keen to not be on her ass at his feet for a second longer than she needed to be. His firm hand closed around hers, and she rose to her feet almost effortlessly.

He was a big man, but she was a big woman.

Clearly, he was packing some serious muscle under his butter-soft leather jacket.

"That's a lot of tree you're hauling there."

"It's not as heavy as it looks," she lied.

He lifted an eyebrow and she knew he wasn't buying her claim. Her backside was still aching and she desperately wanted to rub it. Instead, she put on her professional hat. Not the easiest thing to do with mud splashed up the legs of her oldest jeans and her butt throbbing.

"If you give me a few minutes, I'll clean up and grab the keys to Tea Cutter Cottage for you."

"What about your tree?"

"It's not going anywhere."

"That was kind of my point." He surveyed the yard. "Where are you taking it?"

"I've dug a new site at the bottom of the property."

She didn't go into detail—Flynn would hardly want to hear about her plans for a fruit orchard and a vegetable garden that would eventually feed not only her but her guests—if they chose—as well as her family.

"You're going to kill yourself getting it down there."

Her eyes widened as he started pulling his jacket off.

"What are you doing?"

"What does it look like?"

"But—but you'll get all dirty."

Her gaze took in his expensive-looking brown leather boots, his designer jeans and the black sweater he was wearing.

"I don't mind." He threw his jacket onto the grass nearby, then tugged his sweater over his head and tossed it on top. He was wearing a dark gray T-shirt underneath. It looked as though it was made of silk, which probably meant it was.

"No," she said, shaking her head. "I can't let you ruin your clothes."

"A little dirt never hurt anyone."

He examined the tree for a beat. "The drop sheet was a good idea." He stooped and grabbed the wad of canvas she'd been dragging, separating the corners out and offering her one. "Shall we?"

"No. No way."

"If you don't help me out, I'll have to try to equal your Herculean solo effort and risk embarrassing myself if I fall short."

She stared at him, utterly thrown by his offer and his apparently genuine desire to help her out.

"Okay. If that's the way it has to be," he said with a shrug. He bunched the two corners together again and started to pull the tree forward.

"Stop," Mel said, moving to block his path.

He grinned and offered her a corner of the

drop sheet again. She took it with a frown, which only seemed to amuse him even more.

"Thank you." It came out a little grudgingly and she cleared her throat. "I really appreciate your help."

"It's my pleasure."

She darted him a skeptical look but he didn't look as though he was merely obeying the dictates of some masculine code of honor. He looked thoroughly in his element, as though this really was his pleasure.

Which was just plain strange, given who he was.

"On the count of three?" he said.

She took up the slack on her corner, and on his signal began to heave on the drop sheet. The difference in effort required was profound and she almost fell on her backside again.

"You okay?"

"Yes. I wasn't expecting it to be this much easier."

"I have a feeling I should probably be insulted by that. Do I look that anemic?"

It took her a moment to realize he was joking. She smiled uncertainly. "You don't look anemic at all."

He didn't say anything but he continued to seem quietly amused as they dragged the tree down the lawn, across the garden path, behind

Tea Cutter Cottage and through a gap in the screening trees to the large clearing she'd chosen for her fledgling orchard. Although covered with patchy grass, it had never had a real purpose or design—until now.

She directed him toward the shovel she'd left sticking out of a mound of dirt to the left of the clearing. They came to a halt beside the hole she'd dug that morning.

"Thanks for that," she said, already turning to lead him to the main house so she could get him settled in.

"How are you going to get it in the hole?"

She paused. "The same way I got it out."

Which had been through sheer determination and not a little swearing. But he didn't need to know that.

"Come on, let's do this." He knelt beside the tree and began untying the twine she'd used to keep the hessian covering in place.

She stared at his down-turned head, baffled by his determination to be helpful despite the obvious risk to his clothes and his complete lack of obligation to her. He was her guest, after all. *She* was supposed to be at *his* beck and call, not the other way around.

"I've done this a few times over the years, but it's always a bit heart-in-your-mouth, waiting to see if you've done more harm than good," he said as he tugged at the twine. "It drives me crazy when people plant trees where they think they will look pretty rather than where they'll grow well. A sixty-second conversation with someone in a garden center would have told them that *citrus sinensis* need sunlight, the more the better. How hard is it to ask the right questions if you don't already know the answers?"

He glanced up at her to gauge her reaction and suddenly it hit her.

"You're a gardener."

The amused look was back in his eyes again. "You say that like it's a miracle. Or at least about as likely as Bigfoot being real."

"Sorry. It's just not what I expected."

He nodded thoughtfully. "Let me guess. You had me pegged for a polo player, right? Maybe a yachtsman?" He spoke with an exaggerated British accent.

She smiled before she could catch herself. "Something like that."

"My mother is a keen gardener. She recruited me as her slave when I was a kid, and I've been getting my hands dirty ever since."

Mel dropped to her knees and pulled her penknife from her pocket, making short work of the knots he'd been tugging at without much success. He gave her a wry look and she shrugged apologetically.

He turned to inspect the hole she'd dug before glancing at her in an assessing way. "Would it offend you if I offered some advice?"

"I guess it depends on what it is."

"The hole isn't big enough. You want the soil around the roots to be a little loose and aerated, so the tree can grow new feeder roots easily."

"You're lucky I don't slap your face," she said, deadpan.

She immediately felt a dart of alarm. She'd always been a bit of a smart-ass—impossible not to be growing up with a father and a brother who took no prisoners when it came to teasing and pranks—but her quick tongue had consistently gotten her in trouble with her ex. Owen had hated it when she said something provocative or racy or pithy. He'd wanted her to be discreet and elegant and sophisticated, not mouthy and cheeky.

She waited for Flynn to signal that she'd overstepped the mark with her off-the-cuff response. Waited for the friendly smile to fall from his lips or for his blue eyes to turn cold. But he simply smiled at her appreciatively before pushing himself to his feet.

"I was wondering where your sense of humor had gotten to."

She stared at him as he pulled the shovel from the mound of dirt. "Excuse me?"

"Your sense of humor. You always used to make me laugh."

Her lips twisted. She knew what this was about. "You mean because I jumped in the fountain at the Hollands' party?"

Flynn had started to dig, widening and deepening the hole, but he stopped to consider her. Almost as though he understood exactly how brightly that incident burned in her memory.

"I was under the impression that you fell in. And I didn't think it was particularly funny until you took your bow. Hamish Greggs was an idiot for letting go of you. I hope he groveled at your feet the next day."

She smiled grimly. "The Hollands 'forgot' to invite us to their black-and-white ball. I guess they were afraid I'd take a dive into their koi pond."

"You're kidding?" Flynn looked incredulous. Then he frowned. "I knew there was a reason I never liked them."

For a moment she thought she'd misheard him, but the disgusted expression on his face was undeniable.

He didn't blame her for the incident. He didn't think she was vulgar or stupid or attention-seeking or clueless because she'd set out to help a woman in distress and wound up in the fountain. He didn't think she'd gone out of her way to cause trouble. He was sympathetic. Maybe even supportive.

The shovel hit a rock, the metal ringing loudly, and she realized she was simply watching while her guest sweated over a hole in the ground. She shook her head, wishing she could shake off the past as easily.

"Here. I should be doing that," she said, striding forward.

"If it gets to be too much for me I promise to send up a flare."

"You're my *guest*." She reached out to grab the shovel from him.

"What are you going to do? Wrestle me for the shovel?" he asked.

"I was hoping you'd realize I was right."

"Would it help at all if I told you that I'm enjoying myself? That I've had a really shitty couple of weeks and that digging a nice big hole and getting some dirt under my nails is exactly what the doctor ordered?" His tone was light but there was something in his eyes that told her he wasn't joking.

She let her hand fall to her side and retreated from the hole. "Okay. If you insist."

He set to it again, his biceps flexing powerfully as he drove the shovel into the earth. Mel watched him, twitchy and uncomfortable with being forced into the role of spectator.

"You're about to break out in hives, aren't you?" he asked after a couple of minutes.

"I'm used to doing things for myself."

He drove the shovel into the ground and left it there. "Then you'll be pleased to know I'm done."

Mel bit her lip and looked at him, aware that there was a very real chance that she was coming across as a surly ingrate. "I do appreciate the help. You've been incredibly generous...."

He waved a hand, effectively dismissing her words. "Let's get this baby in the ground where she belongs."

She didn't even bother arguing with him this time. Between the two of them they lifted the tree upright so it sat on its root ball. She squatted to get a grip on the roots, digging her gloved fingers into the dirt and clay, while Flynn did the same on the other side of the tree.

"Okay. One, two, three," she said.

They both lifted and shuffled toward the hole at the same time.

"Slowly," Flynn said as the tree started to slide into the hole.

Mel shifted her grip to the trunk to try to control its descent, earning a face full of leaves for her efforts. She felt rather than saw the tree hit bottom and sat back on her heels with a relieved sigh. Flynn did the same on his side of the hole.

After a beat he leaned to one side so he could make eye contact with her around the foliage.

"Thanks for letting me help."

She couldn't help smiling. "Thanks for insisting."

He pushed himself to his feet and then they filled in the hole and watered the tree into its new site.

"There. Done," Flynn finally said, thrusting the shovel into the earth one last time.

Mel pushed a stray curl out of her eyes and considered her orange tree. In its new position, it would get close to eight hours of clear sunlight a day. With a bit of luck, she might even get fruit this summer.

Reaching out a hand, she patted the trunk affectionately. "Over to you. Show us what you've got, baby," she said quietly.

Then she remembered she had an audience. When she glanced at Flynn, he was trying to hide a smile.

"Okay. So I talk to my plants occasionally," she admitted sheepishly.

"I read my tomatoes Shakespeare one year."

"Yeah, right." She squinted at him, sure he was making fun of her.

"I did, I swear. My mother's housekeeper swore her grandmother used to do it and got bumper crops."

"And?"

"I think I should have gone for one of the comedies instead of the Scottish play."

Mel's laugh was loud and heartfelt.

Flynn grinned, then checked his watch. "Whoa. It's nearly eleven. I'd better get going. I'm supposed to be doing the final inspection on Summerlea."

"You bought it? Oh, wow."

Usually the local grapevine was good for gossip, but she hadn't heard a whisper about the old estate being sold so she'd simply assumed that Flynn and Hayley had walked away from their inspection unimpressed.

"It's going to be a money pit, but I couldn't let Edna Walling's last great design slip through my fingers."

Mel couldn't hide her surprise. It was one thing to know how to transplant a tree, but to know the name of a long-dead, highly influential garden designer took his interest in gardening to a whole new level.

"What's wrong? Having visions of polo ponies again?" he asked wryly.

"No."

But he was right—she was. Mel was the first to admit she had some pretty set ideas about what people with money were like. She'd learned them firsthand at the feet of her husband and her in-laws. She'd seen the hypocrisy, the judgment, the insularity. She'd absorbed the politics, the values, the social mores. She knew where women of a certain income bracket liked to shop, who they allowed to cut their hair, how they preferred to keep their bodies lean and slim. She knew where the men lunched, the football clubs they supported, the charities they were happy to fund in return for a piece of the glory.

She'd assumed Flynn was like the rest of them, but apparently she'd assumed wrong.

He checked his watch again. "I'd really better get going."

"I'll walk you up." It was the least she could do after he'd saved her considerable effort and offered her what was clearly expert advice.

They walked side by side in silence. Mel wracked her brain for something innocuous to say, but the edgy feeling was back now they didn't have the task of transplanting the orange tree to occupy them. She snuck a look at him out of the corner of her eye but he seemed perfectly at ease.

"I can give you your key now if you'd like," she said. "Save you from having to collect it later."

"Sure, if that makes life easier for you."

"I was trying to make life easier for you."

They were approaching the house and Flynn

stooped to collect his jacket and sweater. He washed his hands on the garden tap at the bottom of the stairs as she raced into the house to grab the keys.

"You're not in Red Coat this time, I'm sorry. I had a previous booking, so you're in Tea Cutter, the cottage we passed on the way to plant the tree," she said as she descended the steps to rejoin him.

"I noticed there was another car in the parking lot. Interlopers."

She smiled at his small joke and handed the key over. "Good luck with your inspection. When do you take possession?"

"Next weekend."

She raised her eyebrows. "You don't muck around."

"You know what they say, life's short. It suited the vendors to have the sale go through quickly and it suited me."

He pulled his car keys from his jeans pocket and she realized she was holding him up.

"Take notes on the orchard grove for me." She took a backward step to signal she was letting him go. "I'm basing my new orchard on memories of my last visit to Summerlea so I might quiz you on it later."

He lifted an eyebrow. "Are you admitting to

shamelessly ripping off my new garden's design, Ms. Porter?"

"Um…yes?"

He laughed. "I'll take some photos for you." He turned to go, then swung back. "Unless you want to come to the inspection with me?"

It was her turn to laugh. "Sure. I could give you advice on your renovations. Tell you how a pro would do it."

"I'm serious. I'd actually appreciate hearing your opinion."

He *was* sincere, she could see it in his face. Once she got past her surprise, her first impulse was to say no—she'd gotten into the habit of saying no to a lot of things during her marriage, for a number of reasons—but it had been ten years since she'd seen the gardens at Summerlea. It would be beyond helpful to see how Edna Walling had designed the orchard and how the garden had matured.

Mel hesitated for a moment, then caught sight of her muddy jeans. She was caked from the knees down, her sweater blotched with yet more muck. The Lord only knew what was going on with her hair—something bad, she suspected, because it rarely behaved itself.

"Thanks for the offer, but I'm not really fit to be seen in public right now."

She indicated her muddy clothes.

"It'll only be me and the real estate agent. No film crews or paparazzi."

She opened her mouth to issue another polite excuse.

"All right. If I wouldn't be in the way," she heard herself say. "I'd love to come."

"Do you need to lock up?"

"I do. I won't be a tick."

She went into the house to secure the front door and grab her house keys, and all the while a voice in her head screamed at her to go back and tell him no, thank you, and send him on his way. The voice told her he was simply being polite, that he couldn't possibly really want her tagging along, that even if they'd had a perfectly nice, perfectly normal conversation, she was bound to say or do something wrong because that was what she always did.

She ignored it, because it was her husband's voice, and her mission over the past twelve months had been to get him out of her head now that she'd gotten him out of her life.

An ongoing challenge, obviously. But she was getting there.

Coat in hand, she pulled the door closed behind her and started down the stairs. "I'm ready."

CHAPTER FOUR

"WHEN WAS THE LAST TIME you saw Summerlea?" Flynn asked as he reversed out of the driveway.

Mel glanced at the man sitting beside her. "I guess about ten years. I attended the last open garden weekend they held."

"Really? So did I." He shot her a speculative look and she knew he was wondering if they'd crossed paths all those years ago.

She was almost certain they hadn't. Even though she hadn't known a Randall from a rhododendron then, she would have noticed him if she'd seen him. He was a strikingly handsome man, and she'd been twenty-one and constantly on the lookout for anyone of the opposite sex who was taller than her. He would have stood out as prime flirting material to her younger self.

"All the tea tree benches are gone," he said as he turned out of her street. "The roses are a thorny mess. And the herb garden is a flat-out disaster."

"I loved that herb garden," Mel said, remembering its pleasing mix of orderly English box hedge, sandstone paving and flourishing herb varieties. Edna Walling was famous for designing garden "rooms," and in Mel's opinion the herbal one had been among the most beautiful of the "rooms" at Summerlea.

"I'm telling you all this so you can be prepared," he said. "The old girl ain't what she used to be."

"I'll brace myself."

A silver car was parked beside the open main gate when they arrived. A portly, middle-aged man emerged from the driver's side and waved them onto the grounds. The gravel driveway was rutted and choked with weeds, and the car dipped from side to side as Flynn drove slowly past the house to where a dilapidated double garage stood.

"Okay. Let's go see what I've gotten myself into," Flynn said.

Mel unfolded herself from the low bucket seat and followed him as he walked down the driveway. The real estate agent was huffing and puffing his way toward them, his face already flushed with exertion.

"Spencer."

"Flynn. Good to see you again." The other man's grin was broad as he greeted Flynn. As well it might be——Flynn had guaranteed this man a very healthy payday by buying a property that had to be well into the millions.

"This is Mel, a friend," Flynn said easily.

"As you can see, Flynn dragged me away from the garden," she said when the other man glanced at her muddy clothes.

"More power to you. Draw the line at wielding the lawn mower myself, and even then I usually pay one of the local kids to do it." The agent switched his focus to Flynn. "I'm sorry to do this to you, but we've had a bit of an emergency come up and I need to cover another agent's open home. If it suits you, I thought I could leave you with the keys so you could look around at your leisure, then drop the keys at the office either today or tomorrow."

"Sure. No problem," Flynn said.

"Terrific, much appreciated. I hate having to bail on you like this but there's no one else available to fill in."

Mel drifted away as Flynn and the agent talked business for a few minutes. She was studying the bare branches of what she suspected was a flame azalea when Flynn joined her.

"The keys to the castle," he said, holding out his hand to reveal a chunky collection of keys, many of them old-fashioned skeleton keys.

"I hope he told you which one opens the front door."

There were at least twenty keys on the ring. Flynn looked alarmed for a minute before singling out a key that had been marked with an asterisk.

"What are the odds?"

"Are you feeling lucky, punk?" she asked, doing her best Clint Eastwood impersonation. "Well, are you?"

He grinned. "Let's see."

There was a new energy in him as he led the way toward the house. She studied him surreptitiously. She'd always thought of him as the epitome of sophistication—unfailingly well dressed, never at a loss. Yet right now he looked like a little boy on a visit to Disneyland.

He glanced her way and caught her looking. She racked her brain for something to say so he wouldn't think she'd been ogling him.

"I've never been inside Summerlea before, even though I think I've probably attended four or five open gardens over the years."

"You weren't missing much. I think Brian and Grace saved all their passion for the garden. Not that the place doesn't have good bones. They're just really well hidden."

They'd arrived at the foot of a set of six wide, brick steps. Mel tilted her head and shaded her eyes against the morning sun to examine the facade of the house. Built from the same mellow red brick as the steps, the house boasted a deep porch, with twin stained-glass doors for a suitably grand entrance. Matching bay windows lit the rooms on either side of the entrance, and wood fretwork decorated the eaves.

Flynn started up the steps. She followed him across the chipped and broken terra-cotta tiled porch. He glanced at her as he slid the key into the lock, eyebrows raised with comic trepidation.

"Dum, dum, dummmm." He turned the lock. The door opened with a mechanical snick.

"Phew," he said, but she knew he'd never been seriously worried.

Another thing she'd never expected of Flynn Randall—he was playful.

He stood to one side and gestured for her to precede him into the house.

She stepped into the front hall, breathing in the smell of damp and dust. She paused to give her eyes a chance to adjust to the dim interior. After a few seconds the world assumed shape and form again and she took in the wood-paneled walls, scuffed and discolored wooden floors and the high ceiling with its ornate, elaborate cornice and moldings and original light fittings.

"The living room's through here," Flynn said, directing her to the right.

She entered a large, light room. To her right

was a large bay window, its curve fitted with a seat, to her left a rather grand marble fireplace. The carpet was a faded Axminster floral. Darker patches near the walls and in the center of the room indicated where furniture had once sat. The far wall was punctuated by a series of French doors that looked out over the garden— not original, Mel suspected, but they offered a great outlook over the house's best feature.

"So. Am I nuts or what?" Flynn asked, and she realized he'd been watching her as she inspected the room.

"It needs a lot of work."

She glanced around the room again. The chimney breast was streaked with smoke stains, a sure sign that the chimney was either blocked or poorly constructed. There were two large, dark marks on the ceiling, which almost certainly meant a leak, and even from across the room she could see the rot in the French door frames.

"But you were right, it has great bones. This could be a very special house—once you've poured the equivalent of the GDP into it."

He laughed, then glanced around, his expression wryly self-aware. "Don't I know it."

He crossed the room to inspect the fireplace, crouching to peer under the mantel. His jeans stretched tightly across his thighs, revealing powerful muscles. Mel caught herself looking and glanced away, frowning.

"I might go check out the garden," she said.

"Sure. Take your time. I want to take some notes, start to get my head around the size of the renovation."

She crossed to the French doors and tried the handle. It gave beneath her fingers and she stepped out onto a paved patio area. Her shoulders dropped a notch the moment she felt fresh air on her face and she headed for the garden proper, feeling like a dog that had been let off its leash.

Her memories of the garden had blurred over the years, like slightly out-of-focus family snapshots, and she discovered it again as she walked. The herb garden, with its box-hedge border grown wild and woolly, and its pavers obscured by weeds; the lily pond, complete with bridge, and the water beneath a tangle of weeds. The rose garden, with its arbors and unkempt rows of roses.

She found the orchard where she'd remembered it, in the far southeast corner of the property. The trees had all grown enormously, and Mel guessed they hadn't been pruned in years. Long grass grew between them, and there was evidence of some sort of fungus on the peach trees. Sadness swept over her as she remembered how beautiful this place had once been, how much pride Brian and Grace had taken in maintaining a certain standard. It must have burned to let things slip this much as their aging bodies failed them. And now they'd had to give up their precious garden altogether.

She'd been exploring the orchard, making mental notes for her own more humble project for nearly twenty minutes, before it occurred to her that Flynn might be waiting for her at the house.

She started navigating her way through the garden, her stride long and urgent. Panic fluttered in her chest. He'd be angry with her for keeping him waiting and wasting his time. He'd be wondering why he'd bothered asking her to come, regretting his impulsive invitation. She'd be lucky if he hadn't simply driven off and left her to find her own way home.

She was aiming for the side patio entrance when she spotted Flynn leaning against the low stone wall near the rose garden. He lifted a hand in greeting and she altered her trajectory and joined him at the wall.

"I'm so sorry. I lost track of time," she said. "I was trying to work out what sort of fruit trees you've got down there and I guess I just got carried away—"

"Relax. I only got here myself. I've been exploring the outbuildings."

He said it easily, with a shrug of his shoulder, and it took a moment for it to sink in that he meant it.

He isn't Owen. You don't have to answer to anyone anymore.

Sudden, hot tears pushed at the back of her eyes. She recognized the reaction for what it was—a hangover from her marriage, a mental shortcut her mind had slipped into out of habit—but the last thing she wanted to do was bawl like a baby in front of Flynn.

She ducked her head, letting her hair fall over her face, and did her damnedest to stop the tears from falling.

"So have you successfully ripped off all the best design elements from my orchard?"

"Absolutely." Her voice sounded a little thick and she cleared her throat. She used the excuse of pushing her hair behind her ear to wipe a tear from her cheek. Then she took a deep breath, blinked a few more times and forced herself to make eye contact with him.

Like a normal person.

"You said outbuildings, plural. So there's more than the garage?"

His gaze swept over her face. She tensed, but

when he spoke his tone was even and utterly casual.

"Yep. There's a little dark building I suspect was once a dairy. And way over in the north corner there's a rusting monster of a shed, filled with enough old garden tools to start my own kibbutz."

"Really? I wonder if Brian and Grace realize they left them behind?"

"I'm going to talk to Spencer about it later, but I suspect they figured they wouldn't be needing them in a retirement village."

"No, I guess not."

Since he didn't seem inclined to leave yet, she leaned against the wall beside him and tried to regain her equilibrium. She stared at the toes of her work boots, angry with herself and a little scared. She'd thought she was over the worst of her divorce. She'd survived the dark early days, held her head high through the ugliness of the settlement, and now she had her own place, her own life, her friends and family around her.

So why was she slipping into old behaviors? Why, out of nowhere, had she suddenly lapsed into Old Mel?

Old Mel, who had run herself ragged trying to be good. Old Mel, who had developed the act of effacement into an art form.

"I know it's a jungle at the moment, but it's still bloody beautiful."

Mel glanced at the man sitting next to her, pulled out of her introspection. He was gazing over the land, the edges of his mouth curled in an almost smile. She turned to consider the view, taking in the sweeping lawn and the nearby stand of silver birches, the overgrown garden beds with their flowing, natural lines, and the distant winter skeletons of a stand of oak trees.

It *was* a jungle—overgrown and unruly, unbalanced and messy. But it was also calm and green and real.

The churning in her stomach slowed. She took a deep breath, let it out again.

"It's not bad," she said, her tone deliberately low-key.

Flynn gave her a dry sideways look. Despite everything, she found herself smiling a little.

"It's a shame about those benches," he said, his eyes on the view once more.

"There's a guy at the farmers' market in the village sometimes. I don't know his name, but he works with local timber and driftwood."

"When's the next market?"

"It's the first Sunday of every month, so you just missed it."

"Huh."

They lapsed into a companionable silence.

Then Flynn gave a sigh and pushed himself to his feet.

"I guess I'd better hand the keys back," he said with obvious reluctance.

"Don't worry, it's only ten days or so till settlement."

"That's ten whole sleeps. Pure torture."

Mel's laughter burst out of her, as unexpected as his comment. He was like a kid with a new toy.

Or someone fulfilling a lifetime dream.

She studied his profile, intrigued by the idea. "You've always wanted this place, haven't you?"

"I believe the correct word is *covet.* And yes, I have. I have coveted the hell out of this place ever since I was old enough to understand who Edna Walling was and how freaking amazing this design is."

"Well, congratulations. That's very cool. It's not every day a man gets his lifelong dream."

By unspoken accord, they turned and started walking toward the house.

"True. So why do I have this cynical voice in my head saying 'Be careful what you wish for'?"

"Don't listen to that voice. Stick a sock in its mouth. There's nothing wrong with this place that you can't fix."

He was silent for a long moment, then he gave

her a warm look. "Thanks for coming with me today, Mel. I appreciate it."

There was a shadow in his eyes as they found hers. For the briefest of moments he looked almost sad. Lonely, even. Then he was busy pulling his car keys from his pocket and checking his phone for messages, and the moment had passed.

Mel scoffed at herself. The man walking beside her had everything. He was handsome, wealthy, successful, respected, sought after. No way was he lonely.

As if.

FLYNN KEPT UP A steady stream of conversation as he locked Summerlea and led Mel to his car. He talked about some of his plans for the house, the state of the lawns, the contents of the toolshed he'd discovered. As they drove to her place, he talked about the weather, the local village, her business. He tap-danced his ass off, keeping things light and breezy.

Anything to keep her smiling and laughing and engaged.

She'd been close to tears earlier. She'd looked so wounded, so abject as she'd apologized for keeping him waiting. For long seconds he'd been sure she was going to lose it, and he'd been on the verge of offering her a shoulder or a handkerchief or a word of comfort. Then she'd pulled herself together and it was as though the moment had never happened.

Except it had.

There had been that other moment when they were transplanting the orange tree, too. He'd made that crack about Hamish Greggs being an ungrateful ass and she'd stared at him as though she couldn't quite believe her ears. As though no one had ever said anything even remotely supportive to her about that night.

It was beginning to dawn on him that perhaps Owen Hunter was a bigger dick than Flynn had ever believed. He'd never had much time for the guy—it seemed to him that Owen was always on the make, always desperate to flash his wealth around and assert his social superiority—but he'd never considered Hunter truly malicious. Until now.

Flynn had always been pleased to see Mel when he ran into her over the years, even though they'd never really had a chance to get beneath each other's social veneers—a brief conversation at so-and-so's charity fundraiser or what's-his-name's cocktail party was hardly conducive to forming a deep understanding of another human being. But he'd liked the *sense* of Mel that he'd garnered from those superficial meetings.

He didn't like the thought that Owen had put

that wounded look in her eyes. Didn't like to think about what a man might do or say to a woman to make her so tentative and wary.

Mel unclipped her seat belt the moment he pulled to a stop in her guest parking area.

"Thanks for letting me poach some ideas. I promise not to rip them off too slavishly." The nervousness was back. She was practically humming with it.

"Thanks for keeping me company."

She gave him that uncertain smile again, then reached for the door handle. "Enjoy the rest of your stay."

She slipped from the car and shut the door firmly behind herself before he could think of an excuse to keep her talking. By the time he climbed out she was halfway to the house, her stride brisk.

He stared at her rapidly retreating back, wondering. Then he grabbed his gear and made his way through the garden to Tea Cutter Cottage.

He might like Mel, but she was none of his business. His dance card was full to overflowing with his father's illness and Randall Developments. And now, of course, he could add the beautiful, impractical, expensive white elephant that was Summerlea to the list.

As what had happened with Hayley had so

brutally illustrated, he was not in a position to be interested in a woman.

He let himself into the cottage. He dropped his bag in the bedroom, then walked to the kitchen and put the kettle on. Five minutes later, he opened the rear door and sat on the steps that looked out over the garden. The temperature had dropped a little, but he simply turned up the collar on his coat and curled his hands around his coffee cup.

For the first time in a long time, he had nowhere to be, and no one relying on him for anything.

He stayed on the step for a long time.

TWO WEEKS LATER, Mel exited the local bakery and collided with a wall of hard, male chest.

"I'm so sorry—" She looked up into Flynn's blue eyes and forgot the rest of her apology. "Oh, hi."

"Hi. How are you doing, neighbor?"

She glanced over his shoulder, expecting to see Hayley, but he appeared to be alone. Again.

"I'm good, thanks." She straightened her sweater, wondering why she always seemed to be at her worst when she ran into him. Last time she'd been covered in mud, this time she was covered in paint splatter. Then a thought occurred. "You're here to pick up your keys, aren't you? Summerlea is yours."

He held up a chunky key ring and gave it a triumphant shake to confirm her guess.

"Congratulations. That's great. Are you staying the weekend?"

"I am. Although it's going to be interesting."

He lifted the shopping bag he was holding and she saw he'd bought what looked to be a month's supply of candles in all shapes and sizes. It took her a moment to join the dots together.

"You don't have power?"

He shrugged sheepishly. "Some idiot forgot to have the utilities connected. So I'm camping out, old-school style."

She frowned. "You know the temperature is going to drop into the low single figures overnight, right?"

"Brian and Grace didn't quite get around to installing central heating, so I'm not missing out on anything there. But there's a woodpile the size of a small country behind the garage so I figure I'll be right."

All very well for him to say, but he had no idea how cold it got here on the peninsula sometimes. Without all the concrete of a city to hold the heat of the day, the nights could be bitterly cold. Recently, Mel had had to resort to using two quilts on the bed as well as her electric blanket to keep the chill out.

"Come and stay in one of my cottages," she said impulsively. "I've only got two bookings this weekend, and you can have your choice of Tea Cutter or Windrush. It'll be my housewarming present to you."

"Thanks for the offer, but I'm actually kind of looking forward to camping out. I'm about to go buy some cheese and wine, and I'm going to hunker down in front of one of the fireplaces and pretend I'm living in another century."

He almost made it sound attractive, but she knew better. She gave him a dry look.

"I'll leave the key to Tea Cutter under the front door mat if you change your mind in the middle of the night."

He laughed. "Ye of little faith."

"What can I say? I'm a pragmatist. A pragmatist who likes to be warm."

A woman with a stroller was approaching and Mel touched Flynn's forearm to alert him to the fact. Together they moved out of the woman's path so they could continue their conversation.

"How's the orange tree?" Flynn asked.

"I was a little worried after the first week but I found new growth on a couple of the branch tips yesterday. I figure that's a good sign." She looked to him for confirmation, since he clearly knew far more about these things than she did.

"It is. You might want to give it a gentle feed with something organic, too. Help it establish a new root system."

"Thanks. I will."

She suddenly became aware of how close they were. Somehow, in moving aside for the stroller, they'd also moved together, and she could see the small crease marks at the corners of his eyes and the smile lines around his mouth. If she inhaled deeply, there was a very real chance her breasts would brush his arm.

Quickly she took a step backward, something close to panic tightening her belly.

"You probably have tons to do. And I need to get back to my painting," she said.

"What are you painting?"

"The bathroom." She took another step backward. "Good luck with your campout. The key will be under the mat if you need it."

"It's generous of you, but I won't."

He was watching her with the same very focused intensity that she'd noticed at Summerlea two weeks ago. She made a big deal out of shuffling her bags around before offering him a small farewell wave.

"See you around."

She turned and walked away. It wasn't until

she passed the butcher's shop that she remembered her car was parked in the opposite direction. She glanced over her shoulder, but Flynn was still in front of the bakery, his phone in his hand. Feeling like a teenager, she took the long way around, past the supermarket and through the parking lot until she'd done a loop and could approach her car from behind.

You're an idiot.

It was true, for more reasons than she cared to count, not least of which was the fact that her heart was pounding out a fast, heated beat beneath her breastbone.

She threw her bags into the back of her car and climbed in. It was tempting to lie to herself and put her body's reaction down to the fact that she'd taken a completely unnecessary walk around the block, but Mel knew better. Standing so close to Flynn for those few seconds, she'd suddenly remembered that he was a man and she a woman and that it had been a long time since she'd felt the warm press of another body against her own.

On one hand, she understood why it had happened. He was handsome, after all, and he'd been nice to her. A woman would have to be dead from the neck down not to respond to his strong, very male body and natural charm.

The thing was, Mel had thought she *was* dead

from the neck down. But apparently she wasn't. For the past year, she'd been in survival mode. She'd done what needed to be done to keep her head above water and no more. There had been a certain comfort in her batten-down-the-hatches mentality—she hadn't asked too much from the world, hadn't risked herself, hadn't expected too much from herself.

But now the nonessential parts of her life appeared to be coming back online. The parts that got lonely and horny and enjoyed flirting and laughing with a man. How…strange. She'd honestly thought she would never be interested in a man again. Naive, perhaps. Or maybe it had simply been a way to get through those hard first months. Whatever the reason, the notion that she might be ready to reenter the world of male-female relations made her feel more than a little anxious and panicky.

Because even if her body was ready, her mind wasn't. Not even close. It would be a long, long time before she was ready to trust a man again.

She forced herself to take a deep breath and calm down. She was freaking out over nothing, over nobody.

After all, on the most basic of levels, even if she had felt the stir of desire as she stood next to Flynn and registered his body heat and looked at his mouth and inhaled his scent, it wasn't as though anything would come of it. The man was in a relationship with someone else, a beautiful, sophisticated woman from his own world. The chances of anything happening between her and Flynn were nonexistent.

Her thoughts slowed as her anxiety receded and common sense returned. A long time ago, before Owen, before she'd been stripped of her confidence and sense of herself, she'd enjoyed sex. Not indiscriminately, but it had been a normal, healthy part of her life. It wasn't exactly a miracle that her sexual self was rising from the ashes of her marriage in the same way that so many other aspects of her self had. Her sense of humor. Her pride. Her determination. It was a good sign. A sign that she was healing.

Feeling more rational, she started her car and headed for the certainty of home.

CHAPTER FIVE

FLYNN BREATHED IN THE COOL winter air as he walked toward the house later that day, allowing the fact that he was here and this was real and that he was actually doing this to sink into his bones. Yes, restoring Summerlea was going to be a huge challenge, but it was doable. It was definitely doable.

He'd spent the past few hours completing a slow, painstaking tour of the garden. He had a list as long as his arm of basic maintenance issues to attend to, and he mentally allocated his free time to tasks as he climbed the stairs. It didn't take a rocket scientist to know that it would take him a long time to turn things around here, doing it piecemeal, when his schedule allowed. A lot of people would simply throw money at it and let other people make the problems go away, but Flynn hadn't bought Summerlea to delegate. Once, he'd hoped to spend his life making other people's gardens beautiful, livable and sustainable. He'd given that dream up, but Summerlea offered him a different outlet for his passion.

Some people might call it a sop, and maybe it was. But it was his sop, and he was bloody well going to give it his all.

He kicked his shoes off inside the door, then padded around the house in his socks, washed his hands and finally carried the groceries he'd bought for dinner from the kitchen to the living room. He lit half a dozen candles, then set a match to the fire he'd laid earlier. Flames licked up the kindling and flared along the logs and he felt a very primitive sense of satisfaction.

Me man, me make fire.

Smirking at his own idiocy, he turned his thoughts to dinner. He'd bought a range of goodies—a truly indulgent picnic, really. A round of brie, gourmet crackers, olives stuffed with almonds and feta, tiny bell peppers filled with goat's cheese, salty cashew nuts, a long, thin loaf of Afghan bread slathered with garlic, triple-smoked ham. For dessert, he had a slab of fruit and nut chocolate, and he had a choice of either an Australian shiraz or a New Zealand pinot noir to accompany his feast.

He was unwrapping the creamy-looking round of brie and contemplating which bottle of wine to open when he heard what he thought was a knock at the front door. He stilled, head cocked to one side. Sure enough, after a few seconds the knock sounded again.

He walked into the hall, baffled as to who it might be. The only people he knew in Mount Eliza were Mel and Spencer, the real estate agent. Given the way Mel had retreated when he'd bumped into her in town, he figured the odds were good it was Spencer. Which was a bummer, for a number of reasons.

Then he opened the door and recognized Mel's tall, athletic silhouette in the deeper gloom of the porch.

"Mel. Hey," he said, genuinely surprised.

"Oh. You're here." She made a nervous gesture with her hand. "When you didn't answer, I thought maybe you'd gone out. I was just going to leave these here for you...."

For the first time he registered the two lanterns and a bottle of what looked to be kerosene at her feet.

"I found these in my shed when I was tidying up this afternoon and thought of you," she explained.

"I think that's the nicest thing anyone has said to me all week."

She smiled, then moved away. Her car keys jingled in her hand. She was about to run again.

"Hang on to them for as long as you like."

She started to take another step backward but he reached out and caught her wrist.

"Not so fast. Before you go rushing off again, I need to make an unmanly confession—I have no idea how to light one of these things."

Her wrist was warm in his hand. He could feel her pulse beneath his fingertips.

"They're pretty simple." She tugged lightly on her wrist and he let her go.

"Does that mean you won't come in and have a glass of wine with me and show me what to do?"

She glanced over her shoulder, almost as though there was someone waiting for her in the car. For the first time it occurred to him that maybe there was, that maybe she had somewhere else to be.

Someone else to be with.

She was an attractive woman, after all. Young, single. The odds were good that the first guy with eyes in his head had snapped her up once her divorce was finalized.

"Unless I'm stepping on someone else's toes?" he asked.

"No. I just— Sure, I can show you how to light them."

He noticed that she'd avoided responding to the rest of his invitation. He grabbed one of the lanterns by its wire handle and held the door wide while she collected the second and the bottle of kerosene. She entered the house and he gestured for her to head into the living room. Firelight cast a warm glow over the room, while the few candles he'd lit created their own small pools of light.

"Do you have matches or a lighter?" Mel asked as she placed her lantern to the left of where he'd set up his camping gear.

He pulled the box of matches from his hip pocket and handed them over. She knelt in front of the first lantern, carefully pouring kerosene into the tank below the wick. A strand of her long, curly hair slid over her cheek and she pushed it back impatiently. She put the lamp together, then lifted the glass shade. A match flared to life in her hand and she applied it to the wick. It took immediately, burning with a bright blue-and-orange flame before settling down. She slid the glass into place and a warm glow spread out from the lantern.

"That's more like it. Much more civilized," he said.

Mel glanced at him briefly, her mouth curved into that uncertain smile of hers. Then she shifted to the second lantern and repeated the process.

While she was occupied, he opened the bottle of shiraz and poured wine into two of the plastic tumblers he'd bought along with his other supplies that morning.

"There you go," Mel said as the second lantern came to life. "When you want to shut them off, just lift the glass and blow out the flame. They can be a bit smelly, so make sure the room stays ventilated."

She pushed herself to her feet and he held out the glass of wine. She shook her head immediately. "I can't."

"Somewhere else to be?"

"Not exactly…"

"Giving wine up for Lent?"

She smiled slightly. "No."

"Then have a drink with me. It's my first night in Summerlea and, while I don't have anything against swilling a whole bottle of wine on my own, as a rule I prefer company."

She hesitated for a moment longer before taking the glass. "Thank you."

"Have a seat," he said, waving toward the array of pillows and rolled-up bedding he'd fashioned into a couch of sorts. "I can offer you a pillow, or a rolled-up sleeping bag and sleeping pad. Nothing but the best."

She looked as though she wanted to say no again—no doubt she'd planned to simply stand there and gulp down her wine before making a bolt for the door—but after another one of those maddening hesitations she crossed to the fire and knelt to the right of the hearth, her wine in one hand. He'd set the chopping board on top of an old crate he'd found in the kitchen and he crouched there now and cut the brie into bite-size wedges.

"You should know I have victuals as well as wine," he said, sliding the chopping board toward her. "This is a quality establishment."

"I can't eat your dinner."

"Trust me. There's plenty. My eyes are bigger than my belly. Always have been."

He started peeling lids off deli containers until the peppers, olives and ham were arrayed in front of her. He added the bread, crackers and cashew nuts then reached for his wineglass. Holding it high, he offered a toast.

"To Summerlea, and camping out, and finger food." He leaned forward to clink his glass against hers.

She frowned, but didn't say anything. He waited until she'd taken a mouthful before nudging the cheese toward her.

"Eat something. I dare you."

Her gaze shot to his face, startled, and he raised his eyebrows. After a few seconds she grabbed an olive, popped it into her mouth and bit down almost defiantly.

He felt a ridiculous surge of triumph. She was staying. For now.

He tried to think of something to say that would put her at ease. His gaze fell on the lanterns. "So did you do much camping when you were younger?"

"Yes. Every summer, pretty much. It was the only way we could afford a family vacation."

"Where did you go?"

"Dad likes to fish, so we always had to be near water of some kind. Lake Eildon, Eden, Merimbula, Wilson's Promontory."

"Did you like it?"

She thought about it for a moment. "You know, mostly I did. At the time I thought I didn't. But in hindsight, those holidays were some of the best times we ever had as a family."

"Did you sit around the campfire holding hands and singing 'Kumbaya'?"

"Why? Are you about to break into song?"

He laughed. "Hardly." He tore off a hunk of bread and passed it to her before tearing a second hunk for himself. "I always wanted to go camping when I was a kid but Mom hates sleeping rough. Which is pretty funny, given how much she loves gardening. She always says that if there's no hot and cold running water, she's not interested."

"Mostly, I agree with her. But I'm prepared to

make an exception every now and then. There are some parts of the world you can't see without roughing it."

She was starting to lose the tense, wary look around her eyes. Flynn settled against the rolled-up sleeping bag. The fire was really throwing out some heat now. Or maybe it was the wine warming his belly. Either way, he could feel the week's worries slipping away.

"Tell me, have you ever had to deal with a blackberry thicket?" he asked.

"Yep. Got the scars to prove it, too."

"I've got a huge one on the western boundary. About five meters long by two meters thick."

She whistled. "Impressive."

"I know received wisdom is to poison them, but I'm not a fan of using chemicals in the garden if I can avoid it."

"You're thinking of digging it out?"

"I guess I am, since that's the only alternative."

She grimaced. "Horrible job. I did it once. It's not just a matter of cutting it back, you have to dig the roots out—and you have to dig deep, too. Anything you miss will sprout again in spring. Took me months to get on top of mine."

"Yeah, I'm anticipating a battle. I'm trying to work out whether I should tackle it first or prune the orchard."

"Blackberries, definitely. Those bad boys will take over if you let them go. I tell you what, I'll drop my brush-cutter off for you tomorrow. That'll break the back of it above ground for you, at the very least."

"That'd be great, thanks. But only if it won't be leaving you high and dry."

She waved a hand to indicate she wasn't fussed, then helped herself to some ham. She re-settled with her legs stretched out to the side, her tumbler of wine within easy reach. The firelight struck auburn notes in her dark hair, and the heat had put a bloom in her cheeks. Of its own accord, his gaze slid below her neck to where her fuzzy blue sweater covered her full, round breasts.

He dragged his gaze away. He hadn't asked her in for a drink so he could stare at her breasts— even if they were very, very nice.

"So, have you got any ideas for how you're going to renovate the house yet?" she asked.

"Not a single one."

She laughed and shook her head. "You're such a gardener."

"Guilty as charged. I have a friend who's an interior designer. I might let her loose on it."

She raised her eyebrows. "Won't Hayley have something to say about that?"

He shouldn't have been surprised that she assumed he and Hayley were still a couple. After all, five weeks ago they'd arrived arm-in-arm to stay in one of Mel's cottages together. But he was, and it took him a moment to formulate a reply.

"Hayley and I aren't seeing each other anymore."

"Oh. I'm sorry to hear that." She took a big gulp of her wine, her swallow audible. Her free hand smoothed down her thigh before gripping her leg above her knee. Tightly, if her white knuckles were anything to go by.

"It's okay, Mel. I didn't invite you in so I could jump your bones." He'd meant it half as a joke, half as reassurance, but she only grew more tense.

"I should go," she said abruptly. She set her glass on the hearth and stood. She seemed impossibly tall viewed from his prone position, with her features limned by firelight and her curls a halo around her face and shoulders.

"Okay," he said, more than a little baffled by how quickly their conversation had shifted. He swallowed the last of his wine, then stood and led her to the door. The cold night air was a shock after the coziness of the living room.

"Thanks for the drink," she said as she moved past him to the porch.

"Thanks for bringing the lanterns. And for being my first visitor."

She rolled a shoulder, brushing off his gratitude. "Have a good night."

She disappeared into the darkness. He stood in the doorway listening to her retreating footsteps. After a while there was nothing but silence, then he heard the faint, distant sound of a car starting. He shut the door and returned to the living room, where he threw more wood on the fire and poured himself another glass of wine. Then he stretched out, his head supported by the sleeping bag.

He couldn't work her out. Every time he saw her she seemed to be walking on eggshells—when she wasn't backing away at a million miles an hour. He'd practically had to hold her at gunpoint to get her to accept a glass of wine.

Yet she'd gone out of her way to bring him the lanterns tonight, and he bet if he arrived at her place at three in the morning, he'd find the key to Tea Cutter Cottage beneath her doormat.

He thought about how she'd looked, standing above him a few minutes ago outlined by firelight, and acknowledged to himself—at last—that he found her attractive. Very attractive.

He always had.

And maybe he'd lied when he'd said he hadn't invited her in to jump her bones.

If he closed his eyes, he could still remember in vivid detail how she'd looked rising out of the fountain at the Hollands' that night, her gown glued to every curve and hollow of her body. Over a year and a half had passed, but that moment was still etched in his memory as though it was yesterday.

That didn't mean he was going to do anything about it. No matter how sexy her tall, athletic body was. No matter how compelling he found her soft gray eyes and wide, mobile mouth.

Someone had hurt Mel Porter. Quite badly, if he was any judge. She was vulnerable. Maybe even a little broken.

He was the very last thing she needed in her life. As he'd proven so thoroughly with Hayley, he was not a good bet in the romance department right now. He had too much on his plate, too much uncertainty in his world, and he didn't want to set up expectations that he wasn't going to fulfill again. At best, he was good for some no-strings sex and some laughs, but Mel was not fling material. Not by a long shot.

He took a long swallow of wine and told himself it was a good thing she'd gone home.

By the time he'd finished his third glass, he had almost convinced himself it was true, too.

MEL CHASTISED HERSELF the whole drive home. She'd known taking the lanterns to Flynn's place had been a bad idea. From the moment she'd spotted them in her garden shed this afternoon she'd been at war with herself, going back and forth over whether she should drop by Summerlea and offer them to Flynn or not.

She'd been worried the gesture would come across as sucky or ingratiating, as though she was desperate for Flynn to like her. In the end she'd convinced herself that if she dropped them off and didn't try to parlay the brief contact into anything further, there was no way he could misconstrue her intentions as anything other than what they were—a friendly, neighborly gesture.

Then he'd asked her to show him how to light the lanterns, and the next thing she'd known she had a glass of wine in one hand and a piece of brie in the other.

Not what she'd anticipated, although she'd be lying if she pretended that she hadn't enjoyed their conversation—until the moment he'd revealed he and Hayley had broken up.

A hot flush of embarrassment washed over Mel as she remembered the way she'd bolted for the door after he'd made that crack about jumping her bones. With the benefit of hindsight it was clear to her that he'd seen her tension and had been trying to put her at ease—and she'd responded by behaving like a scared rabbit.

Very sophisticated and adult. God, she was an idiot. She should have listened to her first instincts and simply stayed away from Summerlea and Flynn Randall.

She threw her keys onto the kitchen counter as she entered the house and crossed to the sink. Pouring herself a glass of water, she drank deeply. The empty glass thunked loudly against the counter as she set it down with too much force. She stared out the window past the dim reflection of her own features.

The world outside was dark and still. In contrast, she was buzzing with adrenaline, her head filled with mixed-up thoughts and half-acknowledged emotions.

She'd read the self-help books. She knew this was all standard fare for a woman recovering from psychological abuse. Knew, too, that it would take years for her to regain her confidence fully. If she ever did. It was a day-by-day battle to recover herself. Hour by hour.

Weariness washed over her. She was so sick of feeling anxious and uncertain. So sick of always doubting herself and second-guessing her every move.

Once upon a time, she'd been fearless. She'd been brave and confident and bold. She'd set off for London with two pairs of jeans, a pair of boots, half a dozen T-shirts and less than a thousand dollars in her bank account. She'd thrown herself into the adventure of travel—picked fruit, pulled beers, cleaned houses, packed boxes—done whatever it took to make enough money to live and move onto the next new place. She'd made great friends, had amazing experiences. Then she'd met Owen and fallen in love. The ultimate adventure. Or so she'd thought.

She'd come home and become Mrs. Melanie Hunter, and bit by bit, Mel Porter had slowly ceased to be, thanks to a concerted campaign by her husband to try to turn her into something other than what she was.

I want her back. I want to be that brave and confident again. I want to laugh without looking over my shoulder to see who is judging me. I want to just be.

She'd been trying. She'd been silencing the voice in her head whenever it started in on her—the voice that sometimes sounded like Owen, and sometimes like his mother. Mel had been doing her best to reconnect with her family and her old friends. She'd even been making a point of doing something impulsive every now and then, the way she used to before second-guessing herself had become a way of life.

She had no idea if any of it was making a difference, but she didn't know what else to do, either.

Her gaze shifted, focusing on the ghostlike reflection in the window instead of the yard outside. The woman staring back at her looked so sad and lost that she felt an instinctive surge of compassion for her.

You'll get there. Don't worry. You'll muddle your way through.

Turning away, she flicked off the light and walked to her bedroom. The familiar bedtime routine of washing her face and brushing her teeth was infinitely soothing, a form of behavioral valium, and she climbed into bed and pulled the quilt high around her shoulders.

Rather than give her whirling thoughts more oxygen, she very deliberately called up an image of her orchard-to-be.

Her brow furrowed with concentration, she began to plan her design. After a few minutes, her brow smoothed out.

Not long after that, she slipped into the forgetfulness and comfort of sleep.

THE FIRST THING Mel remembered the next morning was that she'd promised her brush-cutter to Flynn so he could tackle his blackberries.

She groaned, covering her face with her hands.

Everything in her rebelled at the thought of facing him again after her undignified retreat last night. There was no way he didn't know why she'd left—she might as well have hung a sign over her head with the words *I'm sexually aware of you* glowing in hot pink neon, the way she'd scrambled for the exit the moment he'd mentioned he was single.

He probably doesn't expect to see you, anyway. He probably thinks you made an off-the-cuff offer and won't be surprised if you don't follow through.

She seized on the idea the moment it registered. People made offers all the time that they didn't follow through on. *Come over for dinner sometime, we'll have to catch up, blah, blah.* It wouldn't be the end of the world if she simply… forgot to take her brush-cutter over to Summerlea.

Except, of course, that it would make her a big old yellow-bellied scaredy-cat. A cowardly custard who made excuses for herself instead of facing up to the world. Last night, she'd stood at her kitchen sink and grieved for the bold, adventurous, confident woman she'd once been. The only way she was going to get her back was to start challenging herself, pushing herself to move past all the little safety mechanisms she'd built into her life to protect herself and please her ex-husband.

She threw off the sheets and rolled out of bed. Then she showered and breakfasted and went out to collect the brush-cutter from the shed. She checked the oil, filled it with fuel and switched the bump-feed line head for the brush-cutting blade. Then she put all the necessary accessories together in a recyclable bag and loaded it into her car. She was about to head over to Summerlea when both sets of her guests appeared to hand in their keys and extend their thanks for a relaxing stay. She directed them to local cafés with reputations for good breakfasts and handed out winery trail maps and a guide to the Tyabb antiques market in case they wanted to see a little more of the area before heading home. Then she girded her loins and drove over to Summerlea.

She collected the brush-cutter and accessories and did battle with the rusty gate latch before marching up the path. Her boots sounded very heavy and loud on the porch as she crossed to the front door.

She knocked, the sound echoing inside the house. Flynn didn't answer immediately and she rested the brush-cutter on the porch and knocked again. When nothing but silence greeted her, she walked around the house to double-check that his car was still there. It was.

He was obviously in the garden somewhere, even though it was still early. She could leave the equipment on the porch for him to find later. It was the perfect win-win—she would have fulfilled her obligation without having to look him in the eyes after last night's cut and run.

Sure, why not do that, you big old wuss? Then you could swing by the supermarket on the way home and grab enough canned food and bottled water so that you don't have to leave the house for the next six months.

She sighed. This being-brave, reclaiming-her-old-self business was hard work. Hoisting the cutter over her shoulder, she headed into the garden.

He'd mentioned the blackberry thicket was on the western boundary, so she headed there first. She walked along the sweep of lawn and onto a meandering forest path. She heard Flynn before she saw him, a colorful string of swear words floating to her on the breeze.

She found him in a small clearing that was dominated by a huge, bristling wall of blackberry bushes. The scattering of cut canes at his feet suggested he'd already launched his assault, but for the moment he was standing with his head bowed, a pair of hedge shears and thick gardening gloves at his feet as he examined a scratch on the back of his bare hand.

She took a deep breath. "Hi."

His head snapped around, the frown sliding from his face when he saw her. "Hey."

Even though her toes were curled inside her boots with self-consciousness, it was impossible not to feel warmed by the welcome in his eyes.

"You're up early," she said.

"I've never been good at sleeping in."

"Me, either. Is it bad?" she asked, gesturing toward his hand.

"I'll live." His gaze shifted to the brush-cutter slung over her shoulder. "If that's what I think it is, I may have to kiss your feet."

"I told you I'd bring it over."

He didn't say anything and she knew they were both thinking about the way she'd bolted last night.

She cleared her throat. "Have you, um, used one of these before?"

"Only as a line trimmer." He crossed to her side as she lowered the head of the cutter to the ground.

"It's pretty simple. You prime the engine here, then use the pull cord. It usually starts the first time, but if it doesn't, try priming it again. Here, I'll show you."

He moved closer, his shoulder brushing hers as she angled the motor so he could see the priming button. She tried to ignore the smell of his deodorant as she pumped the primer a few times, then pulled the cord. The engine sprang to noisy life.

"Look at that. More reliable than my car," he said.

Out of the corner of her eye she could see that he was smiling, but she didn't dare look directly at him. She couldn't. He was standing too close.

"So this is the throttle, yeah?" he asked, pointing to the orange control halfway down the shaft. "And I assume this is the safety stop switch?"

"Exactly. I brought you some protective gear, too. The blade kicks up a lot of debris."

She handed the brush-cutter over and watched as Flynn put the harness on so that the strap ran diagonally across his chest, the weight of the machine balanced near his hip. He frowned, adjusting it first to one side of his body, then to the other.

"It's sitting a little high," she said. "You're taller than me."

"I'm not sure an inch really counts."

"I thought inches always counted with men. Sometimes twice." She had no idea where the comment came from, but it was out her mouth before she could catch herself.

He let out a crack of laughter.

"Sorry," she said automatically.

"What for? For being funny?"

It was on the tip of her tongue to say yes. Owen had hated her smart mouth. "Women don't tell jokes," he'd once told her. "It's unfeminine. And let's face it, you need all the help you can get in that department."

She'd gotten used to guarding her words, in the same way that she'd gotten used to thinking twice before she did anything.

"If you stand still, I'll adjust that for you," she said, indicating the harness.

She stepped closer. The adjustable buckle lay low on Flynn's belly, above the waistband of his jeans. Her fingers brushed hard stomach muscles through his sweater as she lifted the strap away from his body.

"Can you take the weight off the harness for a moment?" she asked.

He did so wordlessly, lifting the brush-cutter so the harness hung loosely. She fed more strap through the buckle, lengthening the harness by a good couple of inches.

"There. That should do it."

She made the mistake of looking up before she moved away. His blue eyes, clear and sharp, seemed very bright this morning as they looked into hers. As though he could see all the way through to her soul.

"Thanks, Mel."

Flustered, she bent to collect the safety equipment, passing over the hearing protectors and face mask.

"I feel like I should be terrorizing teenagers in *Friday the 13th*," he said as he pulled on the mask.

"Trust me, five seconds from now you'll be grateful for it."

He engaged the throttle experimentally before moving in on the blackberries for an experimental pass, the brush-cutter buzzing like an angry hornet. She stood to one side, watching his technique. After a few seconds she strode forward and touched his shoulder to get his attention.

He turned his head, eyebrows raised in question.

"Sweep it in more of an arc," she yelled over the noise of the engine. "And it spits stuff out to the left, so if you keep stepping right, you should avoid walking into anything."

He gave her a thumbs-up. She retreated again and watched as he followed her advice. After a few seconds he glanced at her for feedback and she gave him an okay signal.

He let the brush-cutter slow to an idle and pushed the safety mask high on his head.

"Thanks for this. You're a lifesaver."

"Hang on to it as long as you need it. And it's four-stroke, so if it runs out of fuel it takes plain unleaded."

"Noted, thanks." He hesitated a moment, then took a step toward her. "Listen, Mel—"

The sharp ring of a cell phone filled the clearing. Flynn looked rueful. "You ever wonder what we did before these things?" he asked as he slid a sleek handset from his back pocket.

"We waited till Monday."

He smiled faintly. "Yeah, we did, didn't we?"

He glanced briefly at the display and the smile faded from his mouth, his gaze sharpening as he took the call.

"Mom," he said into the phone.

Mel turned away, not wanting him to think she was eavesdropping.

"How long has he been gone?"

His tone was unexpectedly curt and she glanced back at him. His expression was stony, his body tense as he directed all his energy to the phone call.

"Have you called the police?"

She frowned. It sounded as though there had been a break-in. Or maybe someone was lost.

"Don't worry about that. Call them. I'll be there as soon as I can. And Mom, don't worry. We'll find him, I promise." He ended the call.

"I have to go. Sorry." He started shrugging out of the harness. His face was pale, his lips pressed into a thin, straight line. Clearly, whatever was going on was an emergency.

She stepped forward, hand extended. "Here, give it to me. I'll pack all this up and leave it in the garage so you can tackle the job another time."

"Thanks. I appreciate it, Mel." He handed the brush-cutter over, but hesitated before heading off.

"Go. Seriously," she said, shooing him off with her free hand.

"I owe you."

She shooed him off again and he smiled briefly before turning on his heel and heading for the house, his stride long and urgent. Within seconds he'd disappeared around the bend in the path.

She collected his gloves and hedge clippers, stowed the safety gear back in the bag and hoisted the brush-cutter over her shoulder. She walked toward the house, wondering all the way what could possibly have happened to make him so tense and worried so quickly.

Whatever it was, it was obviously a private matter. Otherwise he would have said something.

She was approaching the house when she heard a high-pitched mechanical whine. Both her father and brother were mechanics and she'd absorbed more than her fair share of know-how from them over the years. The whine sounded exactly like an old-style starter motor failing to catch. Again and again the motor protested, but the engine didn't fire. She dumped the equipment by the front steps and hurried around the side of the house.

Flynn was propping up the hood of the Aston as she approached, his movements tight with frustration and urgency as he leaned over the engine.

"Flynn."

His head came up and she tossed him her car keys. He caught them automatically, his hand closing around them in a tight fist.

"It's not what you're used to, but it's got a full tank. Get it back to me when you can."

The relief in his face said more than any words ever could. "How will you get home?"

"It's five minutes away, and I have these things called legs. Go," she said, shooing him off for the second time that day.

He surprised her by taking a sudden step toward her and dropping a quick kiss onto her cheek.

"Thank you."

He was gone before she could respond. She could still feel the warmth of his mouth against her skin as she shut the hood. She checked the ignition and wasn't surprised to see his keys were still dangling there.

She locked the car, then took the brush-cutter around to the garage and propped it in the nearest corner, along with the safety gear. Then she walked home, his keys heavy in her pocket.

CHAPTER SIX

FLYNN PUSHED THE SPEED LIMIT all the way to the city. Every few minutes he checked his phone to make sure it was still working. It was, which meant that the reason it hadn't rung was because his father was still missing.

According to the short conversation he'd had with his mother, his father could have been gone from anywhere between five minutes to over an hour. She'd been in the garden, and it wasn't until she'd gone inside to use the bathroom that she'd realized he was gone.

Flynn's hands tightened on the steering wheel. He reminded himself that his parents lived in a leafy, highly affluent neighborhood, so the risk of his father walking into harm's way was minimal. The odds were good that he hadn't gone far. It would simply be a matter of combing the nearby streets.

They would find him. Of course they would.

Then they would have to deal with the implications of this incident and what it meant for the future.

His parents had downsized from the family home to their current, more modest house twelve months ago after his father's initial diagnosis, and his mother had reduced some of her social and charitable activities, but essentially they were still living a normal life together. Obviously, that would have to change if his father could no longer be trusted with an unlocked door.

Flynn sighed. It was inevitable that at some point in the progression of his father's illness tough decisions would have to be made, but he'd hoped that they'd have a few more years before they had to start curtailing his father's freedoms.

He was only minutes from his parents' place when his phone rang. He snatched it up, driving one-handed even though he was probably breaking half a dozen laws.

"We found him," his mother said. "He went to buy milk, but he thought we were still at the old house and he got confused. I've already called the police and told them." His mother's voice was thin and worried.

"I'm five minutes away, Mom."

"Okay. All right."

He tossed the phone onto the passenger seat and sent up a small prayer to the universe that his father was safe and sound. He pulled into the driveway not long after. His mother opened the door as he walked up the path. She looked pale but calm and he lay a hand on her shoulder.

"You okay?"

"I am now. If anything had happened to him…"

"I know."

He hugged her, then she led him to the conservatory, where his father was ensconced on the window seat, one elbow resting on the sill. He was gazing out into the garden, his face slack, his gaze utterly vacant.

Something hard and painful twisted in Flynn's chest. His father looked so empty. So absent.

Then his father registered their presence and suddenly his eyes were alive with awareness and intelligence again as he turned toward them.

"Flynn. Your mother told me she called you. I wish she hadn't."

"She was worried."

"I know. But I would have found my way home eventually."

Flynn didn't bother arguing with him. He sat next to him on the window seat and his mother drew up a chair at the table.

"When was the last time you saw the specialist?" Flynn asked.

His father made a vague gesture, looking to his mother to answer the question.

"Three months ago."

"Maybe we should make another appointment," Flynn suggested.

His father shifted beside him restlessly.

"What's wrong, Dad? You don't think so?"

"Whatever you think is best."

Flynn exchanged glances with his mother. "You get a say, too, Dad."

His father met his gaze, his own eyes bleak. "He's not going to tell us anything we don't already know." He stood. "I've got a headache. I'm going to lie down."

He left the room without a backward glance. The conservatory was profoundly silent after his exit.

"We need to talk. All of us," Flynn finally said. "We need to sit down and hammer out what he wants while he can still tell us."

"I know, but surely it's not necessary to subject him to that yet?" Her eyes pleaded with him.

"He's going to deteriorate, Mom. There's no get-out-of-jail-free card on this—it's going to happen. And if we don't take the opportunity to talk now, while he's still able to rationalize and make decisions, then we're doing him the biggest disservice of all."

A single tear slid down her cheek. Flynn stood to go to her but she held up a hand.

"I'm okay." She took a deep breath, then let it out. "I know you're right. Of course you're right. The sooner we hash this out, the better it will be. We'll all know how things are going to be and we can get on with living."

She forced a smile. "Would you like a hot drink? Something to eat? You must have missed your lunch, rushing to us like this."

"Something to eat would be good." He stared at the floor after she'd left the room. He felt bone-tired. Utterly exhausted.

After a long moment he pushed himself to his feet and went to the kitchen to help his mother.

MEL WAS IN THE kitchen cleaning up after making lasagna for dinner when she heard the sound of a car engine in her driveway. She crossed to the sink and looked out the window as Flynn drove her car beneath the carport at the back of the house.

She glanced at the clock—it was a little after six o'clock—then dried her hands before crossing to the door and walking onto the rear porch.

Flynn was getting out of her car. She called to him, "I wasn't sure if I'd see you again today."

"I wanted to get your car to you."

"Hang on, I'll grab my shoes and come down," she said, searching for her gardening clogs in the dim shadows beside the door.

"How about I come to you? It's the least I can

do." He walked to the bottom of the stairs and started to climb.

"I hope you didn't rush back. Like I said, I didn't need the car for anything."

When he arrived at the top of the stairs she saw that he was holding a bottle of wine. He offered it to her, along with her car keys.

"I really appreciate the loan," he said.

She reached for the car keys but didn't take the bottle from his hand.

"Mel…"

"If I'd wanted to rent my car to you for a bottle of wine, I would have said so at the outset. But I didn't."

"Fine. I'll drink it, then. Have you got a bottle opener and a straw?" There was a dark undercurrent to his light words.

She searched his face and saw that he was tired and worried. "Come in," she said, stepping to one side.

He shook his head. "I've already imposed on you enough for one day. But I appreciate the offer."

She reached out and pulled the wine bottle from his grip. "Come in."

He was silent for long enough she thought he was going to decline. Then he stepped past her, entering her house. She shut the door behind him and waved him toward the kitchen table.

"Grab a seat."

She collected two wineglasses and the bottle opener while he pulled up a chair. She crossed to the table and slid the glasses and the bottle onto the table in front of him.

"Have you eaten?"

"You don't need to feed me, Mel."

"Have you eaten?" she repeated.

"Not for a while." She grabbed a bag of corn chips from the cupboard, then she sat opposite him and reached for the bottle opener.

"Knock yourself out," she said, indicating the bag.

He smiled faintly and reached for the bag, tearing it open and taking a handful of chips. She poured the wine and slid a glass his way.

He lifted his glass to his mouth, but after a second he set it down again without drinking.

"My father has early-stage Alzheimer's disease."

It was the last thing she'd been expecting him to say and it took her a moment to process his words. "I'm so sorry. How long…?"

"He's been diagnosed for about a year now. But he's probably been deteriorating much longer." He sighed. "He went missing this morning. Just wandered off without telling anyone. That's why I had to rush to the city." He rubbed his forehead tiredly.

"But you found him, right?"

"Yeah. He's okay."

"How old is he?"

"Fifty-nine."

"That's young."

Flynn nodded. "Yeah. It is."

"It must be tough on your mom. On all of you."

He nodded again. He looked so defeated. If he were anyone else—a friend, a family member—she wouldn't hesitate to pull him into her arms. Instead, she nudged his glass toward him.

"Drink your wine. You look like you need it."

He swallowed a big mouthful. Then he looked at her, his eyes dark with unexpressed grief. "I don't want to be the one who takes away his freedom. I don't want to be his jailer."

"To keep him safe, you mean?"

"I know someone has to do it. I know it has to happen. But I don't want to be the one who says no to him."

She thought about it for a beat, trying to understand, trying to find a way through this for him.

"I guess it's a bit like parents with children," she said slowly. "It's always a balancing act between what they want and what's good for them."

Flynn blinked rapidly and brushed the back

of his hand across his eyes. "Sorry. Usually I'm good with all this. I guess I'm just tired—"

"I'd be a basket case if this was happening to my family."

"What makes you think I'm not?"

"I don't know. Your high level of competence and compassion, maybe?"

He smiled slightly. "Got you fooled, haven't I?"

She eyed him seriously. He had had her fooled. She'd thought he was living a blessed life. But he was as human and frail as the next person.

"Would you like some lasagna?" she asked.

It took him a second to switch gears. "That depends on whether I'm stealing your dinner or not."

"Absolutely not—you're stealing tomorrow night's dinner. I always cook for two. Saves cleaning up. Plus it means I only have to come up with three meal ideas a week."

He smiled. "In that case, lasagna sounds great."

She crossed to the counter to collect cutlery and place mats.

"I'll do that," he said when she returned to set the table.

"Thanks. Push all that junky stuff to the other end." She'd been doodling with some ideas for the orchard earlier and there was a stack of scrap paper and a fistful of pens and pencils cluttering the table.

She busied herself at the oven, using a knife to check that the pasta layers were tender before sliding the dish from the rack.

"You've been working on your orchard design."

She saw that Flynn was studying one of the rough sketches she'd made that afternoon. "Butchering it, more like. Design is definitely not my forte."

"What's the problem?"

"Apart from the fact that I really suck at thinking in three dimensions, you mean?"

"Apart from that."

She cut the lasagna into two portions and slid one onto each plate.

"I want to include a vegetable garden into the design, but I can't work out how to integrate it with the orchard."

"Right. That's what these boxy things are. Garden beds."

She shot him a look. "Are you making fun of my stick drawings?"

"Only a complete boor would dis a woman's stick drawings when she was about to feed him lasagna."

"Exactly."

She ferried the dishes to the table. "You might want to give it a moment to cool."

"So, do you want to use the whole clearing for the garden?" he asked.

She saw that he'd grabbed one of the scraps of paper and taken up a pencil.

"I don't see why not. It seems stupid not to use all the available space."

"The thing with incorporating different design elements into the one space is about making sure they either complement or contrast with each other...."

He quickly blocked in the cottages and the surrounding pathways and trees, creating a site plan.

"Is that all from memory?" she asked, impressed.

"Sure. Obviously it's not to scale, but it's an idea."

"It's bloody close to scale. It's amazing."

She studied him and his sketch intently as he added the orange tree and shaded in a few other details. Bits and pieces of information came together in her mind. His gardening expertise, the way he'd spoken about "incorporating design elements," the way he'd rendered her garden plot in a few easy pencil strokes...

"I thought gardening was a hobby for you. But you've had training, haven't you?"

He glanced at her and smiled briefly before returning his focus to the page. "Three years of horticulture and landscape design. I even had my own design firm for a while."

"What happened to it?"

"I folded it." He shifted in his chair, angling the piece of paper toward her a little more as he added ideas onto the page. "I think the key to making this work might be materials, and making a virtue of the demarcation between orchard and garden. How do you feel about using railway ties to create a series of interlinked garden beds? Keeping things really rough and rustic?"

He was playing it very cool, but there had been something in his eyes when he'd talked about his business.

"Why did you fold it?" she asked.

"Dad got sick. So, railway ties, yes or no? Thumbs up or thumbs down?"

She sat back in her chair. "You gave up your business for him?"

He shrugged. "It was always going to happen. Randall Developments is a third-generation business. You don't walk away from that kind of legacy. When Dad retired I would have stepped into his shoes. In that respect, Verdant Design was always a pipe dream."

He said it so calmly, so rationally. As though he'd simply swapped one make of car for another instead of abandoning something he obviously loved and changing the whole course of his life.

"You still haven't answered my question about railway ties."

She wanted to ask more questions about the business, about him. She wanted to understand, because suddenly he was a lot more than a handsome face and a hard body to her. Suddenly he was a person with depth and flaws and unimagined character.

But he was clearly uncomfortable with her probing, so she dropped her gaze to the paper between them.

"I have absolutely nothing against railway ties. In fact, I'm rather fond of them."

"Good. How about we think about something like this…."

He filled in detail, describing his ideas so she could see it the way he obviously did in his mind. She asked questions, made suggestions, and at some point realized their lasagna was stone cold. She heated both portions in the microwave while Flynn finessed his design and they both studied his finished sketch while they ate.

"You're really good at this," she said after he'd explained the simplest way to construct the raised beds.

He shrugged modestly.

"I mean it. This is actually going to be beautiful, and not just some utilitarian jumble."

"I'm glad you like it."

"You're a dark horse, Flynn Randall."

"Thank you. I think."

She studied him. He studied her in return and slowly it dawned on her that neither of them had spoken for a while. The nervousness that always seemed to dog her when he was around returned, all guns blazing, and she pushed her chair back with a screech of metal legs on linoleum.

"Dessert," she said. "Would you like dessert?"

He checked his watch. "Actually, I need to think about heading to Melbourne. What's the best taxi service to use down here?"

"I'll get you a number."

She kept a card from a local driver in the business-card holder beside her phone and she started rifling through it. She could feel him watching her and self-consciousness turned her fingers to thumbs. She almost jumped out of her skin when the phone rang on the wall beside her.

She reached for the receiver while continuing to search. "Mel speaking."

"It's me," her sister said. "I need a favor. Rex just dropped the phone charger down the toilet and Jacob's got a big job tomorrow and his phone is practically dead. Can we borrow your charger?"

"Sure. Want me to drop it by?" Mel's sister's husband, Jacob, was a plumber, and she knew he needed his phone when he was out and about during the day.

"I'm already in the car. I'll come grab it," Justine said.

"Okay. See you soon."

Mel put down the receiver and glanced at Flynn. "Sorry. That was my sister, Justine. She's got a toilet-bowl-meets-phone-charger emergency."

"I hate it when that happens." He sat with one elbow on the table, his big body relaxed, his blue eyes watching her. She dropped her gaze to the holder and gave a silent sigh of relief when she spotted what she was looking for.

"Bingo."

Now he could call his taxi and she could stop feeling like an idiot.

"Thanks." He pulled his phone from his pocket as she passed the card over.

She cleared away their dishes while he spoke to the cab company, giving herself a stern talking-to all the while. Yes, he was an attractive man. A surprisingly *good* man. Yes, they'd had a nice hour or so together and there seemed to be a buzz of mutual attraction between them. But that didn't mean anything was going to happen. It was stupid to let herself get so jumpy over something so small and everyday.

"Ten minutes," Flynn said when he ended the call.

She wiped her hands dry and folded the tea towel over the oven handle. "Good. Great. I'll go put the porch light on so they know which house it is."

"I should probably wait outside, anyway," he said.

"Sure."

She led him to the front door, flicking on the outside light before opening the door and stepping outside.

It was chilly and she automatically crossed her arms over her chest.

"You don't have to wait with me, it's too cold," Flynn said with a frown.

"I'm fine." For some reason she was having trouble maintaining eye contact with him.

"Thanks for tonight, Mel. For everything. I really appreciate it."

"Thanks for my new garden design."

Two sets of headlights cut through the night as the taxi and her sister arrived from opposite directions. Her sister turned into the drive while the taxi parked out front.

"That was fast," Flynn said.

"A new record," she agreed. Her shoulders relaxed a notch. Sixty more seconds and he would be gone.

"Before I forget, don't buy any plants for your garden without talking to me first, okay?" Flynn said. "I know a few guys who can help you out with wholesale plant stock."

"Oh, okay. Thanks. That'd be great."

He reached into his pocket and pulled out his wallet, sliding a business card from one of the slots. "Email me with a list of anything you're thinking of and I'll run it by my contacts."

"I will." She looked at his card, running her thumb over the raised lettering of his name. When she glanced again Flynn was watching her, a warm, intent look in his eyes.

"I'll see you later, Mel." He leaned close, aiming a kiss at her cheek.

She was so startled by the unexpected gesture she flinched and his mouth dragged across her cheek an inch or so before winding up somewhere near her ear.

"Sorry. I wasn't expecting…" She laughed, the sound high and horribly nervous.

For God's sake, Porter, it's just a kiss on the cheek.

"Then I'll give you fair warning this time."

She went very still as his hands landed on her shoulders and he leaned forward again. This time his kiss landed square in the middle of her left cheek.

"Look after yourself, Mel."

She watched as he stepped away. Justine was coming up the walkway and they crossed paths, Flynn giving her a small smile as he passed her by.

"My God. Who was *that?*" Justine asked the moment she hit the porch. Her sister shared the same slim, slight build and straight dark hair as their mother and her grin was wide and curious as she waited for Mel to answer.

"His name is Flynn Randall. He's the guy who bought Summerlea."

The interested, speculative look dropped from her sister's face like a rock. "The rich guy?" She said *rich* as though it was a dirty word. "What was he doing over here?"

"Something came up for him today and I helped him out."

Justine's mouth thinned. "Don't do it, Mel. Don't get sucked in by another one of those I-own-the-world assholes."

Mel frowned at her sister's motherly tone. "I'm not getting sucked in by anyone. He's moved into the area, I was helping him out. He's interested in gardening, I'm interested in gardening. That's all it is."

"Gardening."

"Yes. Gardening."

"Are you sure?"

"Just, if you'd seen me scuttle away from his house the other night when he told me he'd broken up with his girlfriend, you would know exactly how ridiculous this conversation is."

"What were you doing at his house?"

"My God, you're nosy. Has anyone ever told you that?"

"I'm protective. There's a difference."

"You don't need to protect me. That's my job."

"Okay. Just make sure you do it this time."

Mel flinched. Justine's face creased with instant contrition.

"Jesus. Sorry. I'm not sure where that came from."

Mel did. Her sister had urged her to walk away from her marriage half a dozen times before Mel had finally bitten the bullet and done it. But it was always easier to make big, brave calls from the sidelines. Especially when you hadn't been demoralized by years of put-downs and criticisms.

"I need to dig that charger out for you," Mel said, pivoting on her heel and heading into the house.

Her sister followed her, watching from the study doorway as Mel stuck her hand down the back of the desk to try to pull the charger from the outlet. She could just reach it with her fin-gertips.

"I'm sorry," Justine said after a moment.

The plug was wedged in too tightly and Mel couldn't get a good grip on it. She dropped to her knees and crawled under her desk, yanking the damned thing free. When she emerged, she looked at her sister.

"I know I made mistakes, Just. If I had it to do over, there are about a million things I would change. But I don't need you judging me as well. I've got enough of that going on in my own head, without you joining in."

"I didn't mean it like that. I just get so angry on your behalf sometimes."

Mel stood and handed the charger over. "I know. And I appreciate your concern. But you don't need to worry about me. I've learned my lesson. Believe me. No one will ever do that to me again."

Mel had made a vow to herself in the early weeks of her separation. It had been a painful time as she'd struggled to come to terms with how much of herself she'd given away during her marriage. Sitting with her new self-awareness, looking back over the past six years with wiser, sadder eyes, she'd made a promise—never again would she put herself in another person's power the way she had during her marriage.

Never.

Justine nodded. "I believe you."

They walked to the door. Justine put her arms around Mel and gave her a hug. "I really am sorry."

"Forget about it. It's okay," Mel said.

And it was okay. Her sister had been a rock in the aftermath of her marriage; she could hardly blame Justine for wanting to protect her from future hurts, even if the only person who could ever really do that was Mel herself.

"Thanks for the charger. I'll pick up a new one tomorrow and get this back to you ASAP," Justine said as she started down the steps toward her car.

"No worries." Mel stood on the porch in the cold for a while after her sister had driven away. It was strange, but out of all the things that her sister had said, the two things that lingered were Justine's comment about Mel not protecting herself and the disparaging reference her sister had made to Flynn, calling him an "I-own-the-world asshole." Standing in the cool darkness, Mel felt…not *guilty,* but close to it for not correcting her sister's assumptions. Flynn had shared a meal with her as well as offering her a window into matters that were clearly deeply important to him. He might be wealthy, but he wasn't an imperious asshole. He was open and interested and friendly and talented and creative and incredibly generous, given what he'd sacrificed for his father, and she felt as though she'd betrayed him by letting her sister's disparaging comment slip by.

I like him.

It was a fairly obvious realization, but it hit her like a slap. It was one thing to be attracted to him—she figured that was simply about being female and having eyes in her head—but to *like* the man behind the gorgeous face…that was a different matter entirely. It felt much more dangerous and threatening, especially after the conversation she'd had with her sister.

Unsettled, she reentered her house, heading for the kitchen to check the possibilities for dessert. Instantly, she spotted Flynn's keys, sitting on the counter. She'd forgotten to give them back to him.

Oh, well done, Porter. Well done.

CHAPTER SEVEN

THE FARTHER HE GOT from Mel's place, the more Flynn felt like a dick. He couldn't believe that he'd elbowed his way into her home and proceeded to dump all his crap on her. Every time he thought about how he'd almost cried he squirmed in his seat. Sure, he'd redeemed himself a little with the garden discussion afterward, but still…

She'd been great about it, hearing him out and offering her thoughts and feeding him, but that was beside the point. He felt as though he'd rolled over and displayed his soft underbelly to her like a beseeching puppy dog.

Was he really that desperate for a little comfort and companionship? This was the sort of behavior that had wound up with him hurting Hayley. He needed to get a grip.

Although, in all fairness, it had taken him a long time to tell Hayley what was going on with his parents. They'd been sleeping together for well over a couple of months before he'd shared his father's diagnosis with her. It wasn't information that he bandied about, out of respect for his father's privacy and dignity. But with Mel, he'd let it all hang out. He wasn't sure why.

Staring out the taxi window, he thought about the calm, serious way she'd watched him as he'd told her about his parents. She had a very warm, real presence. He'd felt…safe with her. Maybe that was why he'd spilled his guts so unceremoniously.

Or maybe you wanted her to hold you to that spectacular bosom of hers and offer you a different kind of comfort.

He shifted again, but there was no denying the fact that he was very attracted to Mel. His mouth thinned into a grim line. He'd like to think he had a little more finesse than to try to whinge and whine his way into a woman's bed, but the evidence was definitely stacked against him.

He was still brooding when the taxi pulled up in front of his town house in Kew. He handed over the fare and was sliding out of the cab when his phone rang. He took the call as he pushed the car door shut.

"Hi. I feel like such an idiot— I forgot to give you your keys."

It was Mel, her voice low and slightly breathless over the line. "Keys. Right." He patted his pocket, and sure enough there was no telltale bulge beneath his hand.

Damn.

He was vaguely aware of the taxi driving off into the night as Mel spoke again.

"You left them in the Aston Martin and I locked it up and brought them home with me and meant to give them to you.…"

He turned and considered the locked door to his town house. "Don't worry about it."

"But you'll need your house keys, won't you? I can bring them up to you. Give me your address and I'll be there as soon as I can."

"You're not making a two-hour round trip to bring me my keys. I've got a spare with the neighbors, and it wasn't as though I was going to be able to drive the Aston Martin into work tomorrow, anyway. I'll organize a courier to pick them up in the morning."

"I'm so sorry."

"I'm the one who ran off like a moron. I'll give you a call tomorrow to let you know when to expect the courier, okay?"

"All right."

He hesitated, tempted to apologize for the gut-spilling and associated other self-indulgences of the evening. Then he decided that he should quit while he was ahead.

"I'll see you later, Mel," he said.

He ended the call and glanced at his neighbor's window. There was a light on downstairs.

With a bit of luck they'd be home. Otherwise he'd be forced to catch a cab to his parents' place for the night.

Luck was with him and he was soon letting himself in with his spare key. He sent Mel a quick text, just in case she was worrying. She responded immediately:

Phew. Load off. Will get keys to you tomorrow.

He started composing a return text and then caught himself. He'd imposed himself on her enough for one day. Time to give the woman a break.

It didn't stop him from thinking about her as he got ready for bed.

The way she'd thrown her car keys at him with no questions or caveats.

Her sympathetic patience as he'd talked about his father.

The admiration in her gaze as she looked over the design he'd sketched for her.

That moment this morning when she'd been adjusting the harness on the cutter and her fingers had brushed his belly and she'd looked up, straight into his eyes.

Mel Porter was one out of the box. Funny, smart, kind, generous—and, of course, sexy as hell.

Last night he'd decided that she wasn't fling

material because there was a vulnerability in her that demanded patience and commitment that he simply didn't have to offer at the moment. But it hit him suddenly that he'd gotten it completely ass-about. The reason Mel wasn't fling material wasn't because she was vulnerable, it was because she was a keeper.

One night with her would never be enough.

It was the last thought he had before he drifted off to sleep.

MEL WOKE IN muffled darkness, covered in sweat. Her legs were bound, she couldn't breathe.... She flailed and kicked and suddenly was fully awake, in her bed, the sheets wrapped around her legs, the quilt over her face. She batted it away, kicked her legs free and reached for the bedside light. Golden light shone up the wall and she blinked. Her heart was pounding away, her pulse vibrating in her neck. She moved to the edge of the bed and stood, shivering in the cold with her clammy skin. She grabbed a towel from the ensuite, stripped off her pajamas and rubbed herself down. She found a fresh pair of pajamas in the chest of drawers and pulled them on. She straightened the covers, then got into bed on the opposite side, where the sheets weren't damp from her panicky sweat.

She lay on her side, legs curled up, doing her

best not to read too much into the nightmare. She'd had a lot of them in the early days after she and Owen separated, and she'd thought she was past them.

Apparently not.

Fragments from her dream floated back to her: Owen sitting beside her in the car, hands tight on the steering wheel, his silent, oppressive anger pushing her into her seat; Owen yelling at her, again, for getting it wrong, pacing up and down in their bedroom; her standing in a ballroom full of beautiful, glittering people, yet feeling utterly isolated and alone.

A delightful highlight reel from her marriage, although she'd left out a couple of doozies. Maybe they were still lurking in her subconscious somewhere, waiting to disturb the rest of her night. Lucky her.

She wondered idly what had come first—her becoming entwined in the bedclothes, or the dream with all its attendant memories of how trapped she'd felt in her marriage. Chicken or egg, dream or entanglement.

It probably didn't matter. And perhaps it was timely for her to remember exactly how bad it had been, given the arrival of Flynn in her life and the conversation she'd had with her sister tonight. Perhaps it was a damned good thing for her to revisit exactly how powerless and trapped she'd felt. She'd been bound to her marriage in so many different ways—by expectation, by her vows, by pride, by her inability to fully comprehend how ugly things had become between them, by crippling self-doubt that had been fed by years of her husband's criticisms, large and small.

Like water on a rock he'd worn her down until she'd started to believe the things he said to her. That she was stupid. That she was responsible for his failure to make headway with his political ambitions. That she deliberately went out of her way to anger him. That she'd never even tried to learn how to fit in with his world.

She sighed heavily. So much anger and unhappiness. For both of them, really. She wondered if Owen was any happier now that he was free of the wife who had "done nothing but hold me back." She doubted it, because he would always have his rapaciously ambitious mother's voice in his ear, urging him to be better, do better, and Diana Hunter would never be satisfied. Ever.

Mel almost felt sorry for him.

Almost.

Finally she drifted off to sleep. When she woke again it was morning. Judging by the state of the bedcovers, she'd barely moved. She showered and wrapped herself in her Thai silk dressing gown before making her way to the kitchen.

She was trying to decide between porridge or peanut butter toast when the doorbell rang. She answered the door to find Flynn standing there.

"Flynn," she said, her voice high with surprise.

"Hi. I hope it's not too early."

His gaze drifted over her dressing gown. She was instantly acutely aware of the fact that she was naked underneath.

"No. Of course not. You're here for your keys, right?" she said, one hand instinctively lifting to the neckline of her robe to ensure it wasn't gaping immodestly.

"Yeah. When I thought about it again this morning I realized there was no point sending a courier when I needed to get the car sorted out, too, so I grabbed a couple of hours to make it happen." He gave her what could only be described as a polite smile.

She stepped away from the door, waving him inside. "Come in."

She led him to the kitchen and grabbed the keys off the counter, handing them over. "Would you believe they were sitting there all night and I forgot to give them to you?"

"Thanks." He offered her another polite smile.

She frowned. Maybe she was reading too much into things, but he seemed different. More distant. Less warm. Not that that was a bad thing, all things considered, but it seemed out of step with the way they'd parted company last night. The way he'd kissed her cheek. The way he'd looked at her.

"Also, I was hoping there was a mechanic you can recommend locally. My regular guy's in the city and I don't particularly want to have Gertie towed all that way."

"There are a couple of workshops in the village. Barry Cassidy has a good reputation. And the other guy is my father."

"Well, that makes it easy. Obviously I'll go with Barry Cassidy."

Her mouth curved up at the corners. "Naturally. That seems like the obvious choice."

"That's what I was thinking." His smile was more genuine this time and some of the stiffness had gone from his face.

"You want Barry's number?" she asked.

"Sure. But I guess I might as well speak to your father, too."

"Good plan. I don't know why I didn't think of that."

Flynn pulled his phone out and took her father's number down as she reeled it off.

"In all seriousness, my dad is a good mechanic. He does a lot of work with classic cars—he and my brother restore them as a hobby. I would have mentioned him to you earlier but I figured you probably had some NASA-trained mechanic in the city somewhere."

"As I said, I do have a guy but I believe he may have skimped on the NASA training."

"It's so hard to get good help these days."

"Tell me about it." His gaze dipped below her face for a second and she crossed her arms over her chest, conscious of the fact that she wasn't wearing a bra.

"So, um, how did you get down here this morning?" she asked. She could feel her heart beating out a hectic, nervous rhythm against her breastbone.

"I borrowed Dad's car. He doesn't drive anymore. I've been putting off selling, so at least it's earning its keep this week."

She nodded, thinking about what he'd said in relation to the conversation they'd had last night. "It's what you were talking about last night, isn't it? Taking away his freedom. I guess selling his car would really drive home the fact that part of his life is over, wouldn't it?"

The tight look came back to his face. He cleared his throat. "Listen. About last night." He shifted uncomfortably. "I wanted to apologize for dumping all that stuff on you…. That was really uncool."

It took her a second to process what he'd said and another second to put it in context with his behavior this morning. The polite smiles, the distance, his general awkwardness.

He was embarrassed for having let down his guard with her last night.

She propped a hip against the kitchen counter and studied him. "Let me get this straight. You're apologizing for caring about your father?"

"No. I'm apologizing for spilling my guts all over your kitchen table."

"Yeah. See, I happen to think they're the same thing. You're allowed to feel upset, Flynn. You're only human."

He shrugged uncomfortably.

"This is one of those male things, isn't it?" she asked.

"I feel a little uncomfortable talking on behalf of my entire gender, but it's definitely a Flynn Randall thing. I don't generally go around blubbering."

"You didn't blubber last night."

"Sure."

"You know, if you were my brother, I'd punch you right now."

He looked a little startled. Then a slow smile curled his mouth. "Then I'm glad I'm not your brother."

"You should be. I pack a mean punch. The bruises last for days."

"Now you're just trying to scare me."

"How am I doing?"

"Might need a little more work."

"Okay. I'll get back to you."

"You do that."

His phone beeped. He pulled it out to check it. She could tell by the way his face shifted into more serious lines that it was work.

"I need to keep moving," he said. He sounded tired.

"Busy day, huh?"

"They don't really come in any other size these days."

They walked to the door and faced each other across the threshold.

"Good luck with the car," she said.

"Thanks. And thanks for these." He indicated the keys.

He turned away.

Before he could leave, she took a step forward and touched his arm. "Flynn."

He paused, half turning toward her.

"Everyone has tough stuff, you know? Everyone. I don't even want to think of all the times I've lost it over the past year or so. It's called being human. And I certainly don't think any less of you because of it. Okay?"

They looked into each other's eyes for a long beat.

"Okay," he said. Then he smiled, a sweet, small, very sincere smile. "Thanks, Mel."

The urge to touch him in some way—even just his hand—was so strong that she took a step backward.

"Go make another million. Quickly. The world's bankers need you."

She was very aware that she was using humor to diffuse the sudden tension between them and she suspected he was, too.

"If you insist."

He started down the stairs. Mel shut the door so she wouldn't stand there like an idiot watching him walk away. Then she went to the kitchen to make herself peanut butter toast. The way she would if this was a normal day and she'd had a normal conversation with any old person.

"Fake it till you make it" had always been one of her favorite sayings.

FLYNN THOUGHT ABOUT his conversation with Mel as he drove into Mount Eliza village to locate her father. She was smart and she was funny and she always surprised him. He liked that about her.

He also liked how she looked in silk.

Fine, sleek silk in variegated shades of blue that clung to every line of her body. He'd taken one glance at her and known she didn't have a stitch on underneath. The realization had played havoc with his self-control the whole time he'd been talking to her.

He went over the reasons why it would be bad to start anything with her as he pulled into a parking spot at Village Motors, but the old arguments felt as though they were wearing a little thin now. What he felt for her was far more than simple sexual curiosity or interest. He was drawn to her on every level. Which meant that whatever happened between them wouldn't be a repeat of Hayley.

And it might be the best thing that had ever happened to him. Granted, the argument that the timing was bad still held a lot of water, but like Summerlea, Mel was unique. A one-off, never to be repeated. And he'd already decided that even if the timing couldn't be worse, he wasn't walking away from Summerlea.

He was starting to feel the same way about Mel. He glanced up at the building and pushed thoughts of Mel to the back of his mind as he got out of his car. Perhaps he was getting conservative in his old age, but he didn't think it was appropriate to be thinking about ways to get Mel into his arms, his bed and his life while he was introducing himself to her father.

Village Motors occupied a double block, with a wide roller door leading into a workshop occupying the left side of the property and a small office area filling the right. A plastic sign above a glass-fronted door identified it as Reception. He entered and breathed in the smell of engine grease and metal. A counter bisected the room. On this side were a couple of beaten-up chairs and a table with some much-thumbed car magazines, while the other side boasted a desk with a young girl tapping at a computer.

"Hi. Can I help you?" she asked as he approached the counter.

"I hope so. I need someone to take a look at my car. It'll probably need to be towed over, but it's local. Mel Porter is a friend and she recommended you guys."

"Oh, Mel. Cool," the girl said. "I'll get Mike so you can tell him what the problem is." She stood and disappeared through the door to the workshop. She was back in thirty seconds with a tall, muscular, dark-haired man hard on her heels.

Flynn would have recognized Mike Porter as Mel's father in a crowd of thousands. Clear gray eyes sitting above a nose similar to Mel's regarded him neutrally. The shape of his face, the way he held himself—the family resemblance was startling, despite the thick horseshoe mustache that bracketed his mouth.

"Mike Porter. How can I help you?" He offered Flynn his hand.

"Flynn Randall. I'm having some trouble with my '65 Aston Martin. Your daughter, Mel, said you might be able to help me out."

Mike frowned slightly. "Randall. You're not the bloke who bought Summerlea, are you?"

"That's right."

"Mel mentioned you the other day. So, what's going on with your Aston?"

Mel had been talking about him, had she? Interesting.

"I think it's probably the brushes in the starter motor. I've had trouble with them before. The engine is turning over but not starting."

"Starter motor trouble for sure," Mike confirmed. "Where is it? Stacy mentioned something about you needing a tow?"

"It's over at Summerlea. Is there a local tow-truck service I can use?"

Mike made a dismissive gesture. "Since it's local and it's only the starter motor, there's no need to tow. Leave the keys with me and I'll swing by and take a look at it this afternoon. If it's the starter motor, I can unbolt it and bring it here to work on it. If it isn't… Well, we'll cross that bridge."

"Great." Flynn slid the key to the Aston free from the ring and handed it over.

"Mel said you've got a bit of a green thumb."

"That's right."

Mike shook his head. "Gotta say, I don't get it. If I had my way the whole yard at home would be concrete. No mowing, no weeds."

"I suppose you'd paint that concrete green, too, huh?" Flynn asked.

Mike's mouth twitched at the corners. "I hadn't given it that much thought, but I probably would."

"You know there's that artificial grass you can get now, right? Stays green all year round. It's a whole level up from green concrete."

"I'll bear it in mind." Mike glanced over his shoulder toward the workshop. "Leave your details with Stacy, I'll be in touch."

"Just so you know, I may not be able to pick the car up again this week. So if it does need a tow in, you might be stuck with it over the weekend."

"We can deliver the car to you in Melbourne if you like. We do that for a few of our customers."

"Yeah? That would be a load off, I don't mind admitting."

"Consider it done. Thanks for the business, Flynn." Mike gave him a nod before heading back into the workshop.

Flynn passed his business card to Stacy, grabbed a Village Motors card from the stack on the counter and exited to the street.

At least he knew where Mel had gotten her dry sense of humor. He crossed the pavement to his father's car, thinking about the fact that Mel had mentioned him to her family. It was deeply pathetic, but he wished he could have asked what else Mel had said about him, apart from the fact that he'd bought Summerlea and was into gardening.

How old are you exactly?

It was a good question. The thing was, Mel made him feel young and stupid again.

He was still trying to work out whether this was a good thing or not when his phone rang, sucking him into yet another work issue, and, as usual, everything else in his life got pushed into the background.

CHAPTER EIGHT

FLYNN WAS SNOWED UNDER for the next few days, working to beat the deadline for a tender on a government housing project. He was still shoveling his way through his in-tray on Wednesday when his assistant stuck her head in the door.

"Flynn. I've got Mel Porter on the phone. She's delivering your car and wondered where you'd like it parked. Shall I direct her to your spot or tell her to leave it in guest parking?"

He'd been hunched over his desk going over a specification chart but he straightened immediately. "Mel?" he repeated stupidly.

"That's what she said."

He was unprepared for the flood of pleasure and anticipation he felt at the thought of seeing her again. "Put her through."

She returned to her desk and a few seconds later his phone rang.

"Mel."

"Hi. Sorry to disturb you. I only wanted to know where you would like the car parked but your secretary insisted on putting me through to you."

"Why are you delivering my car? I thought some guy named Jimmy was going to do it?" He'd spoken to Mike the previous afternoon to make the arrangements.

"Jimmy has the flu and Dad didn't want to hand your $300,000 car over to a pimply-faced eighteen-year-old who's seen *Ferris Bueller's Day Off* one too many times."

He grinned and sat back in his chair. "I can only applaud your father's excellent judgment. How far away are you?"

"About ten minutes. Your secretary mentioned something about guest parking."

"Turn into the entrance to the underground garage. The guest parking is immediately on your right. Reception's on the ground floor. Let them know when you arrive and I'll come down."

"You don't need to do that," she said hastily. "You're busy. I can drop the keys at Reception and leave you to it."

"Or you could have lunch with me."

"You don't need to buy me lunch."

"I want to."

She was silent for a long moment. Probably trying to come up with an excuse.

"You must be busy," she said lamely. "I don't want to mess up your day."

"I'll see you in ten minutes, Mel."

He thought for a minute after he'd hung up, then buzzed his secretary. "Mary, what's the name of that new Spanish place everyone's talking about in St. Kilda?"

"The Lexington Hotel?"

"That's the one. Can you get me a table for two for twenty minutes from now?"

"What about your one o'clock?"

"I'll move it."

He sent an email to reschedule his one o'clock, then grabbed his jacket and wallet and headed for the door.

"I'll see you later, Mary," he said as he breezed past her desk.

She looked astonished. Probably because he almost never had lunch, unless it was a business meeting. He took the lift to the underground garage and walked up the ramp to where the guest parking was located. He'd been waiting barely a minute when Mel pulled in. She saw him and gave him a confused little wave before driving into a parking spot and turning off the engine.

"What are you doing down here?" she asked as she unfolded her tall body from the car. She was wearing dark jeans and a black turtleneck beneath a short red woolen coat, her hair loose over her shoulders.

She looked great.

"Waiting for you in case you tried to bail on my lunch offer."

She frowned and he pointed a finger at her.

"Tell me it didn't cross your mind."

Her expression became a little sheepish.

"Busted," he said.

"You don't have to take me out to lunch just because I'm dropping off your car."

"I know I don't. Come on, we're having Spanish in St. Kilda."

He plucked the keys from her hand. She hesitated a moment before circling the car to the passenger door.

"Nothing fancy," she said. "I'm not dressed for fancy."

"It's lunch and it's Spanish. Jeans are fine."

She slid into the car and reached for her seat belt.

"How did Gertie behave?" he asked as he reversed out of the parking spot.

"Like a dream. It's a beautiful car. Some people might say too beautiful to have such an ugly nickname."

"She's earned that nickname, don't you worry," he said as they shot up the ramp and out into the street. "The number of times she's broken down on me…"

She gave him a curious look. "Maybe you should get something more reliable then."

"I couldn't do that."

"Why not?"

"Because that would mean admitting defeat. Besides, we all have our flaws, right?"

He could feel her watching him and he took his eyes off the road to glance at her. "What?"

"Nothing." She shifted her gaze to the front.

"I hope you're hungry," he said. "This place is supposed to be good."

"I could eat."

They talked about her garden for the remainder of the short drive. Flynn found a parking spot close to their destination and ushered Mel into what looked like an old-school pub. Inside, however, the building had been gutted. The traditional wood bar and sticky carpet had been ripped out and replaced with concrete everything. The floor was polished concrete, while huge feature concrete arches marched down one side of the room, and on the other side a vast concrete bar dominated the space. The seating was equally modern—white Saarinen tulip chairs with alternating acid-yellow and hot-pink cushions—and the art on the walls was edgy and abstract, with big slashes of black with dripping red and more acid-yellow.

It was incredibly noisy and filled with a laughing, well-dressed crowd—trust-fund kids who didn't have to work, minor celebrities and businesspeople who still had time for long lunches. Not exactly the venue he would have chosen for what he hoped would be an intimate lunch with Mel.

A thin, austere-looking woman approached, arching an eyebrow. "Can I help you?" she asked, her tone implying she would prefer to do anything but.

Flynn had been eating in places like this since he was in short pants and he ignored her attitude. "Table for two. Under the name of Randall."

She perked up predictably at the mention of the *R* word and they were soon being whisked to a small side table. It was only when he was seated opposite her that he saw how tense Mel was. Her gaze bounced around the room uneasily, and when the waitress returned with their menus she ducked her head and murmured her thanks.

He frowned, watching her rather than the waitress as the other woman launched into a lengthy rundown of the day's specials and the wine list. Mel made a show of listening, but he could tell she'd tuned out.

"Thank God," he said the moment the waitress left. "That was like listening to the *begat* part of the Bible. Corn-fed spatchcock begat braised witloof begat roasted baby beets begat brandied goat's cheese—"

She choked on the mouthful of water she was swallowing.

"Are you all right? Should I come around and Heimlich you?" he offered.

"I don't think you can Heimlich for fluids." She coughed.

"Good point." He watched sympathetically as she finally got a grip.

"You okay?"

"Yes."

Her daze darted around the restaurant again, almost as though she was checking to see if anyone was watching. Her fingers pleated the edge of her linen napkin, folding it back and forth, back and forth.

"Do you have any idea what you'd like?" he asked.

"I'm not sure...."

He asked if she wanted wine but it was very loud thanks to all the concrete and she had to ask him to repeat himself twice. Over at the bar, a woman laughed, the sound not unlike an excited hyena.

He looked at Mel. She had her best game

face on, but his gut told him she was deeply uncomfortable. Hell, *he* was uncomfortable. He'd
wanted to treat her, to give her a nice experience
and, yes, to show off a little. Instead, he'd landed
them in the middle of the sort of trendy, pretentious eatery he usually avoided like the plague.

He made eye contact with her across the table
and decided to take a gamble.

"Okay, I'm just going to put it out there," he
said, leaning forward so he could be heard over
the din. "There's this really great burger joint
around the corner from the office. They make
their own relish and instead of buns they use—"

"Let's go," Mel said, already reaching for her
coat.

He laughed. "That bad, huh?"

"I really like burgers."

She was being diplomatic, he knew. They
stood and he helped her into her jacket. The
waitress approached and he told her that they'd
changed their minds. His hand on the small of
Mel's back, he guided her toward the door.

They were almost home free when he felt her
muscles tense beneath his hand. He glanced at
her face and saw that her eyes had gone blank.
For a moment he didn't understand. Then he felt
someone staring at him and glanced toward the
bar.

Owen Hunter stood amongst a group of suits,

a glass of wine in hand, his gaze pinned to them. He looked shocked. And, unless Flynn was wildly mistaken, angry.

Mel lengthened her stride, reaching the door and exiting into the cool winter air ahead of him. He gave her a moment to compose herself before touching her arm.

"You okay?"

"Yes. Of course," she said, but her voice sounded hoarse, strained.

Flynn's hand found the small of her back again and he guided her toward the car. He waited until she was busy fastening her seat belt before he spoke again.

"When was the last time you saw him?"

"More than a year ago. We pretty much did everything through the lawyers."

There was a question in his mind, one that had been bugging him for a long time. He hesitated to ask it. Then he shrugged. If this attraction between him and Mel was going to go anywhere, there needed to be a certain level of honesty and understanding between them.

"Feel free to tell me to mind my own business, but how did you guys ever get together? I keep trying to picture him not being a complete ass-hat and failing miserably."

Her lips bent into a parody of a smile. "We were both backpacking through Europe. I went for a year when I was twenty-one and stayed for four I loved it so much. I met Owen at the beginning of my last year at a bar in Portugal. I beat him in the limbo competition, and that was pretty much it."

"Again, I can't picture Hunter backpacking, either."

The other man always seemed so aware of his own status, his own importance. Backpacking seemed to be the very antithesis of everything that Hunter appeared to crave and value.

"He loved it. I think he saw it as a challenge. He could make a euro go further than anyone I've ever traveled with." She gave a sharp little laugh.

"What?" he asked.

"I was just remembering how shocked I was when I learned he had money. We got married a week before we were due home, on the beach in Thailand, and he told me that night about his parents and their money and his trust fund. He said he hadn't wanted to tell me before because he wanted to make sure I was marrying him because I loved him and not because of what he could do for me."

Flynn tried to think of something to say that didn't have the word *ass-hat* in it again.

"Must have been a bit of a shock," he finally said.

Another grim smile from her. "I thought I was

in my own version of *Pretty Woman*. I mean, it doesn't get much better, right? Working-class girl goes overseas, meets incredible guy, falls in love, and it turns out he's rich as well. Cinderella, eat your heart out."

He started the car and pulled out into traffic.

"The bit they don't tell you in the fairy tale is all the stuff that happens after the happily ever after," Mel continued after a short silence. "Like when Richard Gere's friends won't accept Julia Roberts because she doesn't know all the rules, and how Cinderella wasn't the type of girl King and Queen Charming wanted their son to marry."

He flicked a look at her. She was gazing out the window, an infinitely sad expression on her face.

"I'm sorry."

She glanced at him, surprised. "For what?"

"For asking the question."

She shrugged. "It's not your fault that the answer is so sucky."

They were both silent for the remainder of the drive to the burger place. He turned to face her once he'd pulled into a parking spot.

"Just so you know, this place has no ambience, unless you count graffiti gouged into the tabletops and a few old Coke posters. On the plus side, there's no concrete and not a single waiter with an attitude. Plus the burgers are awe-inspiring. I recommend the burger with the works, but I'm a pig like that."

Mel smiled faintly. "Are we talking egg and beetroot?"

"And pickles, and caramelized onions."

"I'm in."

He ordered while she slid into a booth toward the rear of the restaurant. He slid in opposite her and they immediately bumped knees. She shuffled along the seat and he did the same, and still they bumped knees.

"Okay, these booths were clearly made for midgets. I think we need some strategy here," he suggested. "Staggered knees. It's the only way this is going to work."

"Staggered knees?"

He reached under the table and found her knee. He guided her left knee to the right of his, then did the same with her right knee so that they were effectively interwoven.

"Oh, staggered knees. Why didn't you say so?" she said. Then she started laughing.

He watched her, a smile playing about his mouth, aware that she needed the tension release.

"Sorry. That just tickled my funny bone."

"You have a great laugh," he said.

Her gaze slid away from his and she reached for the straw dispenser. She pulled a straw free and fiddled with it, and he could almost see her casting about, looking for a safe topic of conversation.

"I didn't get a chance to tell you—my sister has organized a working bee at my place this Saturday," she said after a few seconds. "I showed her your plans and she got all gung ho. So, we're going to build my cascading garden beds sooner rather than later."

"It's a pity it's this Saturday, I could have helped."

"Busy washing the cat, are we? Having a violin lesson?" she joked. "My brother tried all of those excuses before my sister nailed him."

A part of him that he hadn't even known was tense relaxed. She was back in form, the bleak look gone from her eyes.

"Your sister sounds scary. And my alibi is water tight—we're having a family meeting to discuss Dad's care."

She immediately sobered. "Because of what happened on the weekend?"

"In part. The thing is, if we don't take the chance to talk to him now, we may lose it forever. This way, we'll at least know we're doing what he wants. Small comfort at the end of the day, but it's something." He realized he was going on about his parents again and sat up a little straighter. "So, have you thought about what you want to grow in your veggie patch yet?"

She eyed him sympathetically. "I don't mind talking about your parents, Flynn. You don't have to change the subject."

Their meals arrived before he had a chance to respond. Mel gave an appreciative whistle as she inspected hers.

"Not bad. And I'm a bit of a burger connoisseur."

"Wait till you taste it."

She took a big bite. "Oh. Wow. I may need a moment alone with my burger. And a cigarette for afterward."

"Please, don't let me stop you."

She closed her eyes as she took another bite. "This is so good. This has to be Melbourne's best-kept secret."

They compared best-burger-ever stories for the next few minutes. As usual, Mel made him laugh. When she wasn't on her guard, she had a wicked sense of humor and a very quick wit. There was a wild energy in her—an impishness—that appealed to him enormously.

On impulse, driven by an imp of his own, he gestured toward her left cheek. "You have something on your face."

"Oh. Thanks." She grabbed the napkin and

gave her cheek a good wipe. She looked at him expectantly. "All gone?"

"Almost, but not quite. Here, let me."

He leaned across the table, hand extended. He was about to touch her cheek when her hand snapped up and caught his wrist. She turned her head to stare at the gob of mayonnaise on his index finger. She shook her head, her eyes dancing with laughter.

"Oldest trick in the book, buddy. The old double-fake face smear. Strictly amateur hour."

"Nearly got you," he said, utterly shameless in defeat.

"Close, but no cigar, my friend."

He grinned, reaching for a napkin to wipe his hands. "I like you, Mel Porter."

The words were out of his mouth before he could stop them. Mel's smile flickered for a moment, then she sat back in her seat and gave him a dry look.

"Second oldest trick in the book—distraction. Don't go thinking you've gotten away with anything, Randall. There will be reprisals, mark my word. So sleep with one eye open."

He thought about pushing it, about declaring himself more openly, but everything in Mel's posture told him it was too soon. He settled back in his chair and smiled at her. He wasn't going anywhere, and neither was she. There was no need to rush this—whatever it turned out to be.

MEL STARED OUT the train window on the way home from the city. Around her, schoolkids played, the boys shoving each other around and checking out the girls, the girls gossiping and texting and checking out the boys.

Mel's thoughts were preoccupied with the man she'd left behind.

I like you, Mel Porter.

The words still gave her a thrill, even though it had been a couple of hours since he'd uttered them.

She liked him, too. More so every day.

She felt the now-familiar dart of anxiety as she acknowledged her own feelings. When she was with Flynn, it all seemed incredibly easy. He was so charming and funny and sweet and sexy. Why wouldn't she want to spend time with him? Why wouldn't she let instinct take over?

Yet when she wasn't with him, reality crowded in. She had no business even thinking about being with someone at the moment. Her head was still way too full with the detritus from her marriage—witness what had happened when they'd run in to Owen in that hideous excuse for a restaurant.

She had literally flushed hot, then cold when

she'd glanced across the dining room and found herself looking into her ex-husband's eyes. The angry, outraged expression on his face had propelled her back in time, back to the days when that look had meant either a lecture or cold silence in the car on the way home, punishment for whatever transgression she'd committed. Laughing too loudly, telling a bawdy joke, drinking too much—she'd been raked over the coals for all of them at one time or another.

Then the insistent weight of Flynn's warm hand on the small of her back had registered and she'd remembered that she was free and that Owen's disapproval and anger meant nothing to her now.

Less than nothing.

Of course, she knew what he'd been unhappy about. He'd done backflips trying to become Flynn's friend, trying to inveigle his way into the Randalls' inner circle. To see Mel there so easily, so effortlessly… He'd be brooding over it for hours, no doubt. Wondering what had been said between her and Flynn, what had been done.

God, she was glad she was free of it. All of it. The pretentious restaurants, the constant low-level anxiety about looking the right way and saying the right thing… It had been exhausting. Six long years of trying to live up to her husband's expectations.

If only she'd thought to ask him to live up to hers.

She'd expected him to love her. She'd expected him to be her friend. She'd expected him to be on her side, to support her. He'd failed to deliver on almost every score.

The train pulled into a station and Mel shook herself. She didn't want to waste more time thinking about Owen. He'd consumed enough of her life.

As for Flynn...

She didn't want to think about him, either, but for very different reasons.

It was too late, however. Her mouth was already curving into a smile as she remembered that stunt he'd tried to pull with the mayonnaise.

Flynn Randall was a goof. She never would have guessed in a million years, but he was. He was naughty and he was cheeky and he was fun.

I like you, Mel Porter.

She gazed out at the passing cityscape as the train left the station.

The feeling is mutual, Mr. Randall. Extremely mutual.

FLYNN SPENT A LONG TIME in the shower on Saturday morning. Head bowed, he let the water wash over him and tried to steel himself for the day ahead.

It didn't matter that his father had agreed to this meeting. It didn't matter that they were all going in with their eyes open, determined to listen and be patient. He didn't want to sit at a table and discuss options for his father's care once he was beyond caring for himself. Flynn didn't want to be rational about something that made him want to bang his head against a brick wall with anguish.

But he would. As would his father and his mother, because the only other option was to bury their heads in the sand, which really wasn't an option at all.

When the hot water finally ran out, he toweled off and dressed. He thought about breakfast but decided he couldn't eat. Feeling heavier than lead, he drove to his parents' place.

His father answered the door, his hair damp from the shower. His gaze was sharp, his demeanor familiar and affectionate.

"Dad."

They exchanged hugs.

"Come in. Rosina's making waffles. Anyone would think it was a special occasion."

He gave Flynn a small, self-deprecating smile as Flynn walked past him and into the house. Then his gaze dropped to the folder in Flynn's hands and his smile flattened. He didn't ask, but Flynn knew he'd guessed what was in the folder:

information on in-home nursing care and other support organizations for late-stage Alzheimer's patients and their caregivers.

"I don't suppose it's too late to cancel and suggest a day trip somewhere instead?" his father said.

"Sure. If that's what you want."

"Oh, nice answer. Leaves me with bugger all room to maneuver."

"I learned from the best," Flynn said as they entered the dining room.

"What did you learn, and from whom?" his mother asked, looking up from arranging a large bunch of camellias in a vase on the cherry-wood sideboard against the wall.

"How to get his own way, and from me," his father said.

"Oh. That. I'd like to think I had a hand in that, too. I'm no slouch at getting my own way, either," his mother said.

"True. Although logic would dictate that it's impossible for two people to both always get what they want all the time," his father said. "Someone has to miss out."

"Agreed—unless they both want the same things." His mother angled her cheek for Flynn's kiss. "There you go, darling—the secret to thirty-odd years of happy marriage, in a nutshell. Find a woman who wants the same things as you."

Flynn was very aware that beneath the banter and lightheartedness there was an edgy undercurrent. He pressed his molars together, wishing he could fast-forward through the next few hours and cut to the part where the hard decisions had been hammered out.

He crossed to the window and his thoughts drifted to Mel, as they were wont to do these days. He wondered if she was up and about yet, and what time her working bee was scheduled to start. Then he thought about the way she'd giggled like an idiot when he'd arranged her knees under the table at the burger place and smiled faintly.

"Would you like a coffee or a tea before we get started?" his mother asked from behind him.

Flynn turned to face his parents. "Tea, thanks."

"How many waffles would you like?" she asked.

"I'm not hungry right now. Maybe later." His gut was too tight to welcome food.

"Okay, then. Let's get this show on the road," his father said decisively, taking a seat at the head of the table. He'd set himself up with a notepad and pen, along with a sheet of printed notes. His reading glasses sat on the end of his nose and he surveyed Flynn and his wife over the top of them, every inch the former CEO of Randall Developments.

Painfully aware that his father's dignity depended on the illusion that he was in control of at least some aspects of his life, Flynn took a seat to his father's left, while his mother sat opposite.

"So, where do we start?" his father asked.

Flynn rolled his shoulders. Then he opened the folder in front of him. "I think we should take this step by step. What needs to be done now, medium term and long term."

His father nodded. "Agreed. You okay with that, Pat?"

"It makes sense."

"So what are our short-term issues?" His father sounded utterly professional, as though this were any other meeting, yet his hands trembled as he shuffled his papers.

A sudden, white-hot surge of anger hit Flynn.

His father was a good man. He deserved far better than the fate that awaited him. He deserved some peace and pleasure, the chance to enjoy everything he'd worked so hard to achieve.

Instead, he was going to fall apart, cell by cell, memory by memory, until he was completely unravelled, his sense of self destroyed.

The urge to smash something, primitive and

fierce, gripped Flynn. His hands curled around the chair's armrests, tightening until his knuckles ached.

For long seconds he simply hung on, riding the wave of his rage. Then the moment passed and he registered that his mother was speaking, talking about ways of making the house safer without his father feeling under lock and key.

He let his breath out slowly and reached for his pen and started taking notes.

CHAPTER NINE

"THIS IS WHY THEY DON'T have girls on building sites. Grooming breaks."

Mel rolled her eyes at her brother as she finished pulling her hair into a ponytail. He was standing next to the pile of railway ties she'd had delivered the previous day, a bored look on his face. Behind him, several cubic meters of topsoil formed a mound in the center of her lawn.

"You're jealous because you cut all your hair off," Mel said as she tugged her leather work gloves on. Once, a long time ago, her brother had had shoulder-length rock-and-roll hair that had been his pride and joy

"Wouldn't go back there for quids." Harry ran a hand over his close-cropped hair. "No muss, no fuss this way. You should try it sometime."

"Oh, yeah, that's gonna happen. Not." She already had man-shoulders and man-height. She wasn't about to compound the issue with man-hair.

She bent her knees and got a grip on the end of the top tie.

"When you're ready," she said to her brother. "Take your time."

Harry gave her a look before getting a grip on the other end. "One, two, three."

They hoisted the beam, straightening their legs so they were both holding the length at waist height.

"Onto your shoulder," Harry instructed. "Two, three."

Mel felt the burn in her arms as she lifted the tie high enough to roll a shoulder under it. The weight settled heavily and she braced the beam with both hands, adjusting her stance to suit.

"Okay, let's go," she said.

They walked along the side of the house and into the garden, passing her father and her brother-in-law, Jacob, on their way to collect their next load.

"That's my girl," her father said approvingly, slapping Mel on the backside with his work gloves as he passed.

Mel grimaced and concentrated on where she was putting her feet. She would never admit it out loud, but there were times when she really, really wished she was a different kind of woman. The kind who was more than happy to kick back and watch men do the heavy lifting because she couldn't possibly measure up. The thing was, she *could* measure up, and she'd never been content to let others do for her. She wasn't about to start now—especially when the men in her family were giving up their weekend to help her. The least she could do was toil by their sides.

Harry led the way past Tea Cutter Cottage and into the clearing that would soon become her new garden. A dozen railway ties were already lined up to one side and she and Harry added theirs to the stack.

"Couple more trips should do it," Harry said.

"Yep."

Mel placed a hand on the small of her back and stretched. Her arms were aching, and her thighs felt a little shaky. And it was barely midday. She was going to be in all kinds of pain by the end of the day.

Harry had already started walking to the front and she trudged after him. They passed her father and Jacob coming the other way, a tie on their shoulders. Mel couldn't resist mimicking her father's gesture, slapping his butt with her gloves.

"That's my daddy," she said.

He barked out a laugh. "You'll keep."

Mel was still smirking when she rounded the house, only to stop short when she realized Harry was talking to somebody, and that somebody was Flynn.

An absurd rush of pleasure hit her as he turned to face her.

"Hey," she said, grinning like an idiot. "Didn't think I'd be seeing you this weekend."

"Like I was saying, she was right behind me," Harry said dryly.

"Hey," Flynn said. "Sorry to barge in. I forgot about your working bee."

He was smiling, but it didn't reach his eyes and she realized he was upset. Deeply so.

Then she remembered he'd had his meeting with his parents today. The one where they discussed his father's future care.

She glanced at her brother. "I'm going to grab a glass of water. I'll be out in a tick."

She didn't wait for Harry to respond, simply caught Flynn's eye and gestured with her head for him to follow her into the house.

The moment they were safely inside and out of her brother's hearing, she turned to face him.

"What happened? Did your father have a bad day?"

"Nothing. Nothing happened. I just—" He shook his head. "Sorry. I don't even really know why I'm here. I got in the car and the next thing I knew I was turning off the freeway." He turned away from her, almost as though he was about to leave.

Mel caught his forearm. "Flynn."

He stilled, then some of the starch went out of his spine. His blue eyes were dark with pain as they met hers. "I don't know if I can handle this, Mel."

Her grip tightened on his arm. "You can. You will."

He shook his head again.

"You'll do it, Flynn. Moment by moment. That's how you get through the bad stuff. One day, one moment at a time."

He started to say something, then he stopped and lifted his free hand to his face, pinching the bridge of his nose.

Fighting tears, if she had any guess.

She acted completely on instinct, closing the distance between them and wrapping her arms around him. He was unresponsive for a long beat, as though she'd taken him by surprise, then his arms went around her in turn.

Her breasts were pressed to his chest and every breath she took was filled with the smell of his aftershave but there was nothing sexual about their embrace. She was offering him a little comfort, and he was accepting it. It was as small and simple as that.

After a few seconds his arms loosened and she took a step backward. Flynn didn't quite meet her eyes and she reached out and gave him a gentle shove on the shoulder.

"Don't," she said. "It's okay to feel overwhelmed. You guys have been dealt a shitty hand."

He shrugged a shoulder, still not meeting her gaze.

She imitated him, one eyebrow cocked. "What's that supposed to mean?"

Finally he looked at her. "There are plenty of people worse off. People in the same situation with money problems and other things going on. In a lot of respects we're bloody lucky."

"So? Is that supposed to make it easier to watch your father disappear before your very eyes?"

"No." He said it heavily, resignedly.

She led him into the living room and waved him into the nearest armchair.

"Tell me what happened."

"I told you, nothing. It was just a lot harder than I thought it would be. And I thought it would be pretty damned hard."

He sat on the edge of the chair, his elbows braced on his knees. Mel sank onto the arm of the opposite chair.

"How was it harder?"

He shrugged impatiently, as though he was irritated by her questions and her pushing, but after a moment he started talking. "It was okay until we started talking about late stage. I don't know how much you know about Alzheimer's..."

"Not a lot. I know there are seven stages." She'd done a few internet searches since he'd told her about his father's condition.

"Then you know more than a lot of people. Late stage is also called stage seven. By then, the patient can't speak, can't walk, can't sit up or even hold their head up unassisted. Facial expressions disappear, except for grimaces. They need help going to the bathroom, getting clean, eating—" His voice quavered and he pressed the bridge of his nose again.

After a long moment he dropped his hand and started talking again. "Late-stage patients need twenty-four-hour, seven-day-a-week care, but right from the start Mom has been determined to take care of Dad at home. The way she sees it, the house can be fitted with everything they'll need, and we can hire agency nurses and caregivers to support Mom. It's completely doable, and it's what she wants."

Mel had a feeling she knew where this was going. "What about your father?"

"He wants to go into a home. He's even picked one out. He doesn't want to be a burden. Doesn't want my mother's final memories of him being changing his adult diaper or wiping spit off his chin."

"What did your mother say to that?"

"Honestly? I've never seen her so angry. She

told him that it was her marriage, too, and that this was happening to both of them. And that she wouldn't be able to live with herself if she let someone else care for him. She said that she didn't care about shit or spit, she cared about him, and she was going to be there with him to the bloody end because she loved him." Flynn's eyes were shiny with tears as they met hers. "That's almost a direct quote, by the way."

She could see the pride in his gaze, along with the pain. "She sounds pretty cool, your Mom."

"She's awesome."

"So, who won?"

His smile was grim. "No one. Dad got upset. He said that if this was the last chance he had to make decisions, the least we could do was respect them. Mom told him that just because he was sick didn't mean he got to rule the world. We finally agreed to have a time-out so they could both consider each other's point of view."

"What do you think will happen?"

"Mom will win. I think in his heart my father wants her to. The thing is, he loves her too much to want to be a burden."

Mel blinked away the sudden warmth of tears. It was all too, too sad. When her vision was clear again, she saw Flynn was watching her, a frown on his face.

"I should go. You're busy. I didn't meant to show up out of nowhere like this."

She'd seen him backtrack like this before and understood that he was embarrassed about needing to talk about his feelings. Instinct had bought him here, but pride was about to drive him away.

Men. Sometimes they really drove her crazy.

"Are we friends or not?" she demanded.

He looked arrested.

"Because friends don't make a run for it when there's a working bee in process," she continued.

She tossed him her work gloves. He caught them before they slid down his belly to the ground.

"And friends offer each other a shoulder when it's needed and don't make a federal case out of it."

He eyed her for a moment. She would have given a lot to know what was going on behind his eyes. His mouth turned up at the corners and he nodded slowly. "Okay. Point taken."

"Good."

He glanced down at the gloves. "You know, I was jealous when you told me you were having a working bee this weekend."

"Jealous? Of hauling heavy-ass lumps of wood around and wheelbarrows full of soil?"

"Guilty as charged."

"You're a very strange man, Flynn Randall."

She pushed herself to her feet. "But you should know that I am not above exploiting that."

"Exploit away."

She started for the door. "You are so going to regret those words tomorrow."

"We'll see."

She led him to the lawn, where the remaining railway ties were stacked. There was no sign of her brother and she moved to the far end of the next tie in the pile.

"Let's do this, then. On the count of three," she said, bracing her legs and getting a grip on the end.

Flynn held up a hand, eyebrows raised. "Whoa there. You're not lifting this thing."

"Why not?"

"Because it's too heavy for you."

She grinned at him. "It isn't, you know." She patted her right shoulder with her left hand. "You think these babies are just for show?"

"Mel. These things have to weigh at least a hundred pounds."

"Flynn, I've already carried half a dozen of these today. I think I can handle another one."

He continued to stare at her. She put her hands on her hips and raised both eyebrows, waiting.

Finally he shrugged. "Okay. I can't believe I'm saying that, but okay."

Mel rolled her eyes. "Thank you. Now that I have your permission, can we get on with it?"

"As soon as you put these on."

Her gloves hit her in the chest. Her reflexes weren't as fast as his and they slid to the ground before she could react. She started to object but he shook his head.

"I'm not using your gloves while you go without. Besides, I'm pretty sure I've got some old gardening gear in the trunk."

He crossed the lawn to where he'd parked the Aston Martin in the street. Half a minute later he returned minus his leather jacket with a pair of dirt-stained gardening gloves on his hands.

"Okay, bossy pants. Show me what you've got," he said.

She huffed out a laugh. *"Bossy pants?"*

"You heard me."

She gave him a look that promised payback, then bent her legs and got a grip on the tie. On three they lifted, then she counted off again before they hefted the beam to their shoulders.

"All good your end?" she asked.

"I should be asking you that."

"Get over it, Randall. It's called girl power."

They headed toward the clearing.

"You've really done this six times already today?" he asked.

"At least."

"Remind me never to arm wrestle with you."

She was still smiling when they rounded the last corner to find the men of her family lounging like lizards on the stacked ties. En masse, they made quite the picture: Harry, close-shaved head and bulging arms covered in inky black tribal tattoos, his ears shiny with piercings; her father, equally muscular in a white wife-beater tank top with his dark horseshoe mustache; Jacob, dressed in an old Metallica T-shirt, his hair spiked into a David Beckham faux-hawk, a hand-rolled cigarette dangling from his lips.

They looked exactly like what they were—three working-class men enjoying a laugh in between bouts of hard labour—and she couldn't help but notice the assessing glances they threw Flynn's way.

The men in her family had never rated Owen. They had never said anything to her directly, but she'd sensed the tension whenever they were in the same room as her ex-husband, which, fortunately, hadn't been very often, particularly toward the end. She didn't blame them, since Owen had always either been falsely hearty or smugly patronizing in most of his interactions with them. He'd never tried to simply engage with them person-to-person—probably because he'd not-so-secretly believed he was better than them and that her family was a waste of his valuable time.

Now, she watched as her father, brother and brother-in-law took in Flynn's leather boots and designer jeans and cashmere sweater and felt herself prickle defensively on his behalf.

"You owe me fifty bucks," Harry said to Jacob as they moved to one side to make way for the tie she and Flynn carried.

Mel threw her brother a sharp look, ready to step in if it looked as though he and her brother-in-law were making a joke at Flynn's expense.

Her brother shrugged a big shoulder. "I bet Jacob you'd rope your mate into helping out."

"For your information, Flynn volunteered," she said as she and Flynn set down their tie.

Flynn immediately nodded toward her father. "Good to see you again, Mike."

"You, too. Don't suppose you've met my son, Harry?" her father said, jerking a thumb toward her brother. "And the idiot with the nicotine addiction is Jacob, my son-in-law."

"So, how'd Mel talk you into helping out? Bribery? Threats?" Harry wanted to know as he and Flynn shook hands.

Flynn shot Mel an amused look. "Like Mel said, I volunteered."

"You poor sucker." Harry slung his arm

around Mel's neck and pulled her into a loose headlock.

"Do you mind?" Mel said. She tried to wriggle free, but Harry simply ignored her.

"You should know she's been luring guys to their deaths for years now, making them do stuff they don't want to do. My sister, the siren of Frankston."

Mel gasped with only partly feigned indignation. "Excuse me?"

"Don't play dumb. Remember Peter O'Donnell?" Harry addressed his comments to Flynn. "Idiot went on the Forty Hour Famine with her and passed out during a footy match he was so hungry. Then there was Simon what's-his-name. He painted her name along the side of his car when she broke up with him. Oh, God, and that one who kept playing his guitar outside her bedroom window..." Harry made a pained strangling sound.

"They were all years go," Mel explained for Flynn's benefit. Although, by the looks of things, he was clearly enjoying the Porter family cabaret act. "*Plus,* I didn't ask them to do any of those things. Anyway—" she jammed her elbow into her brother's ribs, but Harry only tightened his grip on her neck "—you're the one who's the biggest man-slut this side of the equator, so you can hardly talk."

"Yeah, except you don't see me roping any of my girlfriends in as free labor."

"Flynn's not my boyfriend, and I didn't rope anybody into anything. Unlike you, you big petrol-head, Flynn happens to enjoy gardening."

She elbowed him again, harder this time, and took advantage of his instinctive flinch to slip out from under his arm. Feeling more than a little hot and flustered thanks to her brother's manhandling, she straightened her top and adjusted her ponytail before glancing at Flynn to see how he was handling it all.

Now that the floor show was over, he was talking quietly with her father about his car, one hand tucked into his back pocket, his posture relaxed.

The last of her protectiveness slipped away as she watched her father laugh at something Flynn was saying. It had only been five minutes, but already the Porter men liked Flynn about five-hundred times more than they'd ever liked Owen.

She frowned. The odds were good that Flynn wasn't going to be spending a lot of time with her family, so working up a sweat over whether they liked him or not was a waste of time—and yet she wanted them to like him, very badly, because she liked him and she wanted other people to see the same good qualities in him that she did.

She turned away, fussing with her work gloves, swiping at the small splinters and other debris on her T-shirt and jeans, thrown and more than a little overwhelmed by her own feelings.

This…*thing* with Flynn was getting out of hand, taking on a life of its own. She'd resisted it every step of the way, yet somehow he was still standing here in her yard, talking and laughing with her family.

She slapped her gloved hands together loudly, a physical expression of her inner frustration and confusion. Four sets of eyes turned to her expectantly and she realized she'd inadvertently drawn everyone's attention. "Who wants to go grab another tie with me?"

She marched toward the house before anyone could respond and, more importantly, before she could do or say anything too stupid.

TWO HOURS LATER, Flynn released the trigger on the circular saw.

He pushed the safety glasses high on his forehead and brushed wood splinters off his forearms as he inspected the cut he'd made.

"All done?" Mel asked from behind him.

He glanced over his shoulder. "All done. Last

piece, too. Now we just have to fill these suckers with topsoil."

"He says as though it's going to be a walk in the park getting all that dirt from one end of the property to the other."

She moved off to talk to her brother-in-law and Flynn's gaze drifted over her body. It was a warm day for winter and she'd long since stripped down to a bright blue tank top and a pair of faded jeans. The stretch knit fabric hugged her breasts and belly, flaring out over her hips. With her cheeks shiny from exertion and a handful of loose curls forming a fuzzy nimbus around her face, she looked like an advertisement for the great outdoors. Full of life and sexy as hell.

His gaze gravitated to the thin strip of bright orange satin visible on her left shoulder. It wasn't the first time he'd noticed Mel's bra strap today—it had been playing peek-a-boo with him on and off all afternoon—and it definitely wasn't the first time he'd gotten a little lost inside his own head as he imagined her generous curves cupped in tangerine lace and silk.

He suspected he should probably be trying to rein in his schoolboy fantasies, but sometime during the past few days he'd decided to accept the inevitable where Mel was concerned. He was falling for her—hard. He'd tried in the past to make himself fall for women and failed, and he figured it was probably just as futile to try to stop himself from falling, too.

So here he was. Falling.

Where he was going to land was anybody's guess because Mel was still a closed book to him. Sometimes he was sure they were on the same page. Others he had no idea what she was thinking or feeling. To say it was driving him crazy was something of an understatement.

"How you going with that last piece?" Harry called.

Flynn jerked his attention to the here and now. "Ten seconds." He pulled on his gloves before lifting the shortened tie from the twin sawhorses and carrying it to where Harry and Mike were using a plumb bob and spirit level to line up the final wall of the last garden bed. They worked together to ensure it was in line and level, fixing it in place with big coach bolts that had been weather-treated to resist corrosion.

"Excuse me, fearless leader," Harry said to Mel once they'd finished. "When might your faithful servants expect to be fed?"

"Mom said she'd make sandwiches. I'll call and let her know we're ready to eat." Mel pulled her phone from her pocket and dialed.

Flynn admired the length of her athletic legs

as she propped her butt against one of the completed walls while she waited for her call to connect.

"The eagle has landed, Mom," she said into the phone.

She listened for a few seconds before bursting out laughing. As always, the rich, full sound made Flynn smile in response. Mel shot a mischievous look at her brother. "Mom says you're more of a vulture than an eagle, Harry."

"Tell Mom she's a riot. And if I'm a vulture, she's a turkey."

Mel dutifully relayed his message to their mother. She was grinning fit to bust when she hung up. Flynn had a sudden image of her as a kid, mischievous and full of beans, more than ready to give as good as she got.

It struck him suddenly that this was the first time that he'd seen Mel truly carefree, her habitual wariness completely absent. Clearly, she felt safe with her family.

And, perhaps, with him?

"What's so funny?" Harry asked suspiciously.

"Mom said she's going to accidentally drop all the cheese-and-pickle sandwiches on the floor as payback," Mel said as she pocketed her phone.

"Are we talking Mom's floor? Because everyone knows you could perform surgery on Mom's floor. *Your* floor, on the other hand…"

They continued to bicker cheerfully, Jacob and Mike throwing their two cents in when the mood struck them. Flynn watched from the sidelines, enjoying the interplay and this rare insight into Mel with her guard down.

"What's this I hear about me being a turkey? Harold Neville Porter, you ought to be ashamed of yourself."

A slim woman of average height entered the clearing bearing a tray piled high with sandwiches. He guessed she must be in her early fifties, although she was dressed like a much younger woman. Her sweater was red and tight, the V-neck cut low, and her jeans fitted snugly from thigh to ankle. Her hair was a color somewhere between caramel and blond, and she was wearing the kind of makeup his own mother usually reserved for big occasions. Large gold hoops dangled from her ears, while a series of chunky metal bracelets clanked at her wrist.

"Easy with the Neville, Mom," Harry said with a grimace.

"Easy with the ugly poultry references, Harold," she said.

"You started it with the vulture thing," Harry said.

"Now, now, children. Let's not argue when there are sandwiches to be eaten," Jacob said, stepping up to take the tray from Mel's mother's hands.

"Thank you, Jacob," Mel's mother said pointedly. Then she glanced past his shoulder and caught sight of Flynn, her brown eyes suddenly bright with curiousity. "Hello. I don't think I know you."

"This is Flynn, Mom. Flynn, this is my mother, Valerie."

"Nice to meet you, Valerie."

"Please, call me Val." She smiled, her gaze sweeping his body in a disconcertingly thorough survey.

Out of the corner of his eye, Flynn saw Mel frown.

"Did you bring anything to drink, Mom?" Harry asked.

"The cooler's in the back of the car."

Harry sighed and headed for the path.

"Can you grab some serviettes from the kitchen?" Mel called after him. "Second drawer down to the left of the dishwasher."

"Sure. Anything else you need while I'm at it? Shoes shined, your taxes done?"

Mel didn't respond, which struck Flynn as being a missed opportunity. He glanced over and caught Val giving Mel a big thumbs-up, accompanied by what he could only describe as a salacious wink and a gesture in his direction. Unaware that she was being observed, Mel frowned and shook her head, a signal that Flynn guessed was meant to inform her mother that she was barking up the wrong tree. Val's mouth turned down at the corners and she mouthed the words *Why not?* at Mel. At which point Mel caught his eye.

He offered her his best innocent smile and watched as a tide of pink washed up her face. She turned away and started fussing pointlessly with the garden tools. He decided to take it as a hopeful sign.

A few minutes later Harry returned with a cooler full of canned drinks. Val placed both the cooler and the tray of sandwiches together on the grass and Mike, Harry and Jacob dropped to the ground and dove in. Flynn loitered, waiting until Mel sat before oh, so casually taking the spot beside her, feeling about as suave and sophisticated as a fourteen-year-old with his first crush, and probably just as obvious.

"So what do you do, Flynn?" a voice asked from his other side and he realized Mel's mother had nabbed the spot next to him.

"I work in property development."

"Help yourself to a sandwich before my son hoovers them all up," Val said. "The Porter family motto is He Who Hesitates is Lost. You'll starve if you hang back."

She waited until he had his mouth full before hitting him with her next question. "I believe I've heard Mel mention that you bought Summerlea recently. That's a big project to take on."

Flynn swallowed before responding. "I figure if I take it bit by bit, I'll eventually get things under control. And if that turns out to be completely delusional, I can always call in the pros."

"So you like a bit of handyman work, do you?" Val asked.

"I'm more of a gardener, to be honest. But I'd like to think I'm not completely useless with a power drill."

"You should talk to Harry. He does some handyman work on the side."

"Mom." Mel's voice held a not-so-subtle warning.

"Thanks, I will," he said, shooting Mel a look to let her know he didn't mind her mother's suggestion. He was new to the area, and he'd much prefer to have someone he knew working with him than a random tradesperson he'd plucked from the phone book or the classifieds.

"And are you married, Flynn?" Val asked, nibbling delicately on the crust of a chicken salad sandwich.

Mel choked and he glanced at her in enquiry.

"Need me to Heimlich you again?" he asked.

"No," she said, her eyes watering.

He grabbed a can of Coke from the cooler. Pulling the tab, he passed it to her. When he returned his attention to Val, her expression indicated she was still waiting for his answer.

"I'm not married," he said.

"Ah. Divorced, then?"

Mel sighed loudly. "Mom. I swear—"

"How else am I supposed to get to know people if I don't ask questions?"

"I don't know—maybe you could wait until it comes up in conversation?" Mel suggested.

"As if Flynn's going to talk about his divorce with a total stranger."

"Thank you for making my point for me," Mel said.

She successfully changed the subject after that, and once the sandwiches had been polished off Val went home. After twenty more minutes of lounging in the warm winter sunlight, they roused themselves and started the first of many trips transferring the topsoil from the front lawn to the garden beds.

By five o'clock Flynn was sweaty, sore and covered with grit. It had been a while since he'd worked with his body and hands for a full day and he had a new respect for Mel after watching her toil alongside the men without once letting up. As the time edged toward five-thirty he began to wonder when, exactly, the apparently

indefatigable Porters were going to call it quits.
He heaved a silent sigh of relief when her father
dug his shovel into the garden bed with an air
of finality.

"Right, that's it. It's getting dark and cold and
I need food," Mike said.

No one was about to argue. Between the five
of them they returned Mel's tools to the shed,
then Mel ushered them all into her kitchen and
distributed beers. Harry sat back in his chair and
made an appreciative sound as he swallowed
his first mouthful. Flynn had to agree that an
ice cold beer had never tasted quite so good before, probably because he knew he'd bloody well
earned it.

"Okay, dinner is on me. Fish and chips. Who
wants what?" Mel asked.

She had a notepad in hand and a smudge of
dirt on her cheek. He watched in amusement
as she proceeded to decipher the barrage of re-
quests from her family before finally fixing her
gaze on him.

"What's the burger situation like?" he asked.

"Good fish-and-chip-shop standard, verging
on very good at times."

"Hook me up with one of those, then, thanks.
And a couple of dim sims."

"Fried or steamed?"

"Fried. Of course."

"I knew you were all right," Harry said as he downed the last of his beer.

Mel made a couple of phone calls, and twenty minutes and a round of beers later their food arrived, delivered by Val, and a woman who looked so much like her that she could only be Mel's sister, Justine, and two little boys.

Introductions were performed over the rustle of fish and chips being unwrapped and the booty portioned out. Flynn learned that the taller, skinnier boy was Eddy and the younger, wide-eyed boy was Rex, and that Mel's sister was not going to be as easily won over as her mother, if her coolly assessing glance was anything to go by.

There was much laughter as they ate, most of it in response to the constant one-upmanship Harry and Mel seemed to thrive on. Flynn guessed that Justine was naturally the quieter of the three siblings, but after a while she loosened up and started to toss the occasional comment into the mix. Val and Mike played umpire, laughing readily when they inevitably became the butt of the joke, while Jacob kept up a sly, clever commentary that was so dry Flynn sometimes almost missed the laugh.

It was a noisy, informal, relaxed meal, a far cry from the dinners he usually shared with his parents. He knew from comments his mother had made from time to time that they'd never intended for him to be an only child, but luck had not been on their side. Sitting around Mel's crowded kitchen table, he couldn't help thinking that there was a lot to be said for a large family.

For starters, he'd have someone to talk to about his parents without having to worry that he was boring or overburdening them. Someone who was as invested as he was, someone he could trust implicitly.

The thought killed some of his buzz and he sat back and slid his half-finished beer onto the table. His thoughts circled to this morning's meeting and suddenly the room seemed too crowded, too noisy, too filled with stories and memories that he didn't understand or share.

A warm hand landed on his knee and he glanced up to find Mel leaning toward him.

"I meant to ask, are you staying at the house? Because you're welcome to one of the cottages tonight."

Her gaze was steady, and he could feel the warmth from her hand clear through to his bones.

"I hadn't given it much thought, to be honest. I guess I'll stay at Summerlea. Don't really fancy the drive to Melbourne tonight."

"Stay here. You'll have a proper bed and central heating. The last thing you want to do is have to build a fire and crawl into your sleeping bag after the day we've had."

"Sleeping bag? Who's sleeping in a sleeping bag?" Val asked.

Mel's gaze was apologetic as it met his and he couldn't help but smile.

"I haven't got any furniture yet," Flynn explained. "I've been camping out in the living room until I get something sorted."

"Then Mel's right. You should stay here." Val said it as though it was set in stone, a high priestess handing down an edict.

"That's it, Mom's spoken. No turning back now," Justine said with mock solemnity.

Flynn decided to let it ride for the moment. In truth, he quite enjoyed camping out at Summerlea. It gave the endeavor a boy's-own-adventure feel that helped distract him from the enormity of the job he'd undertaken and offered him a very delineated break from his life in the city.

It wasn't long before it became clear that the youngest members of the family were heading toward cranky territory.

"Bedtime for you, my little friends," Justine announced to her squabbling boys. "Time for us to go."

It quickly became a mass exodus. Flynn shook hands with all the men and kissed Mel's sister and her mother goodbye, then he was alone in the kitchen, surrounded by silence as Mel walked her family to their cars.

He glanced at the mess they'd made and began clearing the table, stacking plates and screwing the paper from the fish and chips into a tight ball. The dishwasher was full of clean dishes, so he left the stacked plates and glasses on the draining board and wiped the table.

He paused to check out the series of photographs stuck to the fridge door—a picture of Rex and Eddy, another of Val and Mike, a couple of postcards from various places in Europe. Just visible behind one of them was a shot of Mel in a pair of cut-off denim shorts and a tank top. Her hair was a wild spill around her shoulders, her face creased with laughter. Harry stood next to her sporting rock-god long hair, one arm looped around her shoulders.

Flynn's gaze traveled over Mel's long, muscular legs before finding her face. She had such a great smile. Like her laughter, it held nothing back, shouting to the world that she was open and accessible. Although the latter was probably more an illusion these days than reality. At thirty-one, Mel was far more battle-hardened than the girl in the photograph.

He heard the door open and close. He turned away from the fridge as Mel appeared. Her gaze swept the table and counter, and she gave him a grateful smile.

"Thanks for clearing the table."

"Thanks for dinner."

"Thanks for working like a dog for me all day."

"Thanks for letting me barge into your family working bee."

She laughed. "I'm all out of thanks. Would you like a coffee instead?"

"Thanks."

She laughed quietly at his little joke as she took the jar of beans from the pantry.

"So, are you going to give in to the lure of civilization and stay in one of my cottages or are you going to go back to your man cave?" She glanced at him in order to gauge his reaction.

"I think I'm going to suck it up and brave the sleeping bag."

"Then there's no help for you." She gestured dramatically with her free hand. "I officially give up."

"Do you?"

He hadn't meant it to sound like a challenge, but that was the way it came out.

The coffee canister hit the counter with a loud thunk. The instinct to make a joke so they could move past the moment was strong. Almost undeniable.

He didn't want to push her.

And yet, he did, too. He was falling. It would be nice to have some idea where he might land.

So he waited.

CHAPTER TEN

MEL WAITED FOR FLYNN to say something—anything—to dispel the sudden tension in the room, but he remained silent. It was going to be up to her, then, to get them past this moment. This moment that had been heading their way for weeks now.

"You take sugar, right?" Her voice sounded a lot huskier than she would have liked. Almost sultry.

"I do."

He was barely an arm's length away, one arm propped on the counter as he watched her. Panic—excitement?—sent adrenaline surging through her bloodstream. She took a deep, calming belly breath.

"Is it that scary, Mel?"

She met his eyes. She intended to cover, to protect herself, but the truth popped out. "Yes."

"Okay." He sounded disappointed. "Then perhaps I should go. If that's what you want."

She stared at him, the right words forming

in her mind but somehow not making it out her mouth.

"The thing is, I've always had a bit of a crush on you. Even when I shouldn't have." He said it lightly, but his words hit her low in the belly.

"Me?"

"Yeah, you. I've always loved the way you laugh. The way you smile. The way you hold yourself. Your body."

She blinked. "I had no idea."

"Then I guess I've picked up a few tricks since I was fourteen."

"I think you might have."

He smiled, but his eyes remained serious. He was waiting for her to answer him. To tell him to go—or to stay.

"I don't know what I want," she said.

"Don't you?"

His gaze was steady on hers as he took one step toward her, then another. Her heart clamored against her breastbone as he stopped a scant few inches away. She could feel his body heat, could smell his aftershave and the faintest hint of good, clean sweat. She could see his five-o'clock shadow and the small scar at the very tip of his left eyebrow.

Her gaze slid to his mouth, tracing the sensuous curve of his lower lip. She'd been too confused, too conflicted to allow herself to even think about kissing him before. Now she let herself go there, wondering how it would feel to press her mouth to his, to feel his tongue inside her mouth, to taste him and breathe the same air as him.

Hot desire unfurled inside her, foreign and familiar at the same time. It had been so long since she'd kissed and been kissed.

"You have the most watchable face," Flynn said, his voice very low and deep. He laid his hand on her face, his thumb brushing along her cheekbone, his fingers cradling her jaw.

She swallowed, awash with nerves and lust and anticipation and fear as his gaze slid to her mouth and he drew closer. She closed her eyes and forgot to breathe as his lips met hers and his free arm came around her, pulling her close.

He was strong and warm and male and his mouth moved gently against hers, his kiss provocative and soothing at the same time. Her hands found his shoulders, her fingers gripping muscle and bone. She felt the brush of his tongue against her lips, then he was inside her, hot and wet and demanding, and a part of herself she'd pushed down deep inside came roaring to life.

It had been so long. Too long. And he felt *good*.

She angled her head to deepen their kiss, her fingers clenching into the fabric of his T-shirt, pulling him closer. She slid her tongue along his, tasting him, giving as good as she got. Her other hand slid down his back, exploring the broad planes and angles en route to his waist. When she arrived, she fumbled blindly for the hem of his T-shirt, sucking on his tongue, pressing her hips forward, desperate to touch him skin-to-skin. Finally she slid her hand over his belly. She made an approving sound in the back of her throat as she felt the flex of his stomach muscles beneath her hand. She needed more from him. Much more.

She caught the hand cupping her jaw and pulled it to her breast, closing her own hand over his. He took the hint, his thumb sweeping across her nipple, and she let out a low moan.

She'd forgotten how good this felt. How needful. How beautiful and powerful a man's body felt beneath her hands, how different the textures of his skin were from her own.

Wet heat throbbed between her legs as he plucked at her nipple through the layers of her sweater and bra. She wanted him. She wanted him very badly.

The press of his hips against hers, the silken rasp of his tongue in her mouth, the beautiful friction of his fingers at her breast, the feel of his hard body beneath her hands, the smell of him, the taste of him—she was overwhelmed by sensation, utterly lost.

Her shaking hands found the waistband of his jeans. She popped the stud free and had his zipper down and her hands inside his boxer briefs in seconds. His erection was thick and hard and hot in her hand, his shaft silky smooth. She stroked him, rubbing herself against his thigh at the same time.

She imagined what he would look like naked, how he would feel on top of her, sliding inside her.

She couldn't wait. She couldn't.

She started pushing his jeans down, her hands frantic. He smiled against her mouth.

"Slow down, babe. We've got all night," he murmured. His tone was light, but his words hit her like a slap.

Suddenly she could hear Owen's voice in her head, cold with condemnation and disgust.

Did it ever occur to you that maybe I'd like to take the lead now and again?

It's not a porn shoot, Mel. Do you have to make so much noise?

Could you at least try to pretend you're not always gagging for it? And you wonder why I don't like you talking to other men.

She jerked away from Flynn's kiss, her whole

body tense. She tried to turn away from him but he caught her shoulders.

"Mel. What's wrong?"

"Let me go."

She couldn't look at him. Was too afraid of what she'd see in his eyes. After a few beats he loosened his grip and she pulled away from him.

"Mel. Talk to me. What just happened?"

She could hear the confusion in his voice. The concern. A part of her understood that he hadn't been criticizing her, not really. He'd simply been trying to slow things down. And she *had* been rushing.

She'd been out of control.

But the greater part of her was running for cover, desperate to protect herself. Desperate to pretend she hadn't exposed herself so completely and left herself so open to his judgment and condemnation.

She wrapped her arms around herself. "This was a mistake."

"Then it's the best mistake I've ever made. Up until about twenty seconds ago, anyway."

His words surprised her so much she looked at him. His face was filled with concern, his gaze worried.

"What happened, Mel?"

There was no way she could answer his question, so she simply shook her head.

He sighed. Then he reached for the fly on his jeans. She looked away while he pulled up his fly and rebuttoned the stud, humiliated color burning its way into her cheeks.

He must have thought she was mad—tearing his clothes off one minute, then pushing him away the next. He must have thought she was completely demented. The moment he was decent she turned and led the way to the front door. She couldn't bring herself to look at him once she'd unlocked the door, so she aimed her gaze at his chin instead.

"I'm sorry. That was… I'm sorry."

He stood on the threshold, his body tense.

"Mel. I wasn't criticizing you. In case you couldn't tell, I was having a damned good time. It was meant to be a joke."

"I know."

It was on the tip of her tongue to tell him that it wasn't about him, it was all about her—about how screwed up she was—but she didn't want to start a conversation that she was never going to finish. It was bad enough that she knew how ugly her marriage had become, she didn't need to share the grim details with this man she'd grown to admire and respect and like so much. She didn't want to watch his lust turn to pity. She didn't want him to know how little she'd valued herself.

"Okay. I'll see you later, Mel." Frustration was rich in his voice but she didn't blame him. Why would she? She'd led him on then pushed him away and now she was kicking him out of her house.

Mel shut the door behind him and allowed herself one small moment of weakness as she leaned her forehead against the cool wood. Then she straightened and walked to her bedroom. The sight of her bed made her lip curl. If she wasn't such a head case, she might have been on that bed with Flynn right now, having what had been shaping up to be some of the best sex of her life.

Angry and embarrassed and deeply sad, she stripped off and walked into the en suite to wash away the day's labors. She stepped beneath the shower and washed herself with a businesslike thoroughness. It was impossible to ignore the sensitivity of her breasts and the sense of heavy fullness between her legs, however.

She'd wanted Flynn. Very badly.

She closed her eyes as she remembered the thick length of his erection in her hand, reexperiencing the rush of longing and lust and need. If he hadn't said anything...

But he had, and the bad old stuff had reared its ugly head.

She turned off the water and stepped out.

She dried herself briskly, almost roughly, before walking naked into her bedroom. She was crossing to her chest of drawers when she caught sight of her reflection in the free-standing mirror in the corner.

She stilled, then slowly turned to face herself.

She lifted her hands and covered her breasts, pressing them tightly against her body. Once, Owen had told her that her breasts made him believe in the divine—and yet in the final months of their marriage, he'd told her to lose weight, claiming her curves made even expensive clothes look tacky and cheap.

He'd also told her that she had no idea how to dress or act modestly and that if she couldn't "behave like a lady" he'd have to start attending social functions on his own.

He'd accused her of humiliating him with his peers and colleagues with her overfriendly manner and kept a constant, censorious eye on her whenever they were out together.

And yet he'd never stopped wanting her once they were alone. The moment they were safely behind their bedroom door, he'd always turned to her with desire. It had confused her for so long, the disparity between what he said and what he did—and she'd hated herself for wanting him in return, for clinging to the last good, functioning, life-affirming thing between them because she'd seen it as evidence that their marriage wasn't beyond repair.

Then things had deteriorated even further and he'd started to run her down in the bedroom, too. By that time she'd been so punch-drunk from years of criticism and disapproval that it had taken the night of the Hollands' party and the ugliness of Owen's anger afterward to awaken her to the fact that her marriage was over.

Well and truly.

Not long after that she'd walked out altogether. The smartest thing she'd ever done in her life.

She turned away from the mirror and crossed to her bed. Last night's pajamas were under the pillow and she pulled them on and climbed beneath the covers. She was tired, but instead of turning off the light she lay frowning at the ceiling, her body as rigid as a board.

She'd ruined things with Flynn. All these weeks they'd been dancing around one another, an invisible question hanging between them. Would they, wouldn't they? She'd answered the question tonight, unequivocally. *No.* A resounding, screwed-up, messy no.

She wouldn't see him as much now. Against the odds they'd become friends, but tonight would change all that. Sex always did—even if it was only half-assed, abortive sex that didn't quite come off.

No more drop-in visits. No more gardening sessions. No more laughter.

If only she'd met him seven years ago. If only—

She closed her eyes. Then she reached out and switched off the bedside lamp.

"If onlys" were a pointless waste of time. She was who she was, and he was who he was, and she had ruined things. Nothing was going to change that.

SUMMERLEA WAS COLD and dark when Flynn let himself in. He turned on the lights in the living room and built a fire. There was a bottle of shiraz he hadn't quite finished from the previous week and he poured himself a glass and sat to one side of the hearth, waiting for the fire to start throwing out some heat.

He had no idea what had happened with Mel tonight. Not a single clue. One minute she'd been insatiable, tearing at his clothes, so hot she'd almost blown his mind—and the next she'd been pushing him away, her body tense, her face pale.

And the look in her eyes…

He tossed back the wine. If there was more, he would have drank it, too, but there wasn't so he stripped to his underwear and unrolled his sleeping bag. Lying on the hard floor, he forced himself to face the fact that he'd badly misjudged things with Mel. Or, more accurately, he hadn't listened to his own judgment, because he'd always known she was wounded and still recovering from her marriage, hadn't he? He'd acknowledged that right from the start—and yet he'd pushed and pushed until they'd gotten to the point they'd reached tonight.

Which was, effectively, nowhere.

A part of Mel might want to be with him, but a big part of her also didn't—and Flynn wasn't in the business of forcing his attentions on women. Even ones he liked as much as he liked Mel.

Even when he thought he was falling for them.

It took him a long time to fall asleep and he woke with a sore back. Standing under the shower in the cold and drafty main bathroom, he made a mental note to have a bed delivered during the week. He didn't need or want anything else yet—he'd only have to move any furniture out again once renovations were under way—but the romance of sleeping rough was starting to fade.

So much for a boy's own adventures. He walked naked up the hallway and dressed in the chilly living room. Then and only then did he allow himself to think about Mel again. In the light of a new day, what had happened between them last night didn't seem quite so dire.

Frustrating, yes, but perhaps not quite as end-of-days as he'd let himself believe last night.

After all, there had been almost five minutes of blazing-hot intensity between them before she pushed him away. That had to count for something, and definitely it had to count in his favor.

He was on his way to the garden, still mulling things over, trying to work out what his next step should be where she was concerned, when he opened the front door and almost stumbled over a bag that had been left on the doormat. Frowning, he picked it up and glanced inside. His gray sweater lay neatly folded in the bottom, while his sunglasses rested on top. Vaguely he remembered leaving both items on the rear porch at Mel's place yesterday.

He walked to the top of the steps and looked down the garden path, but there was no sign of Mel. Which made sense. She'd probably dropped by at the crack of dawn in order to avoid running into him.

So much for things looking better in the light of a new day.

He ran a hand through his hair, letting out a heavy sigh. There'd been so many things against him falling for someone at this ridiculously difficult and stressful time in his life, but for whatever crazy reason he was here, in this place, with his feelings and hopes very firmly engaged— and Mel didn't want a piece of him. There was no other way to interpret this morning's gesture.

He walked into the living room and tossed the bag onto the floor. The urge to kick something was so powerful he didn't even bother resisting it, simply aimed and left fly, sending the old wooden crate flying across the room. It hit the wall with a satisfying crack.

It didn't change anything. He still didn't know what to do. Common sense told him to back off and cut his losses. If it were any other woman, he would. But this was Mel, and last night she'd been in his arms…

Frustrated beyond measure, he spun on his heel and went in search of something sweaty and exhausting to do. At least when it came to dirt and plants he knew what was what.

IT WAS RIDICULOUS, but Mel missed Flynn. Ridiculous because she never usually saw him during the week—last week being an exception—and because she was the one who had pushed him away.

The urge to text or call or email him gripped her most of Monday and Tuesday. She ignored it. For starters, she had no idea how she would even begin to start a conversation with him after what had almost happened. She'd groped him then rejected him—she couldn't now call him and pretend nothing had happened.

Could she?

She toyed with the notion all Tuesday night and was still undecided on the subject when she arrived at her parents' place on Wednesday morning. She'd been pressed into service to help prepare the yard for the big anniversary party on Saturday night and she spent the morning weeding the flower beds along the fence line before making a run to the garden center to get some annuals—"instant loveliness," as her mother called them—then planting them. All the while the question of Flynn whirled in her mind. Could she call him? Should she? If she was going to play it cool and pretend nothing had happened, what would she say?

She started scraping the rust and flaking paint off the garage wall in the afternoon in preparation for painting, and by the time she'd reached the halfway mark she still hadn't come up with a single decent conversational gambit with which to break the ice with Flynn.

"You know why? Because you're an idiot," she muttered to herself.

"Sorry? Did you say something?"

Mel looked over to see her mother crossing the patio, a glass of water in hand.

"Just talking to myself," Mel admitted.

Her mother passed her the glass. "It's when you start answering back that you really have to worry."

"Too late."

Her mother grinned and shaded her eyes to inspect her progress. "You know, your father promised he'd do this for me so many times over the years, but it's taken this party before it finally happened."

"Yeah, and he still isn't doing it." Mel couldn't help pointing that fact out.

"True," her mother said reflectively. "But he is paying for the party, which is why I've been able to guilt you into doing this, so, by extension…"

"You should be in politics. You have a sneaky mind." Mel took a big swallow of water then turned back to the garage wall.

"Sing out if you need anything else," her mother said as she headed inside.

Mel's phone rang as she bent to pick up the wire brush she'd been using. She straightened, leaving the brush where it was, and pulled her phone from her pocket. Her heart did something strange in her chest when she saw it was Flynn calling.

"Hi," she said, hoping she didn't sound as pleased—and relieved—as she felt to hear from him.

"Hey. How are things?" His voice sounded so good, so familiar.

"Things are good. Mom's got me on slave duties for the big party on Saturday night. Although I'm beginning to suspect that this is all a ploy to get a freebie renovation."

She waited for him to pick up the conversational ball and run with it the way he usually did, but there was a small, awkward pause before he spoke again.

"Actually, I was calling about your parents' party. Your mother sent me an invitation, and I wanted to check with you before I responded."

Mel blinked. "Beg pardon?"

"Your mother sent me an invitation to her party."

"Holy—" Mel swallowed a curse, turning to glare at the house. She could see her mother moving around through the kitchen window. If she could have, she would have grabbed her by the shoulders and shaken her until her teeth rattled. "I'm really sorry she did that, Flynn. Believe me, if I'd known… I'll tell her to cross you off her list right now."

"Right. Well, I guess that answers my question," he said slowly.

"What question was that?"

"Whether you knew if she'd asked me or not."

She was so embarrassed she could feel heat radiating off her face. It took her a moment to register the disappointment in his voice and longer still to comprehend what it might mean.

"Don't tell me you want to come?" she blurted.

"The thought had crossed my mind."

"Why?" The question came from her gut, fueled by all the doubts and regrets that had been plaguing her since she'd pushed him away on Saturday night.

"You really need me to spell it out?"

There was a faintly exasperated note to his voice, but she knew that if he was standing in front of her that there would also be a smile in his eyes. A wave of relief washed over her, so strong that she felt a little dizzy in its wake.

"I thought the next time I saw you was going to be when we bumped into each other accidentally in the village," she said.

"Did you? And here I was, under the impression that we were friends."

Her heart was going nuts in her chest. She lay her hand over her left breast to try to contain it.

"I thought that maybe, after what happened, I mean, after what didn't happen, that it might be too weird—"

"Because we kissed?"

"Because we almost had sex and I freaked out and kicked you out of my house like a complete psycho beast."

"That's one way of looking at it."

"What's the other way?"

"We kissed."

Inexplicable tears burned the back of her eyes. She pressed her fingers to her lips to stop herself from saying any of the things that were crowding her throat.

"Mel? Are you still there?"

She closed her eyes. "Yeah. I'm still here."

"Good. I'd like to buy your parents something for their anniversary. Any suggestions?"

Mel opened her eyes and glanced toward the house again. "My mother loves those little porcelain dogs and cats. The ones you can buy at the jewelers. Get her as many of those as you can. Half a dozen should do it."

There was a small pause. "So she hates porcelain. Any other nonsuggestions?"

"Just buy her some flowers. She loves flowers."

"Okay. I'll see you on Saturday, Mel."

"See you." She ended the call then stood for a moment, her head bowed. Flynn was coming to her parents' anniversary party. She was going to see him again. And he hadn't given up on her or decided she was too hard or not worth the hassle.

After a long beat, she lifted her head and took a deep breath. *"Mom!"*

Her mother appeared in the door like a jack-in-the-box. "Are you okay?"

Mel marched toward the patio, the better to loom over her parent while she gave her a piece of her mind. "Why did you invite Flynn to your party without telling me?"

Her mother had the grace to look guilty. "I thought it would be a nice surprise for you."

"Did it occur to you at some point that I might prefer not to be surprised? And that if I had wanted him to come I would have invited him myself?"

Her mother reached for the necklace at her throat, pulling the faith, hope and charity charms back and forth across the chain. A sure sign she was nervous.

"Why don't you want him to come? You obviously like the man. And he obviously likes you. Why wouldn't you want him there?"

"You of all people know why," Mel said.

Her mother shut her jaw with a click and dropped her hand. After a long moment she nodded. "You're right. I'm sorry. We just want you to be happy again, Melly Belly."

"I know, Mom. But you can't make me happy,

especially not by pushing me into something I have no idea if I'm ready for or not."

"I thought I was doing the right thing. I thought maybe you just needed a little nudge."

"No."

"Okay. I'll cross him off the list, then," her mother said.

Mel turned and walked back toward the garage. "He's coming."

"But you just said—"

Wisely, her mother didn't complete her thought. Mel picked up the wire brush and resumed her attack on the garage wall. After a few seconds her mother reentered the house.

Mel spent the next hour trying not to feel like the world's biggest hypocrite—because, of course, she was over the moon that she would be seeing Flynn this weekend. But her mother didn't need to know that just yet.

CHAPTER ELEVEN

THREE DAYS LATER, Mel plugged in the final string of fairy lights and stepped back to assess the effect. She gave a nod of satisfaction.

"Not too bad, if I do say so myself."

"Yeah, not too shabby," her brother agreed.

They'd been working since daybreak to transform their parents' yard for the big occasion. Thanks to their labors, fairy lights now hung from every conceivable anchor point—the eaves, the side of the freshly painted garage, along the fence—and pots full of flowering annuals had been borrowed from Mel's garden and placed in strategic locations to cover various domestic uglies like the tap and the grease trap. Assorted outdoor chairs were placed in conversational groupings, and the caterers had set up a long trestle table beneath the covered patio. Later, guests would help themselves to a selection of salads as well as roast lamb and beef, both of which were currently being spit-roasted on a rotisserie located in front of the garage, sending delicious aromas across the backyard.

"I'm going home to get ready before Mom spots us standing around," Harry said, already fishing in his pocket for his car keys.

"Good point."

Officially the party didn't start for another hour, but her mother's sister, Lydia, was notorious for being early, and the neighbors would probably drift over sooner rather than later. Unless Mel wanted to be caught in her dirty track pants and equally dirty sweater, she needed to make a quick exit while she could.

"Two-minute warning, here comes Mom now," Harry said. He ducked down the side of the house just as their mother exited the sliding door to the patio.

"Mel. Thank God. The light's blown on the front porch. Can you believe the timing? Your father's in the shower. Would you mind?"

Mel held out a hand for the lightbulb her mother was already carrying and followed her through the house to the front door.

"I'm still not sure if we've got enough wine. Do you think I should send Harry out for more champagne? And ice. Do we have enough ice?" her mother asked.

Mel handed her the blown bulb before placing her hands on her mother's shoulders.

"Mom. Calm down. You have enough drink to keep the Australian cricket team happy, and we have ice up the yoo-hoo. Why don't you get ready, then sit down and put your feet up for a few minutes and have a glass of wine?"

"I'm not sure. I wanted to make sure the caterers know where to set up the bar. And—"

Mel gave her mother's shoulders a little shake. "Quit it with the excuses. Go get ready. I'll tell the caterers where to put the bar on my way out, okay?"

Her mother looked relieved. "All right. If you insist."

"I do, crazy lady. Now go make yourself beautiful, and I'll see you in half an hour or so."

Mel waited till her mother had disappeared up the hallway to her bedroom before ducking outside to have a quick word with the caterer. Then she escaped before her mother came up with another task for her to do.

She headed straight for the shower when she got home. Standing under the warm water, she allowed herself to think about Flynn again.

She'd been rationing herself, not allowing herself to think too much about him and build too much into the fact that she was going to see him again. It was enough that he was going to be there and that he wanted to be there. Anything else she was going to have to deal with on the fly, because no amount of thinking and double thinking and analyzing was going to change the fact that the future was yet to be written.

She'd laid her clothes out on the bed before she left that morning and she sprayed on perfume before slipping into a matching bra-and-panties set and reaching for her dress. Even though her parents had hired a number of outdoor heaters to try to take the chill off, she'd chosen a fine-knit red wool wrap dress for the party, as well as her black knee-high boots. Both went well with the black coat she'd be wearing. She sat on the bed to roll on stay-up stockings, then she zipped her boots and went to fix her hair. She pulled it into the laziest of updos, pinning it into a loose bun with stray curls around her face. She spent five minutes on her makeup before adding a pair of dangling jet earrings and matching necklace to her ensemble. She walked into the bedroom to check her reflection.

She looked good. And really, really nervous.

She collected her coat from the hall closet, locked the house and drove to her parents'. The street was beginning to fill with cars and she was forced to park near the corner and walk. She shrugged into her coat as she walked, her high-heeled boots clicking on the pavement. The front door was open and she could hear music and voices inside, a sure sign that the party had well and truly started.

She let herself in and started looking for her mother to check there were no last-minute emergencies she needed help with before things really fired up. Mel's progress was slow as she stopped to greet and exchange quick catch-ups with various relatives and family friends. She'd scored a glass of champagne from a roving waiter by the time she made it to the patio, where she finally found her mother.

Dressed in painted-on black trousers and a jade-green silk jacket with a plunging neckline that was only made decent by a black lace camisole, her mother was lit up like a Christmas tree, a glass of champagne in one hand as she held court with her friends. Mel took one look at her and decided she was fine, making a beeline for where she could see Harry and Justine standing near the garage.

"Mom's on fire already," she said as she arrived.

"Tell me about it. Someone needs to remind her to go easy on the champagne," Justine said.

"Why? It's her night. If she wants to get snookered and stagger around a little, she should be allowed to," Harry said, raising his own beer to his mouth.

His gaze was glued to the petite blond waitress who was circulating with a tray of hors d'oeuvres. Mel couldn't decide if it was because he was hungry or trying to pick up, and she decided she didn't want to know. Harry's love life was hair-raising at the best of times.

Justine's gaze slid over Mel's shoulder and a peculiar expression—half surprise, half smug—came over her face. "Look at that. He came."

Mel knew who her sister was talking about, even though she hadn't realized Justine had been privy to her mother's sneaky invitation.

Slowly she turned, her gaze scanning the crowd in search of a tall, handsome, blue-eyed man.

Everything inside her went very still as she found him. He was talking to her father on the patio, a small smile on his mouth. For long moments the world seemed to recede, leaving her with the rush of blood through her veins and the *thud-thud* of her heartbeat as she ate him up with her eyes.

He was wearing a midthigh-length black wool coat, designer jeans, a black sweater and a red-and-black plaid scarf and he looked dark and expensive and stylish and far too handsome. As though he could feel her regard, Flynn glanced up from his conversation with her father and their eyes met across the crowded yard. His mouth curved into a slow smile and he lifted a hand in greeting. Despite everything, a bubble of unalloyed happiness rose inside her.

A few seconds later, he made his excuses to her dad and began weaving his way to her. Mel checked the side tie on her dress and tweaked her skirt self-consciously, wishing she had a mirror to check her makeup.

"Don't worry, your lippy's on straight," Justine said quietly. "You look great."

Mel forced her hands back by her sides. "We're just friends."

She wasn't sure who she was trying to convince.

"And I'm a Teenage Mutant Ninja Turtle. Just promise me one thing, okay? *Be careful.*"

Mel looked into her sister's eyes, registering the warning she saw there, and the concern. "I will. I am."

"Good."

They both pasted on smiles as Flynn slid past the last group blocking his way.

"You poor bastard. I suppose Mom roped you into coming?" Harry said, shaking his head.

"No rope required," Flynn said, his gaze sliding to Mel. "You look great."

"Thanks." She stepped forward, feeling incredibly bold, and put her hand on his shoulder. Then she leaned forward and kissed his cheek. "It's good to see you."

He was watching her very intently as she withdrew and she had a sudden, hot flash of how it had felt when he'd kissed her last weekend. The way he'd held her. The way he'd tasted. She became aware that her sister and brother were watching them with knowing expressions and she gave herself a mental shake.

"Have you got a drink? Let's get you a drink," she said, taking Flynn's elbow and guiding him away from her siblings. "Beer or wine?"

"A beer would be great, thanks."

They joined the crowd at the impromptu bar and she gave him a small, nervous smile. "Bit busy. Won't be a tick."

"There's no rush. Your mom looks like she's ready for a big night."

"Oh, she is. This will be one for the record books if she's got any say in the matter."

Someone jostled her from behind and she was forced to step closer to him.

"How are your parents?" she asked.

"They're good, thanks. It's been a good week."

She could smell his aftershave and she fought the need to lean closer and inhale a big, greedy lungful of the stuff.

"It's good to see you," she said before she could stop herself.

His eyes were warm as they looked into hers. "It's good to see you, too, Mel."

Her aunt and uncle approached before she could say more and she found herself introducing them to Flynn. Then one of her father's work colleagues came over to ask if Flynn was the owner of the vintage Aston Martin her father had worked on, and the next thing she knew two hours had slipped by effortlessly as she watched Flynn win over her extended family.

He gave everyone he was introduced to his sincere and undivided attention, asking questions and making jokes and generally being too damned charming. He talked politics with her very left-wing cousin, Jack, for nearly half an hour and managed to leave him laughing despite the fact that they hadn't agreed on a single issue. He discussed home preserves with her elderly aunt, herb gardens with her mother's next-door neighbor and the property market with Jacob and Justine. When they ran out of seating at dinnertime, he perched on the rim of one of the built-in brick planters along the edge of the patio alongside her and Harry and made appreciative noises about the tenderness of the meat. He went back to the dessert table twice, insisting that Mel at least try the chocolate-mint mousse that had him so enthralled.

After dinner, Mel excused herself to go to the bathroom and fix her lipstick. When she exited the house to rejoin the party, she saw that Flynn had moved from their perch on the planter boxes. She scanned the crowd and finally found him talking with Eddy and Rex, hunkered down so that he was on the same level with them. His head was cocked, his expression open and engaged as Rex relayed a story that, based on his hand gestures, seemed to involve lots of big explosions.

Watching Flynn give his all to her nephews, something sharp and painful tightened in her chest.

He was such a good man. Hardworking, genuine, kind, funny. What he was doing for his parents was plain old-fashioned noble, although she knew he would reject the label vehemently if she shared it with him because he was also modest and unassuming. By some miracle he managed to combine all of the above with a quiet confidence that drew people to him as naturally as the moon drew the tide.

In short, he was a special man.

And he wanted her. Not just for sex, either. He *liked* her. She liked him, too. She liked him in a crazy way. She liked him so much that even acknowledging it in the privacy of her own mind made her palms sweaty with anxiety.

She hadn't intended to feel this way about a man again. Certainly not so soon. But Flynn was here, and unless she was grossly misreading his signals, he wasn't going anywhere soon. Which meant that this yearning, almost painful feeling in her chest wasn't going to go away anytime soon, either.

Suddenly she felt overwhelmed by all the noise and chatter of the party. Picking her way through the crowd, she reached the side gate and slipped through to the front yard. She walked down the driveway and stood on the sidewalk, arms crossed over her chest as she looked out at the darkened street.

The sounds of the party ebbed and flowed behind her. She squeezed herself tightly and reminded herself that once upon a time she'd been brave. She could do this. She could.

She heard the gate open, then the sound of footsteps on the driveway. She didn't need to turn around to see who it was, but she did, anyway.

Flynn's face was half shadow, half light, his eyes unreadable as he approached.

"You okay?" he asked.

"Yeah," she said.

Then, because she was afraid she'd lose her courage and because she'd been aching to touch him again ever since she'd stopped, she closed the distance between them. Three steps, then her breasts were brushing his chest as she angled her head and pressed a kiss to his lips. He responded minimally, almost warily, and she moved closer still, curling a hand behind his neck and licking the seam of his mouth. She could feel how tense he was and after a few seconds he pulled his head back.

"Are you sure?" he asked, his voice low and ragged.

"Yes." She reached for him again, but he was already reaching for her. His lips found hers, his tongue sweeping into her mouth. One hand slid around her waist, the other cupped her backside, hauling her close. She went willingly, wantonly.

He backed her against the side fence and pinned her there with his hips while he slid a hand inside the warmth of her coat, his mouth never leaving hers. Her nipples were already hard but she gasped her encouragement as his hand slid onto her right breast, his thumb gliding over her nipple. She could feel how hard he was, his erection a solid ridge against her belly, and she slid a hand onto the front of his jeans, gripping him through the denim. He pressed himself against her hand, his own tightening on her breast.

"Mel," he said against her mouth.

"Yo. You guys. Mom and Dad are about to start the speeches. Quit playing tonsil hockey and get your asses in here."

It was Harry, calling from the front porch. Flynn lifted his head but didn't release her. It took her a moment to catch her breath enough to respond.

"We're coming," she finally called back.

"*Way* too much information," Harry said before disappearing into the house.

She could feel Flynn's body trembling with suppressed laughter. She rested her forehead on his shoulder.

"Don't. You'll only encourage him."

He pressed a kiss to her temple before taking a step backward. The loss of his body heat was like a blow.

"Come on. Let's go listen to the speeches," he said, holding out his hand to her.

She took it and let him draw her away from the fence, aware of a profound sense of disappointment and frustration. Which was nuts— it wasn't as though they could have made love against the fence in her parents' yard. They would have had to stop at some point.

Flynn opened the side gate and they entered the fray. Everyone was crowded around the patio for the speeches and they found a spot near the corner of the garage that offered them a decent view. Over the next twenty minutes, her parents milked their moment in the limelight for all they were worth. Flynn kept a hold of her hand, his thumb occasionally brushing her wrist in the smallest of caresses. She glanced at him from time to time to see if he was laughing at the same joke she was or to gauge his reaction to something her mother or father had said, and every time she found herself getting lost in his gaze.

And she knew, absolutely, that she would not be going home alone tonight.

IT WAS NEARLY MIDNIGHT when Flynn followed Mel's car home, parking in the street while she turned into the drive and disappeared around the back of the house to park in her carport. He locked up the Aston and made his way to the front door.

He jiggled his car keys as he waited for Mel to let him in. No point lying to himself—he was nervous. A fairly galling admission for a man in his thirty-fourth year. It wasn't as though he was a babe in the woods as far as making love to a woman went, after all.

But this wasn't just any woman he was about to sleep with.

The *chink-chink* of his car keys bouncing in his hand sounded loud in the still night air. He tensed as he heard Mel's footsteps approaching from inside the house.

Don't blow this. Okay? Just...don't. Take it slow, let her take the lead, take all your cues from her.

The door opened, revealing Mel in the golden glow of the hall light.

"Sorry. I dropped my keys on the back porch and do you think I could find them? Turned out they fell inside one of my gum boots. What are the odds?"

She was nervous, possibly even more nervous than he was, and suddenly all of his own uncertainty took a backseat. Before she could say another word, he stepped forward and kissed her. There was a fraction of a moment's hesitation, and then she was kissing him back, her fingers tangling in his hair as she pulled him closer.

She tasted like chocolate and red wine and he went from being partially to painfully erect in no second flat.

So much for taking it easy.

He kicked the door shut before backing her against the wall. Holding her there with his body, he slid his hands inside her coat. He skimmed one hand down her rib cage to her hip, savoring the voluptuous curve, before sliding it onto her backside. His other hand cupped the fullness of her left breast. She made a small, wordless approving noise as he teased her nipple, her hips flexing against his.

They rocked their hips together as her nipple peaked beneath his hand, hard and eager. Impatient to touch her properly, he pulled the cross-over bodice of her dress below her breast and tugged her bra cup down. Warm, silken skin filled his palm and he groaned into her mouth.

She felt so good. Hot and smooth and soft and firm…

He broke their kiss. Desperate to see her, he glanced down. Her breast was pale in his hand, the nipple rosy pink, the deep burgundy of her bra framing the whole.

"Mel," he whispered brokenly, lifting worshipful eyes to her face.

She was beautiful, and so sexy he could barely breathe.

She fisted her hand in his jacket, pulling him close. She kissed him, hard and hot and fast.

"Bedroom," she said, when they came up for air again.

"Great idea."

She strode ahead of him, already shrugging out of her coat. He followed suit, dropping his jacket in the hallway, his scarf in the doorway, kicking his shoes off as he entered her bedroom.

She flicked on a bedside light and reached for the side tie on her dress. One deft tug and it came free. He'd started pulling his sweater over his head but he froze as her dress fell open, revealing her body in all its glory. Those breasts, those hips, those legs…

Her panties matched her bra, her stockings

were stay-ups with lacy tops and her knee-high boots tipped him firmly over into fantasy territory.

Any pretense at self-control went out the window as he moved toward her. They fell onto the bed together, him on top, her legs spreading to accept his body into the cradle of her thighs. He kissed her neck and her chest, then dragged her bra cup down with his teeth and pulled a nipple into his mouth. She gasped and arched into him, her hands sliding down to grip his backside. Lifting her hips, she ground herself against his erection in a sinuous, knowing rhythm.

He slid his free hand onto her stomach, feeling the excited, expectant jump of her belly muscles beneath his fingers as he began to move south. His fingers found the edge of her panties and he traced the lace with his forefinger. Back and forth, back and forth, all the while sucking on her nipple, biting it, soothing it, loving the way she trembled and breathed and shook beneath him.

He slipped a finger beneath the waistband of her panties, delving until he felt the silken brush of hair against his fingers. She lifted her hips in wordless encouragement and he completed the journey, his fingers sliding into wet heat. She shuddered beneath him, spreading her legs wider as he explored her delicate folds with his fingers.

He was so hard it hurt, and when her hands slid to the stud on his jeans and started tearing them open he tilted his hips to the side to provide easier access. He shoved her bra out of the way and shifted his attentions to her other breast as she gained entrance to his jeans. He groaned low in his throat as she gripped him, stroking her hand up and down his shaft. It felt so good he closed his eyes for a moment, savoring the sensation.

"Take these off," she panted, pushing at his jeans with her free hand. "I want to see you."

He rolled to the side and made short work of his jeans and socks before stripping his sweater and T-shirt over his head. He was aware of Mel shedding the last of her clothes, too, and when they rolled toward each other again they were naked.

She took charge, pressing his shoulders onto the mattress as she slid a long leg over his hips. She straddled him, staring down at him with smoky gray eyes. Her cheeks were flushed, her breasts aroused, her nipples wet from his mouth. She reached for his erection and rolled her hips, rubbing herself against him. He covered her breasts with his hands, squeezing her nipples, plucking at them. She smoothed her free hand across his belly and chest, her eyes half-closed as she watched him watch her.

She was primal and utterly feminine and he needed to be inside her. Now.

"Back pocket of my jeans," he said, barely able to string two words together.

She leaned across him to her bedside drawer instead. He took advantage of the situation to tongue her breasts, holding her to him long after she'd found what she was looking for. She shuddered and writhed against him as he suckled her deeply.

"Flynn," she finally gasped.

He released her, letting her rock back onto his hips. A small smile played around her lips as she tore open the foil square in her hands and removed the condom. He watched through slitted eyes as she smoothed the latex onto him with confident, sure hands. Then she rose above him, gripping him in her hand as she sank onto his erection.

She was tight and hot and he almost disgraced himself. Almost. She made a small, needy sound and started to move. He gripped her hips and watched as she bit her lip and closed her eyes and got lost in the sensation rising inside her. When she started to pant and lose her own rhythm, he lifted his hips off the bed and rolled her over, quickly reversing their positions. She stared up at him, her gray eyes pleading with him. He kissed her as he pushed inside her.

"It's okay, Mel, we'll get there," he murmured against her lips.

Then he set himself to the task of proving it to her.

MEL CLOSED HER EYES and bit her lip to stifle a moan as Flynn moved deeply inside her. His mouth was on her breasts, his big, powerful body pressing hers into the mattress, and she was so close, so close…

Inexplicably, his pace slowed, his thrusts becoming more leisurely. She opened her eyes to find him watching her, an earthy, heated knowledge in his eyes. He shifted his attention to her other nipple as his hand slid between their bodies to where she needed him the most. He found her with his thumb and began to tease her with small, gentle circles, the rhythm echoing his leisurely strokes inside her body. Everything in her wanted to come, wanted to strain toward coming, but the message Flynn was sending her with his body was that there was no rush.

No need to strain. No need to race anyone to the finish line.

Joint by joint, muscle by muscle, she allowed herself to relax. Allowed herself to fall into the long, sensuous stroking of his body within hers, allowed herself to revel in the slow, spreading pleasure building between her thighs. She gave herself over utterly to the experience, moaning and twisting beneath him as the need took her, running her hands up and down his big, beautiful body, languishing in his deep, thorough kisses, relishing the way he supped at her breasts, licking and sucking and biting.

And then, suddenly, she was arching off the bed, her climax rolling over her in a huge, pulsating wave, Flynn deep inside her as she cried out his name and forgot to breathe for long, long seconds.

She felt him shudder, felt the hot gust of his breath against her shoulder as he gasped out his own climax. Her fingers gripped his backside as he tensed inside her…and finally relaxed into dead weight, his head dropping onto her shoulder.

She closed her eyes, the better to appreciate the utter satisfaction pulsing through her body. He was still inside her, and she could feel his heart pounding. She ran her hands along his body in a slow, relaxed exploration, smoothing over the muscular planes of his back, shaping his rounded buttocks, discovering the backs of his thighs. After a few minutes he stirred and lifted his weight off her chest. She opened her eyes to find him watching her, a small smile on his lips.

"How you doin'?" he asked.

"I'm doin' okay."

"Yeah?"

"Oh, yeah."

His smile broadened into a grin. She punched him lightly on the arm. "Okay, now you're getting dangerously close to smug territory."

"You know, I think I'm willing to risk it."

He kissed her, his lips gentle. When he lifted his head again there was no mistaking the tenderness in his eyes. He withdrew from her and she watched as he left the bed to dispose of the condom. His backside was solid muscle and she watched the bounce of his butt cheeks with shameless appreciation. When he exited the en suite she was treated to a full frontal and it was all she could do to suppress an admiring sigh.

He had a beautiful body—well proportioned, muscular but not overly so, with long, powerful thighs, a hard, flat belly and the exact right amount of chest hair.

She'd assumed he was going to get straight back beneath the covers, but instead he stopped by the foot of the bed and cocked an eyebrow at her.

"Seen enough?" he asked cheekily.

Busted.

She laughed. Couldn't help herself. "Are you accusing me of ogling you?"

"Yes, ma'am, I am."

He bent and scooped up his abandoned scarf, looping it around his neck. Then he strutted toward her in perfect imitation of a catwalk model, all haughty looks and cheekbones and pout, gorgeously, undeniably, utterly naked bar the scarf arranged jauntily around his neck. When he reached the bedside table, he did a sharp turn and strutted in the opposite direction, working it for all he was worth.

He should have looked ridiculous, but he didn't. He looked spectacular. Gorgeous. Too cute for words. She didn't know whether to laugh, applaud or drag him back into bed, so she settled for grabbing hold of the scarf when he made his second pass by the bed.

"Stop being a tease," she said, using the scarf to reel him in.

"You're the one doing the teasing, making promises with your eyes like that," he said as he climbed onto the bed.

Excitement kicked inside her as he drew back the covers and pressed his body over hers again. She could feel him growing hard against her thighs and answering heat surged through her belly.

"It's only teasing if you don't follow through," she said.

"That's an excellent point."

She slid a hand between their bodies to capture his growing erection. "Actually, I think you'll find this is an excellent point."

He laughed, the sound loud and uninhibited. "I stand corrected."

He lowered his head and started to kiss and lick and suck her neck, even as one of his hands began a slow, sensual glide down her body. She let her head fall to one side, savoring the slide of skin on skin, the feel of him beneath her hand, the wet velvet of his tongue on her neck.

Had she known, deep inside, that it would be like this with him? Was that why it had been so hard to make herself be sensible where he was concerned?

She let go of thought as instinct took over. Right at this moment, nothing else mattered except the need and the want and the desire burning between them. Everything else—the world, the future, the past—could wait.

CHAPTER TWELVE

MEL WOKE WITH A START, very aware of the heavy, warm weight of a male arm wrapped around her. Her first impulse was to roll away, to push *him* away. And then she remembered: this was Flynn lying beside her, not Owen, and she was in her own home, in her own bed, not trapped in an unhappy marriage.

She let out the breath she'd been holding and tried to enjoy the fact that it was Flynn, listening to his steady breathing, remembering last night. They'd made love three times, laughing and talking and teasing each other until need had taken over. Mel couldn't remember ever laughing so much with a man in the bedroom. Not that there was anything laughable about Flynn's body or his lovemaking—far from it. But he was playful and irreverent and self-deprecating and cheeky and—sometimes—daring. It was hard not to laugh and be engaged by and seduced by a man who was so beautiful, knowing, tender and funny, and she'd thrown herself into the experience—into his arms—with complete abandon.

And she'd survived. Lying in his arms the morning after, she had no regrets. Not a single one. But it had never been the sex she'd been worried about. It was what came after the sex that scared the hell out of her.

Flynn stirred behind her, drawing her closer. She tensed. Even though she knew it was completely irrational, she still felt hemmed in and suffocated. She needed some breathing room.

Moving slowly, she eased Flynn's arm from around her waist and rolled away from him. She padded quietly into the en suite and shut the door. She took care of business, then washed her face, wishing she could wash away the shadows of the past so easily. She studied herself in the mirror. She looked tired, her mouth a little swollen. Her eyes were anxious. Worried.

She pulled her hair back from her face and took a deep breath, letting it out. She reminded herself that this relationship was new and fresh, untainted by the dynamics that had ruined her marriage. For starters, Flynn was a far more secure man than Owen had ever been. And, of course, she and Flynn weren't married. They didn't share a bedroom or a home, she didn't answer to him, her fate wasn't tied to him. She was her own person, and Flynn his.

These were all good things to remember, good things to remind herself of.

Drying her face, she opened the bathroom door, ready to slip into bed.

"Good morning." Flynn was propped against the pillows with his arms behind his head, his hair mussed, his eyes heavy from sleep. He looked warm and sexy and *interested,* his gaze roaming over her body.

Her hands twitched with the instinctive desire to either cover herself like Botticelli's Venus or grab something to hide behind. Last night, she'd ogled him shamelessly and he'd done his little catwalk thing, but she didn't feel nearly as brave in the cold light of day. For starters, there was a lot more natural light in the room this morning than there had been last night. Then there was the fact that it had been a while since she'd done a sit-up or an ab-crunch and even longer since she'd subjected herself to a bikini wax. A few hours ago, none of that had mattered, but with Flynn staring at her so openly, every flaw, every feature, felt as though it was under the microscope.

Somehow she resisted the impulse to scuttle into bed. Instead, she squared her shoulders and looked him in the eye.

"Good morning," she said. "Would you like coffee?"

He dragged his gaze to her face, looking rather gratifyingly distracted.

"You should probably know that if you told me you had an invisible jet parked around the corner right now, I'd totally believe you," he said, his tone bordering on the reverential.

She laughed, even as her confidence skyrocketed. "Aren't you a little old for Wonder Woman fantasies?"

"No one is too old for Wonder Woman fantasies." He flipped the quilt back on the empty side of the bed. "Come back to bed and I'll let you use your golden lasso on me."

"Make a girl an offer she can't refuse, why don't you."

She approached the bed, aware of him watching her every move with focused avidity. There was so much admiration and lust in his gaze that it was impossible for her not to be flattered. She climbed onto the bed and began a slow crawl toward him. His eyelids dropped to half-mast as he watched her gently swaying breasts.

"You didn't have plans today, did you?" he asked as she drew closer.

"Nothing concrete."

"Good."

He abandoned his casual posture and reached for her, pulling her into his lap.

Two hours and a shower later, she watched Flynn get dressed as she fastened the back clasp on her bra.

"You know if men had to wear bras they'd have electromagnetic catches and Kevlar cups, right?" he said as he zipped up his jeans.

"Sure. You guys would probably sneak a phone transmitter in there somewhere, too. Maybe even a miniature TV screen."

"Now you're talking. Not that I have anything against black lace, for the record. I wouldn't want you getting the wrong idea on that one."

"Noted. Thanks."

She pulled her red sweater from her chest of drawers.

"So, where am I taking you for lunch?" Flynn asked. "We seem to have skipped breakfast altogether. Not sure how that happened."

"Aren't you?"

"I have a few ideas, but it's all just a blur, really. I may need a play-by-play reenactment later on to refresh my memory."

"Poor you."

He was grinning shamelessly as he pulled her close for a quick kiss. "So, where am I taking you?"

"It's the first Sunday of the month, so the market is on in the village if you want to see what's happening?"

"Great. I've been meaning to hunt down the driftwood guy you mentioned."

They took Flynn's car and were forced to park

on a side street because the shopping center lot was full to overflowing. A series of stalls were set up on the village green and they paid the small entry fee to the Lions Club volunteer at a makeshift booth on the walkway then began a slow trawl of the stalls. A few minutes in, Flynn slid his arm around her shoulders. A rush of emotion welled up inside her as her hip bumped his and they automatically adjusted their gaits to suit.

She'd forgotten how good it felt to spend time with someone who genuinely liked her, someone who treated her with respect and warm affection. Crazy to think that toward the end of her marriage the only place she and Owen had touched voluntarily had been in the bedroom.

The driftwood man wasn't at the market this month for some reason, so they settled on buying a loaf of sourdough bread, a jar of homemade jam and a bag of crisp red apples before finding a table at Pop and Selma's Café. They ordered an omelette and pancakes and ate half each—another couple pleasure she'd forgotten—then walked slowly to the car, talking and laughing.

They sat on the back porch at her place and ate apples and drank coffee, then Flynn drew her into his lap and she discovered how talented he was at getting inside her clothes with the least fuss possible. They tumbled back into bed and it was late in the evening by the time Flynn dressed and left for Melbourne. Mel stood on the porch huddled in her dressing gown long after his taillights had faded into the night, feeling dazed, her body a little tender.

Arms wrapped tightly around herself, she entered her house. It felt empty now that he was gone—a dangerous acknowledgement. She saw the light was flashing on the answering machine as she passed the study on her way to the bedroom. She stepped into the room and hit the play button.

"It's me. Call me when you get a chance, okay?" It was Justine, her voice carefully neutral.

It was too late to call now, thank God. Mel didn't particularly want to fend off her sister's well-intentioned inquisition. Not right now, anyway. She was still coming down to earth after twenty-four hours of amazing sex.

It was more than amazing sex and you know it.

She did, but she didn't want to think about any of that right now. She was already edging her way toward a precipice she'd promised never to approach again. It was enough that she'd let Flynn into her life. The rest she would deal with later.

Much later.

FLYNN COULDN'T GET the smile off his face as he took the freeway back to Melbourne. Mel was…

He didn't have the words. Beautiful, sexy, funny, warm, earthy, challenging, smart, adorable. Okay, he had a few words, but none of them felt adequate to the task of describing how he felt when he was with her. She made him feel *more*. More alive. More aware. More present. She made him want more, too. But he was smart enough to know not to push things with her. Not in that way. Not yet.

So he resisted the urge to call her just to hear her voice before he went to bed, and he resisted the urge to call her first thing the next morning. His self-discipline failed at lunchtime, however, when his inbox chimed and he saw he had a message from her.

Just checking that you got back okay and that Gertie behaved herself.

He pushed aside the marketing brochure he was reading and pulled his keyboard toward himself.

Gertie behaved. I arrived. When can I see you again?

There was a short pause before she responded.

What suits you? I can come up to town if it's easier for you.

With his crazy workload it was easier, and they settled on the following evening—dinner out then back to his place for what he hoped was the night. He booked the local Thai place and made a mental note to change the sheets. Then he dove into work with renewed enthusiasm.

Mel was coming. She was going to stay at his place. She was allowing him in.

He left work on time for the first time in months the following evening. His assistant stared at him as he walked past, coat over his arm.

"Do you have a dinner meeting?" She started checking his diary, a frown on her face.

"I'm going home. I'll see you tomorrow, Mary."

Mel's car was parked in front of his town house when he arrived. He pulled into the garage and collected his briefcase. She was waiting for him on the front doorstep when he exited the garage. He frowned when he saw she was only carrying her handbag.

"You're not staying?"

"I'm not sure."

He wanted to ask what she wasn't sure about, but decided to concentrate on the positive instead of the negative. She was here, and once he had her on the other side of his front door he could get her naked.

He proceeded to do just that and they were nearly an hour late for their dinner booking. Fortunately it was a Tuesday night and the restaurant wasn't overly busy so they weren't forced to go hungry. Afterward, they went back to his place and had coffee before he made love to her on the sofa with the late-night news playing in the background.

He slipped into a doze afterward and woke to find Mel collecting her clothes from the floor.

"Where are you going?" he asked drowsily.

"You should be in bed."

"Come with me and it's a deal."

She hesitated a moment before nodding. He led her upstairs to the bedroom, where he watched, amused, as she pulled her toothbrush from her handbag and proceeded to brush her teeth.

"Prepared for any contingency, Ms. Porter?"

"I like to keep my options open."

It was an offhand comment, but it stuck in his mind as they got into bed together. He curled his body around hers and kissed the nape of her neck and told himself that he needed to chill a little. It was early days with Mel—very early days—and he needed to stop reading so much into everything.

Right now, right this minute, life was good. Only an idiot would throw that away in order to worry about some nebulous future.

He kissed the nape of Mel's neck again, savoring the feel of her in his arms.

MEL WOKE TO THE SOUND of running water. It took her a moment to orient herself to Flynn's town house. She rolled over and pushed her hair away from her face as she remembered last night—Flynn hustling her inside so he could make love to her, Flynn urging her to try his favorite entree at his favorite Thai restaurant, Flynn kissing the nape of her neck before she drifted off to sleep.

She smiled a cat-that-ate-the-cream smile. It had been a good night. And, better yet, she hadn't woken with that horrible, suffocating sensation again. Maybe she was starting to get the hang of this having-a-man-in-her-life-again thing.

"You're awake."

Flynn stood in the bathroom doorway, a towel wrapped low on his hips. She took a moment to appreciate his sheer masculine beauty before responding.

"I *am* awake. I can't believe I didn't wake up earlier. I never sleep in."

"It's only seven-thirty, so don't get too carried away. And I was sneaky getting out of the bed. Like a ninja."

She threw back the covers. "I'd better get

going. I've got some errands to run this morning and a guest checking in this afternoon."

She was very aware of him watching as she got out of bed. Like sleeping together, she was getting used to being naked with him. Slowly but surely.

"Do you mind if I have a quick shower before I go?" she asked.

"Help yourself. To anything," he said.

She dropped a kiss on his shoulder as she brushed past him on her way into the en suite and he slipped a hand around her waist and pulled her back for a more thorough kiss. She felt him grow hard against her thigh and smiled, breaking their kiss.

"Someone's going to be late for work if he isn't careful," she said.

"If I didn't have an eight-thirty meeting on-site…" he said regretfully.

She rubbed her cheek against his and kissed his neck before slipping from his grasp. She took a quick shower, and by the time she emerged he was fully dressed in his suit, looking as crisp and elegant as a *GQ* advertisement.

"Look at you, Mr. Perfect," she said as she watched him strap on his watch.

"Says the sexy naked lady." His gaze seemed very bright and very blue as he eyed her across the bed. "What are you up to for the rest of the week?"

She knew what he was asking—when she was free to see him again. She bought herself a few seconds of breathing room by searching in her handbag for the spare pair of panties she'd tucked into the side pocket, just in case her desire for more of Flynn's lovemaking had proven more powerful than her misgivings regarding staying the night.

"How does your schedule look?" she asked, throwing the ball back into his court.

"I've got a work thing tonight, but Thursday and Friday are free at the moment."

She stepped into her panties and reached for her bra.

"Friday night is good for me," she said.

"Then I'll call you and we'll tee something up." He pulled a coat from the closet. "I have to run, but just pull the door shut behind you when you go, okay?"

"Okay."

They kissed, the feel of his fine wool suit against her mostly naked skin very erotic. His gaze was hooded when he stepped away from her.

"Hold that thought," he said.

She smiled.

He left the room. She was tidying the rumpled

bed when she heard the automatic door on the garage rumble to life. She crossed to the window and a few seconds later the Aston Martin cruised out of the garage and down the driveway.

The town house seemed unnaturally quiet as she sat on the end of the bed to put on her socks. She glanced around Flynn's room as she pulled on her jeans and sweater, feeling a little as though she was invading his privacy but curious about the man who was becoming an increasingly important part of her life.

A scary thought in and of itself.

The quilt cover was a dark charcoal pinstripe, the sheets snowy-white. The bed featured an upholstered headboard in a neutral café-latte color and there was no art on the off-white walls. In fact, the only giveaway that anyone lived here was the pile of books on one side of the bed—a couple of thrillers, and a stack of colorful gardening books, including a biography on Edna Walling.

Mel smiled to herself. Like herself, Flynn was far less passionate about the inside of his home than he was the outside. She went in search of the real Flynn and found it in the rooftop garden, an oasis of potted palms and cabbage trees and other tropical foliage plants, set off with colorful floral displays in hot pinks and oranges and yellows. A sandstone garden seat sat along one wall, and a potting bench held pride of place in the far corner.

She admired the simple yet striking arrangement before reentering the town house and collecting her jacket and handbag. She double-checked that the door had locked behind her and was on the road ten minutes after Flynn had left the house. Traffic was light leaving the city and she pulled into her own driveway an hour later.

She felt an odd sense of relief as she let herself into her house, as though some part of herself that she hadn't even known was on the alert had relaxed. Which made sense—this was her territory, her space. She felt safe here. Not that she'd felt *unsafe* at Flynn's place, but definitely she'd been aware that she was on his turf. One of the many reasons why no matter what happened with Flynn, she would never give up her house or her independence.

She was checking her email for bookings when the doorbell rang. She opened it to find Justine on her doorstep.

"The mountain has come to Mohammed," her sister said.

Mel waved her inside. She'd been dodging her sister's phone calls since Sunday so she'd been half expecting this. "You want a coffee?"

"Sure. I brought muffins. The better to bribe

you with," Justine said as she followed Mel into the kitchen.

Mel turned the kettle on and grabbed a couple of mugs. Her sister propped her hip against the counter and crossed her arms over her chest.

"So? What's going on with Flynn?"

"If I said none of your business would you listen to me?"

"No."

Mel sighed. "We're seeing each other. In case you haven't already guessed. There's not much else to tell."

Justine frowned. "Are you in love with him?"

"It's way too early for that kind of talk," Mel said, even though her heart did a nervous little shimmy in her chest.

"Not for Flynn it isn't."

"What's that supposed to mean?"

"The man is besotted with you, Mel. If you could have seen the way he was looking at you at Mom and Dad's party, you'd know what I was talking about."

"Justine, can we please not read too much into any of this? I'm seeing a man. A really nice, great, lovely man. It feels like more than enough to be happening without piling the labels on."

"So, what, you're winging it?"

"Yep. Taking each moment as it comes."

"And when he gets down on his knee and proposes, how are you going to take that?"

Mel blinked, startled by her sister's comment. "Wow. You are really pushing the boat out today."

"That man is crazy about you, Mel."

Mel shook her head. "We've barely started seeing each other. Stop trying to make this more than what it is."

"It took me an hour to work out that I was going to spend the rest of my life with Jacob. Sixty minutes almost exactly from the moment we met."

Mel shook her head again. "It's not like that between us."

She could hear the strain in her own voice as she tried to convince her sister. The truth was that she didn't want to think about any of the things her sister was pushing her to consider. She was coping—barely—with being intimate with a man again. Being naked with him, trusting him with her desire and her needs. Both big steps after the way Owen had abused that trust. She wasn't up to worrying about bigger-picture stuff, like where her relationship with Flynn might be going, what it might mean.

"Okay," Justine said, nodding. She pushed away from the counter and pulled a white bakery bag from her purse. "You want chocolate chip or blueberry or halvies?"

Mel watched her warily, not convinced her sister would back off so easily. "Halvies sounds good," she said cautiously.

Justine cut the muffins in half and divided the bounty between two plates. She took a big bite of muffin, then fixed Mel with a contemplative gaze as she chewed and swallowed. "For what it's worth, I like him. He seems like a decent guy."

"He's more then decent. He's a great guy."

"But he's still a rich guy. He's still got lots of rich friends and rich parents and all that bullshit hanging over him."

"And?"

Justine shrugged. "Nothing. I just want you to go in with your eyes open this time."

Mel took a deep breath, reminding herself that Justine had been the one she called the night of the Hollands' party. She'd seen Mel at her worst, seen the marriage at its ugliest. She had a right to dislike Owen and all he stood for.

So instead of telling her sister to butt out, she crossed the kitchen and gave Justine a big hug.

"I'm doing okay. I think Flynn is good for me, and I'm smarter now."

Justine's eyes were swimming with tears when Mel let go.

"I want you to be happy so badly, Mel. He seems like a nice guy, but he's not like us. He doesn't know what it's like to have the heating break down and know you're going to have to live on baked beans for the next month to pay for the repairs. He's never had to call the bank to explain why the mortgage repayment will be late. He's used to the best of everything, to having the world at his feet."

Mel thought about what Flynn was going through with his parents, the career he'd given up to take over the family business. "His life isn't perfect, Justine. Far from it. Money doesn't make everything better, and it doesn't turn people into dicks. They do that all on their own." She paused for a beat to give her words a chance to sink in. "Now, can we talk about something else? Anything else?"

Justine sniffed inelegantly and used her sleeve to blot her tears. Then she pushed the plate with Mel's share of the muffins on it toward Mel.

"Eat something. You're making me feel like a pig over here."

Mel dutifully picked up half a muffin, and her sister dutifully recounted a story about Rex and Eddy. The kettle boiled and Mel made them both coffee, and an hour later her sister left, her doubts apparently assuaged.

Mel went into the garden afterward, wishing she could say the same. She'd meant every word she'd said to her sister, but there was still an uneasy feeling in the pit of her stomach. The garden had always been her sanctuary when she was troubled and she tackled the weeds encroaching on the path with a vengeance, deriving a certain amount of satisfaction from restoring order.

She couldn't stop Justine's words from echoing in her head, however. Her sister thought Flynn was crazy about her—*besotted* had been the word she'd used. She'd even made a crack about him proposing, of all things.

Both notions made Mel feel a little ill. She didn't want Flynn to be *besotted* with her. She wanted him to like her and to enjoy spending time with her, and she wanted him to desire her—but she didn't want any of those wants or likes or desires to become too messy or demanding. The same as she didn't want her own wants, likes or desires in regard to him to take on a life of their own. She wanted to feel in control, and she wanted a sense of separation between her and him, a clear demarcation line that allowed her to maintain her life and him his while allowing them both to meet somewhere in the middle.

She certainly didn't want him to propose. Even the thought of getting married again made her dizzy with anxiety.

Calm down, Miss Melodrama. You've barely been seeing the man a week. You are getting way, way, way too far ahead of yourself. Remember what you said to your sister? You're taking it as it comes. Moment by moment, day by day.

Mel refocused on the pathway, shifting along a few feet and tugging at the weeds, tossing them into a pile. After a few minutes, her heart rate normalized.

Her sister may have had good intentions, but Mel could definitely have done without her probing questions and unsolicited observations this morning. She'd already decided not to obsess over what might happen with Flynn, and she needed to stick to that undertaking if this was going to work for her. For both of them.

Resolute, she pushed her sister's and her own doubts away and concentrated on her garden.

CHAPTER THIRTEEN

FLYNN CALLED MEL the following evening when he got home from work. They talked for nearly an hour while he made himself stir-fry chicken and vegetables, discussing her latest bookings and their various ongoing garden projects. As always, her voice sounded sultry over the phone and he found himself remembering key moments from their last encounter as they talked.

Mel stealing one of his curry puffs at the Thai restaurant where they'd had dinner then laughing throatily at his mock-outrage.

Mel on his sofa, a knowing look in her eyes as he popped open the stud on her jeans.

Mel sleeping beside him, her body curled loosely, her hair spread across the pillow and his shoulder and chest.

"Pick somewhere nice and I'll take you out tomorrow night," he said impulsively.

They'd been discussing the soil quality at Summerlea and there was a small pause on the other end of the phone.

"You don't have to take me out."

"I want to."

"You're afraid of my cooking, aren't you?"

"No. I want to show you off."

"To whom, exactly?" She sounded amused.

"Anyone and everyone. What about that French place in the village?"

"Too posh."

He remembered her discomfort when he'd taken her out for lunch at that Spanish place. "Fine. Then we'll go to the local pub. How does that sound?"

"More my speed."

They talked for another five minutes before winding up their call. The thought of the weekend ahead kept his head above water the following day when various loads of manure hit assorted fans. He was wading through the most recent disaster when he glanced at his computer and saw that it was nearly six. He'd planned to leave at six-thirty, but he was savvy enough to know he wasn't even close to being done for the day.

He reached for the phone and called Mel, explaining the issue and telling her that he was going to be late.

"I have no idea what time I'll get down there," he said apologetically. "Do you still want me to come over?"

"Why don't we do this? Give me a call when

you're twenty minutes away and I'll meet you at Summerlea. I'll bring something to eat and we can have a glass of wine and you can wind down and not have to worry about being anywhere."

"It sounds like a lot of trouble. Especially when I'm supposed to be taking you out for dinner."

"It isn't. Drive carefully, okay?" Her voice was soft, concerned.

His chest got tight as he imagined what it would be like having Mel to come home to every night. "I'll see you soon."

He threw himself into work and managed to drag himself away from his desk by eight-thirty. He hit the road, yanking his tie off as he drove toward the freeway entrance. He hit heavy rain halfway there and shook off his tiredness to concentrate on the wet, dark road. He exited in Frankston and hit speed dial.

"Thunderbirds are go," he said when Mel picked up.

"I'll see you in ten."

He was opening the main gate at Summerlea when she pulled up behind him. Even though it was still drizzling, he abandoned the task to approach her car. She wound down her window but before she could get a word out he leaned in and kissed her.

"Hey," he said when he finally came up for air. She looked gratifyingly dazed. "Hey."

"You look good."

"You look tired."

"I'm very resilient. Give me ten minutes and I'll prove it to you." He gave her his best dirty look.

She cocked an eyebrow in challenge. "Okay, then. Your time starts now."

He laughed, striding back to the idling Aston. She followed him up the driveway, parking behind him. He waited while she collected a shopping bag from the passenger seat and they walked up the front steps together. The porch was pitch-black and he swore under his breath as he tried to identify the door key.

"Remind me to get a sensor light installed here," he said.

Mel followed him into the living room and stopped in her tracks as she registered the king-size bed he'd had delivered during the week. The only real furniture in the room, it dominated the left wall.

"Where did this come from?" she asked, bemused.

"The local bed place. I left a spare key out last weekend and organized for them to deliver it."

A selection of bedding, still in its packaging, was stacked on the end of the bed.

"I would have helped if you'd asked," she said.

"I don't want you running around after me."

"But you'll let complete strangers do it?"

He thought about it for a moment. "Okay, I understand what you're saying. But it still feels wrong. I'm willing to workshop it, however."

"Workshop it?" she asked as she started pulling plastic containers from her shopping bag.

"It's the latest buzz word. You don't like it?"

She pulled a face. He reached out and pulled her into his arms. She came willingly, her hands sliding to his backside.

"I promise never to use it again," he said as he zeroed in on her mouth.

They kissed, tongues stroking one another, bodies straining together. He reached for the waist of her long-sleeved T-shirt just as a low gurgle sounded. She smiled against his mouth.

"Was that your stomach?"

"Ignore it," he said, tugging her top up.

She slipped away from his embrace. "Eat your dinner first, while it's hot. Then you can have dessert."

"I'm going to hold you to that."

She finished setting out containers of food and he crossed to the fireplace and laid a quick fire. By the time she'd handed him a plateful of savory beef Stroganoff and a hunk of crunchy garlic bread the fire was blazing. He grabbed the pillows from the bed to serve as floor cushions and poured them both a glass of wine.

"This looks great, Mel," he said as she joined him in front of the fire.

They talked casually as they ate and it wasn't long before he'd wolfed his meal down.

"That was just what the doctor ordered," he said as he pushed his plate to one side. He focused on Mel. "Come here."

"Maybe we should let our dinner settle first."

"In case we get cramps and drown?"

She laughed. "Something like that."

"Get your delectable ass over here."

She placed her wineglass carefully on the hearth and moved toward him. Bracing one hand beside him, she leaned close and laid her lips against his. Her mouth was hot and spicy with wine and he made an approving noise in the back of his throat. Then he put his hand on her shoulder and pulled her off balance and into his arms. She collapsed onto his chest with a muffled yelp.

"That's better," he said, rolling swiftly so that she was beneath him, his body splayed over hers. "Now I've got you where I want you."

"Really?"

"Definitely." He grinned down at her. "Now, about this dessert…"

He reached for the hem of her top and she

shifted to allow him to pull it over her head. His eyes narrowed appreciatively as he took in the almost transparent black lace of her bra.

"Nice."

He lowered his head and began to kiss and lick the curve of her breast until finally he was sucking her nipple through the lace of her bra. She stirred beneath him and he transferred his attention to her other breast, repeating the action. She slid her hands down his back to his sides and then around to the front of his jeans. When she started to fumble with the stud, he caught her hands.

"Uh-uh," he said.

"Sorry?"

"I haven't finished my dessert yet."

He reached out and undid the snap on her jeans. Holding her gaze, he started to peel her jeans down her legs. Her mouth opened ever so slightly and she licked her lower lip. His gaze dropped to her hips. She was wearing black stretch-lace French knickers and he smoothed his hand over her belly and down onto her mound.

"Great presentation. Pass my compliments to the chef," he said.

She swallowed a laugh as he tucked a finger into the waistband and pulled her panties down. He studied her, admiring the paleness of her skin, the taut muscles of her thighs, the dark silk of her hair.

"So beautiful, Mel..."

He swept a hand from her hip to her knee before pushing her thighs wide. He moved lower, settling himself between her thighs. She caught her breath as he pressed a kiss to her inner thigh, following it with an exploratory lick. A shudder racked her body.

"Don't forget to breathe," he murmured.

She dropped against the pillows as he started to tease her with his fingers and tongue and mouth. Stroking her inside and out, he drove her higher and higher until she was mindless with need. She fisted a hand in his hair and pushed her hips toward him, unashamedly demanding everything he had to give. When she came, she cried out, her back arching off the floor, her body as taut as a bow.

She collapsed onto the carpet, as loose as a rag doll. He was so hard it was a wonder he hadn't exploded. He kicked his suit pants to one side and rolled a condom on before laying his body over hers and drawing one rosy pink nipple into his mouth. His erection nudged against her slick folds and she gave a low, needy moan and tilted her hips to accept him. He slid home to the hilt and started to move inside her. She gripped his ass, hips lifting to meet his thrusts.

"Yes. Please, Flynn, you feel so good…."

He whispered in her ear, dirty, sexy words of praise, telling her how she made him feel, how much he loved her body. She shuddered as she came, his name on her lips. A few seconds later he followed her, his cheek pressed against hers.

After laying lax and spent in the flickering light of the fire for endless minutes, they made the bed and drifted into sleep beneath his new down duvet.

He woke with a start to find Mel sitting upright in the bed beside him, the covers pooled around her waist.

"Hey," he said sleepily, reaching out to lay a hand on her naked back. "You okay?"

She was tense and her skin was clammy with sweat.

"Sorry. I think I must have been too hot or something."

She slipped out of the bed before he could respond. Her pale figure was like a ghost in the darkened room as she headed for the door.

"Mel. It's freezing," he said.

"I'll be fine," she said as she walked out the door.

Flynn threw back the covers and walked across to flick on the light. The fire had burned down to embers and he threw some more kindling on before scooping up Mel's T-shirt from the floor. He grabbed a T-shirt for himself from his overnight bag and shrugged into it as he went in search of Mel. He found her in the bathroom, washing her face with big handfuls of water. The room was freezing and she was shivering and covered with gooseflesh.

"You'll catch a cold. Here," he said, handing her the T-shirt.

"Thanks."

She dried her face on a towel before slipping the T-shirt over her head.

"Come here."

He pulled her into his arms, smoothing his hands over her back to try to warm her. It took a moment for her body to relax into his embrace.

"What's going on?" he asked quietly.

"Just a bad dream. Nothing important."

He hesitated a moment. "Anything you want to talk about?"

"No. It was mostly gobbledygook. Bits and pieces of lots of stuff."

She turned her head and pressed a kiss to his throat.

"Your house is very cold." Her hands slid to his backside and she cupped his butt cheeks. "Lucky you're so hot."

She kissed his neck again, opening her mouth this time. His body stirred to life instantly but he was very aware of the fact that Mel was using sex to distract him. She lifted a leg and ran her foot along his calf, pressing her hips against his. He pulled back from her a little so he could see her face.

"Are you sure you're okay?"

She returned his regard, her gray eyes unreadable.

"I'm fine. Really."

She kissed him, urging him close again with her hands on his hips. This time he didn't resist, even though he knew he wasn't getting the full picture, even though he suspected that Mel wasn't *fine*. She clearly didn't want to talk about it, and she clearly also wanted to make love again. He was prepared to follow her lead. For now, anyway.

They returned to the living room and made slow love, firelight flickering over their bodies. Afterward, Mel tucked her body against his back and rested her cheek on his shoulder. A few minutes later she was asleep. He lay awake, watching the fire, thinking.

He knew Mel's marriage had been unhappy. She'd intimated that her ex had been critical, maybe even controlling. The day they'd had lunch together she'd also implied that Owen Hunter's parents had not approved of their marriage and that she'd never fit in with the Melbourne society set.

Not a good picture, any of it. And he could understand why Mel might be gun-shy. He wished he knew more about what she was thinking, how she was feeling, because he was about as committed as it was possible to get. Had been for some time now. For the first time in his life, he was truly in love. Mel was the woman he'd been waiting his whole life to find. Everything in him wanted to sweep her off her feet and put things in motion to start the rest of their lives together.

But only an idiot would ignore the subtle and not-so-subtle signals that Mel was broadcasting. She'd been reluctant to acknowledge their attraction from the very beginning, and even though he'd been hoping that what had happened between them last weekend would have put paid to some of her doubts, it was clear that she was still very much feeling her way as far as their relationship was concerned.

He was going to have to be patient, and he was going to have to let Mel set the pace. It chafed the impetuous idiot boy in him, but at the end of the day, as long as they wound up at the same destination, he was willing to take as circuitous a route as Mel required. Whatever it took.

Because she was worth it. A million times over.

THE NEXT DAY they both woke early. After a quick shower, they walked into the village and bought croissants and *pain au chocolat* from the local bakery and ate them during the walk to Summerlea. He still had her brush-cutter in his garage, and Mel insisted on borrowing her brother-in-law's machine as well so they could tackle the blackberry brambles in tandem. By the time they were finished they had a huge pile of severed canes and a large collection of cuts, scratches and splinters between them. Walking to the house with Mel at his side, his muscles aching pleasantly from a day of physical activity, Flynn had a vision of how the rest of his life could look—the two of them working here at Summerlea, restoring the garden to its former glory, restoring the house, growing together. It felt so close, so achievable, as though he could almost reach out and touch it.

"I was thinking of inviting my parents down next weekend to show them around the place," he said as they stored the equipment in the garage.

Mel shot him a quick, startled look before her expression smoothed into polite interest. "I didn't realize they hadn't seen it yet."

"Between one thing and another, I haven't had the chance to have them down yet. I was thinking we could do a bit of a tour here, then go to one of the local wineries for lunch. What do you think?"

"It sounds lovely. I can recommend a few places for you if you like. I always get good feedback from guests who try the restaurant at Paringa Estate, and I've been hearing good things about La Pétanque, too."

"So which day would suit you better? Saturday or Sunday?"

She gave a funny little shrug. "Sorry, but next weekend isn't great for me. Rex has got this thing at his school and I promised to help out."

"How about the following weekend?"

She pushed her thick plait back over her shoulder. "Don't change your plans on my account. I'm sure your parents are keen to see this money pit that you've bought."

"Sure. But I'd like them to meet you, too," he said.

Her smile was forced. "They can meet me any old time. Seriously, don't put them off for my sake."

He studied her a moment, tempted to push. Then he had a flash of her standing naked and shivering in his bathroom last night, fleeing from a bad dream she wouldn't share with him.

"Okay, sure. Why not?" he said easily.

Her shoulders dropped visibly with relief. Just as well he'd already had a conversation with himself about being patient, otherwise his ego would be in the gutter right about now.

They went inside the house together and, because he couldn't resist, he slid an arm around her shoulders. The tight feeling in his gut loosened as she leaned readily into the contact, resting her head briefly on his shoulder as her arm slid around his waist.

Slow and steady wins the race, he reminded himself.

Slow and steady.

GUILT ATE AT Mel for the rest of the weekend. No matter how many times she told herself she hadn't technically been lying when she said she was busy the following weekend, the reality was that if she'd wanted to, she could have made time to meet Flynn's parents.

And Flynn knew it, too. He hadn't said anything, but she had seen the knowledge in his eyes as he'd accepted her feeble excuse. The urge to tell him that she'd changed her mind, that she'd find a way to be available, gripped her half a dozen times, but each time she balked.

She didn't want to meet his parents. And not only because she didn't have the greatest track record as far as parental approval went, although that was definitely a part of it. She didn't want to meet Flynn's parents because it felt like the first step toward something she didn't want to even think about.

The man is besotted with you, Mel.

Her sister's words kept echoing inside her head. She pushed them away again and again, but every time she looked at Flynn and saw the warmth and tenderness in his eyes her heart did a little backflip in her chest and she knew that he cared for her deeply.

This was serious for him. It was serious for her, too. More and more so. But that didn't mean she was ready to meet his parents. It seemed… too much. Too fast. Too heavy. Too real. The ink was barely dry on her divorce papers. She needed time to adjust, for her head to catch up with her galloping, reckless heart.

She almost felt relieved when he left on Sunday night. She waved him off from her front porch, grateful that she was going to have a few days' reprieve from the intensity of her own feelings when she was around him. Then she went inside and immediately registered how cold and empty her house felt without his warm presence.

Great. He's barely been gone five minutes and you want him back already. Way to keep a grip on things, champ.

She didn't call him the next day, to prove to herself that she could. But on Tuesday she caved and called and wound up agreeing to meet him at his place again that evening. She was pulling up in front of his town house when her phone rang.

"Mel, I'm really sorry. I've had a problem come up here at work. I'll do my best to hose things down, but it's going to be another twenty minutes minimum before I can get away," Flynn said.

"No worries. I'll go for a walk and check out your neighbors."

"I'm really sorry about this." He sounded frustrated and more than a little angry.

"Flynn. It's okay. I get it. You have a big, big company to run. I'll see you when you get here, okay?"

"Okay."

She killed the time by driving around until she found the local supermarket. She knew from conversations they'd had that he was a sucker for pasta so she bought ingredients for one of her favorite dishes, then threw in a bar of fruit and nut chocolate because she knew he liked that, too. She returned to his town house and had just turned on the radio to listen to talkback when she heard the distinctive rumble of the Aston Martin's engine. Flynn gave her a wave as he drove past and she grabbed her groceries and her overnight bag and walked over.

"Hey," he said as he emerged from the garage.

His tie was pulled loose and he looked pale. Her chest tightened. More than anything she wished there was something she could do to lighten his burden.

"Hey, yourself," she said.

They kissed, his five-o'clock shadow rough against her face.

"I bought makings for dinner, in case you didn't feel like going out anywhere," she said as they drew apart.

"You don't have to cook for me."

"It's hardly cooking. Spaghetti with garlic bread crumbs. It's more assembling than anything else."

"Mel. How am I supposed to stick to my guns when you offer me spaghetti with garlic bread crumbs?"

"Give in gracefully. It's the only way to preserve any dignity."

He dropped a quick kiss onto her mouth. "Deal."

He unlocked the door and she followed him into the kitchen.

"Give me five to get out of this suit," he said.

"Show me where your knives are and I'll get started while you're gone," she suggested.

He grabbed a chopping board from beside the oven and opened a drawer to indicate a selection of knives.

"Great. You go do your thing," she said, waving him away.

By the time he reappeared she'd peeled the garlic and was chopping it as finely as possible.

"Olive oil?" she asked, glancing at him.

He'd changed into jeans and a navy hoodie and his feet were bare, his hair even more ruffled.

"Naturally."

He grabbed a tall bottle from the pantry and slid it onto the counter beside her, his shoulder brushing hers. He leaned close and dropped a kiss onto the nape of her neck.

"It's good to see you," he said, his voice very deep.

Heat bloomed between her thighs.

"You, too."

He moved behind her, wrapping his arms around her as she sliced a lemon in half. She smiled as she felt the nudge of his erection against her backside.

"Behave yourself or we'll starve," she said.

He pressed another kiss to the nape of her neck, his whiskers sending a delicious shiver down her spine.

"I'll try, but I can't make any guarantees." He released her then and moved to the wine rack beside the fridge.

"Red or white?"

"I'm not sure. What would you recommend with bread crumbs?" she asked, tongue very firmly in cheek.

"Hmm. Tough call. Something light, something cheeky. A shiraz, perhaps?"

"I bow to your superior knowledge."

He was smiling as he pulled a bottle of wine from the rack. A warm, expansive feeling filled her chest. It was good being here with him like this, knowing that the whole evening stretched ahead of them. Knowing that she would sleep in his arms tonight and drive home to her own house tomorrow.

"Before I forget…"

She waited for him to finish his sentence, and saw that he was lifting a key ring from the hook stuck to the side of the fridge.

"The spare key. So next time you can let yourself in instead of trawling the streets in search of spaghetti," he said.

He held his hand out, the key dangling in the air between them.

CHAPTER FOURTEEN

MEL STARED AT THE KEY for a long beat before shifting her focus to the cutting board.

"I don't need a key," she said, trying to keep her voice as casual as possible as she chopped the remainder of the parsley.

Out of the corner of her eye she saw Flynn's hand drop to his side.

"You don't think it would make life easier?"

"I didn't mind waiting. Besides, this is your place."

"Sure. But I'm happy to share it with you."

She put the knife down and turned to face him, a part of her recognizing that this conversation had been inevitable. Her expectations and Flynn's had always been on a collision course.

"I'm happy to share it with you. But it's always going to be yours," she said carefully. "Just as my place is always going to be mine."

He was twisting the cork out of the bottle but he stopped with the cork only half extracted, setting the bottle on the counter.

"Why do I feel as though we're suddenly have a much bigger conversation?"

"Maybe because we are. And maybe because we should, before this thing between us goes any further."

He frowned slightly. "*Thing.* I didn't realize we were a *thing.*"

"Relationship," she said. It was hard to get the word past the tightness in her throat. "This relationship."

"Okay," he said. "I'm happy to lay my cards on the table. More than happy. This is serious for me, Mel. I want you to be a part of my life."

His gaze was steady and very serious and her heart seemed to expand and contract at the same time. Was it possible to be both thrilled and terrified simultaneously? Because that was how she felt—enormously gratified, and yet also scared to death.

"I feel the same way." Anxiety was making her feel light-headed and she swallowed noisily.

"But you don't want my key?"

"I made myself a promise after Owen and I separated that I would never let myself get trapped in a situation like that again. That I would never put myself in another person's power in that way. That no matter what, I would always hang on to who I am."

"I know your marriage was unhappy. But I'm

still not sure how that relates to you having a key to my place."

"Because if I take your key, you'll expect mine. And then the next thing I know your things will be at my place and my things will be here, and then suddenly we'll be living together.... And I don't want that. I can't do that again." It came out in a garbled rush.

He took a moment before he responded. "I know this has been hard for you, Mel. I know that you weren't looking for a relationship so soon after your divorce. I get that, and I'm willing to wait as long as it takes for you to feel safe about us. Whatever it takes. We don't have to rush into anything."

"Time isn't going to make any difference, Flynn." It was hard to make herself say the words but she had to. Had to make him understand that if things were going to continue between them, there would be certain limitations. "I don't ever want to live with a man again. And I definitely never want to get married."

He didn't move, didn't say a word, but she could see she'd shocked him. It took him a moment to respond.

"Like I said, I'm willing to wait as long as it takes. We can take things one day at a time," he finally said.

"It's not going to change anything. I know

what I want, and what I don't want. I don't want to lose myself to a relationship again."

He stared at her, and she could see the dawning understanding in his eyes as he realized that she was serious. That this was a deal breaker for her.

His gaze dropped to the floor and he lifted his hand to rub his forehead, masking his expression from her for long seconds.

"It doesn't change the way I feel about you. I love spending time with you. I'd like to keep spending time with you," she said quietly.

He nodded but didn't drop his hand. Something big and heavy was sitting in the pit of her stomach. She'd hurt him. Shocked him. He wanted her to have his key. He was serious about her. And she'd hurt him.

"Flynn, I'm really sorry," she said helplessly.

Her gaze fell on the chopped parsley and garlic. Tears burned the back of her eyes. She liked this man so much. But she understood that what she'd said may have killed off any possibility between them, including the ones that scared her.

"If you want me to go, I can go. If you need time to think... I understand," she said.

"I don't want you to go, Mel. That's pretty much the point, really, isn't it?" He lifted his head and looked at her, his blue eyes blazing with intensity. "I'm crazy about you. I don't want you to go anywhere."

Even though she was half-afraid she wouldn't be welcome, she stepped forward and threw her arms around him. His arms came around her at the same time and they held each other tightly.

"Mel…"

She cupped the back of his head and pressed her cheek against his. He was such a special man. So beautiful, inside and out. But she simply could not risk herself again the way she had during her marriage. She'd already come so much further so much faster with Flynn than she'd imagined she could, but she didn't have it in her to go further again. The thought of it alone was enough to push her into genuine panic.

She never wanted to feel as weak and helpless as she had during her marriage, and the only way she knew to do that was to protect herself against everyone. Including Flynn, and including herself.

"I know you don't like talking about your marriage, but you have to know that I would never hurt you, Mel," he said, his voice gruff with emotion.

"I know. And I trust you. But I have to look after myself. That's what I learned from my marriage—that I can't expect anyone else to do that for me."

They drew apart. Flynn still looked shell-shocked. Maybe even a little shattered. She ached for him, wishing she could find the one thing to say that would make everything okay between them.

"Look, if you need time, I can go. I really don't mind," she offered again.

He shook his head. "I just need to get my head around this." He picked up the bottle and yanked the cork out, but he didn't pour the wine into the glasses he'd set out. Instead, he looked at the bottle as though he wasn't quite sure what to do with it.

"I guess what I'm trying to understand is how you see this working between us, if living together and marriage are out of the question," he said after a moment. "What do you see happening between us?"

His gaze was piercing, searching as it met hers.

"We keep doing what we've been doing," she said. "We spend weekends together, nights during the week. It doesn't change anything, it doesn't change what we have together."

"It changes a lot of things, Mel. What about children, for starters?"

She blinked in surprise.

"Or hadn't you even gotten that far yet?" He sounded sad.

She shook her head. "I hadn't. I guess— I hadn't."

She hadn't allowed herself to go there. When she'd first married Owen she'd wanted children, but at a certain point in her marriage she'd become profoundly grateful that she hadn't gotten pregnant.

But Flynn was not Owen, and if she'd stopped to really think about it she would have anticipated this question because Flynn was a man made for family life. The way he cared for his parents, his bone-deep nurturing instincts... He would make a great father.

"I need to check on the garden. Make sure the timer tap is working..."

It was the feeblest of excuses, but she let him go, watching him walk from the room, his shoulders very square. She let her breath out in a rush and pressed her hands to her stomach.

She felt sick. In protecting herself, she'd hurt a wonderful man. A man she cared for a great deal. A man who had become very important to her very quickly.

You may have lost him. You know that, right?

The possibility reverberated inside her, grim and very real. Flynn had had plans for them, hopes. Expectations. She'd seen it in his eyes. He'd even said it—*I want to share my life with you.* And she'd fenced off a lot of those hopes and expectations. She'd corralled him into a relationship that operated on her terms, for her protection.

She closed her eyes, thinking about the confusion and hurt she'd seen in his face. He didn't understand that she had reasons—good reasons—for her decisions. He said he did, but he couldn't, not really, because she'd never told him the truth about her marriage. She'd been too ashamed. And he'd never asked, because he was too good a man to push her into something he knew she found uncomfortable.

She opened her eyes. Then she walked to the counter and poured herself a glass of wine. She swallowed it in one big gulp. The wine warmed her throat before it hit her stomach. She stared into the glass, thinking about what she needed to do.

After a few seconds she put down the glass and went in search of Flynn.

HE DIDN'T UNDERSTAND. That was the bottom line. Flynn knew Mel was scared and wary, but he hadn't understood that her resistance to a relationship ran so deep, and he didn't understand how anyone could close herself off to the future so comprehensively.

Mel had always struck him as being brave and bold. Her laughter, her smile, her earthy sexuality—he'd always thought she was the sort of person who took life by the scruff of the neck and shook it.

Yet she didn't want to live with him. She didn't want marriage. And she hadn't even thought about children.

He sat on the sandstone bench on his rooftop garden and put his head in his hands. He felt as though he'd had the rug—the world—pulled from beneath his feet. All his life he'd waited to feel this connected to another human being, yet Mel didn't want the connection. Or, more accurately, she wanted parts of it. Neatly apportioned parts. The friendship. The sex. The companionship.

She didn't want shared responsibility and domesticity and the sort of deep, abiding knowledge of another person only gained through sleeping in the same bed night after night and sharing both the highs and lows and the grand and the not-so-grand challenges of life. She didn't want children. She didn't want to truly share herself and her life with him.

The worst thing was that he'd known, on some deep, instinctive level, that she wasn't as committed as he was. And yet he'd still fallen in love with her. Hadn't been able to stop himself.

He heard the scratch of dirt beneath a shoe and knew that Mel had come in search of him.

He didn't lift his head immediately, unsure that he could keep the disappointment he felt from showing in his face.

"I want to tell you something, but it's really hard for me to talk about because it's not something I'm very proud of," she said.

Her words surprised him into lifting his head. He met her gaze.

"You can tell me anything, Mel." He meant it, too. He loved her.

She sat beside him on the bench and took a deep breath.

"People always say that it's impossible to understand a marriage from the outside looking in. I never really appreciated how true that was until I left Owen, because looking back over the six years we'd been together, even I couldn't understand how things had gotten so ugly between us. How I'd let them get so ugly. Intellectually, I understand that it happened in increments, that one thing led to another, which led to another. I know that by the time we got to the end of the line, I was so worn down by his disapproval and anger, and his parents' lack of acceptance, and by my own feelings of inadequacy and failure that I believed the things he said to me. My brain can see all that and process it and join the dots. But there's a big part of me that still doesn't understand why I let him treat me so badly."

He drew breath to speak but Mel's hand landed on his thigh.

"Please. Let me get this out. I want you to understand where I'm coming from. Why this is so important to me. And if I stop, it'll take me ages to find the courage again."

He nodded, then realized that perhaps she couldn't see him in the dark.

"Okay."

"Thanks."

She was silent for a long moment after that and he started to think that maybe she'd changed her mind.

"You were there the night of the Hollands' party. You saw what happened with the fountain. In case it wasn't obvious, Owen was furious with me afterward. He didn't talk all the way home in the car, not a single word, and when we got home he made me strip in the front hall. He said it was in case the carpet got wet, but it was really because he wanted to humiliate me the way I'd humiliated him.

"The whole time, he stood there and told me how stupid I was. How I'd shamed him. How every man at the party had seen my body and knew how cheap I was. He told me that I was a laughingstock and that I'd made him a laughingstock. Then he told me to go into the living room and take off my underwear."

He stirred beside her. His whole body was hot and tense as he guessed what was coming next.

"He told me to bend over the arm of the couch, and he screwed me from behind. Then he told me I was lucky he still wanted me."

She'd been staring at the tiles on the terrace, her expression blank, but now she lifted her gaze to his. "And I let him. I let him treat me like that, Flynn."

"Mel—"

"I know what you're going to say. That it wasn't my fault, that he was emotionally abusive, that I was a victim. It's all true. But I still allowed it to happen. I allowed him to talk to me the way other people talk to their dogs. I let him use my body. I accepted his parents' judgment of me. I turned myself inside out trying to please him. Me, Flynn. No one else. That's why I won't live with you. And that's why I will never marry again. Ever."

Flynn wasn't a violent man. He'd been in exactly one real, knock-down, drag-out fight in his life. But if Owen Hunter walked through the door right now, he would take him apart with his bare hands. No hesitation. And he wouldn't stop until the other man was begging for mercy.

The thought of Mel living with someone who spoke to her that way, who used her that way... It literally made him ill. She was so funny and generous and loving and beautiful and sexy. How anyone could fail to love her he didn't know— and how anyone could take her love and turn it against her that way...

It beggared belief.

"It's not your fault." He paused, trying to gather his thoughts. How to explain the gut-wrenching sympathy he felt for her? How to acknowledge the shame he could hear in her voice? How to even begin to express the sadness and anger and regret he felt on her behalf? "Anyone who would treat someone they purportedly love like that is a freaking head case and doesn't deserve to walk the streets. He's an abusive asshole, Mel. And you were his victim."

She nodded, but he wasn't entirely sure that she really believed him. Never had he felt so inarticulate. So out of his depth.

"It's okay, Flynn. You don't have to convince me or fix this for me. I know what it is. I know it better than anyone. I just wanted you to know, to understand. This isn't about you. This is all me. All of it."

He gave in to his instincts and twisted to face her, wrapping her in his arms. She came willingly, her breath leaving her on a little shudder. She rested her chin on his shoulder and he could feel her working hard to control herself.

"Thank you for hearing me out," she said, her

voice thick with emotion. "I know I hurt you to-night. I know I can't give you everything that you want. But I care for you so much, Flynn. So much."

He turned his head and pressed a kiss to her temple. For the first time since he'd known her, she felt fragile in his arms. Funny how a shift in perception could do that. All this time, he'd known she was wounded, but he hadn't understood how deep the wounds went, how profound the damage was. And, also, how strong she was to have rescued herself and rebuilt her life.

I love you, Melanie Porter.

The words filled his mind and his chest but he was smart enough not to let them pass his lips. Now was not the time to burden Mel with his feelings.

He finally understood what he was up against. He'd been so certain that he had only to be patient, to give Mel time to get past her wariness, but her instinct to protect herself went far deeper than wariness. She'd learned a powerful, visceral lesson, and she was determined to never forget it.

Even if that meant keeping him at arm's length.

If he accepted her rules, if he decided to continue with their weeknights and their weekends, he would be condemning himself to enormous frustration. Among other things.

But it wasn't as though he had a choice.

He kissed her temple again. "We should probably make dinner, yeah? Otherwise we'll be gnawing our arms off sometime soon."

She pulled back enough to see his face, her gaze searching. He held her eye.

"I'm not going anywhere, Mel," he said, answering the unspoken question in her eyes.

How could he? He loved her.

"A thousand men would."

"Not this man."

He stood, tugging her to her feet as well. "Let's finish making dinner."

LATER THAT NIGHT, Mel lay in bed beside Flynn listening to his steady breathing. Now that it was safe, she let the tears she'd been holding in all night slide down her face.

She was glad she'd told him, glad that he knew now, but a part of her felt small and ashamed and wrong and incredibly exposed. Flynn had always looked at her with admiration in his eyes. She didn't want his pity. She didn't want him to see her as weak or helpless or a victim. She knew it was inevitable that he would, to a certain extent, because she *had* been a victim, yet a part of her—her pride? her ego?—wanted him only to see good things in her.

She thought about the way he'd held her afterward, the way he'd kissed her temple so tenderly, so gently, and the way he'd made love to her tonight, as though she was the most precious thing in the world to him, and her tears fell faster. More than anything she wished she could give him what he wanted, what he needed. He deserved to be happy. She wished she was braver. She wished she had the courage to throw caution to the wind and leap feetfirst into everything he offered.

A sob rose in her throat and she swallowed it, using her fingers to wipe her tears away. Breathing through her mouth, she took deep belly breaths until she'd calmed herself.

I'm not going anywhere.

He'd said those words to her only a couple of hours ago, so there was no need for her to be lying here crying and grieving over a loss that hadn't happened. He'd heard her, he'd understood her and *he wasn't going anywhere.*

She turned toward him, wrapping her arms around his body from behind, curving her legs to fit behind his. He stirred in his sleep, his hand settling over hers to keep her arm in place. She lay her cheek against his back and inhaled his scent and allowed her body to absorb his calm, solid warmth.

Slowly, by small degrees, she drifted off to sleep. She woke to the feel of his mouth on her breasts the next morning and they had lazy morning sex before Flynn rolled out of bed and hit the shower. She joined him and left when he did, waving out the window of her car as he headed to work in the Aston.

She was aware of a certain tremulous fragility within herself as she took the ramp to the freeway. She reminded herself that while last night had been hard, they'd survived it. Flynn knew where she stood, and he knew why, and he hadn't pushed her away or become angry or demanding or resentful.

They were going to be okay. For the short term, anyway.

She bit her lip as she thought about what she was asking of Flynn in the long term, what she was asking him to give up, then quickly pushed the thought away. Tomorrow was tomorrow. Right now—*today*—things were okay. That was what she needed to concentrate on.

CHAPTER FIFTEEN

THE NEXT MONTH SLIPPED through Mel's fingers like water. She spent every weekend with Flynn, and at least one night during the week. They worked in the garden at Summerlea, pruning the orchard rather brutally, and Flynn insisted on helping her plant her new vegetable garden, even though she told him she could easily do it on her own during the week.

Flynn was late getting home twice when she stayed with him in Melbourne, but he didn't raise the subject of the spare key again, even though she half expected him to. He didn't touch on any subjects that might make her uncomfortable. He continued to call her on the nights they weren't together, he sent her emails, he made love to her with a single-minded devotion that never failed to drive her wild.

He was perfect. Not once, not by a slip of the tongue or a sideways glance or a hesitation, did he let on that he wanted more from her than she was willing to give, and yet the sense that there was something looming on the horizon—a crisis, a reckoning, an ultimatum—kept growing inside her.

She told herself that when the flash point came she had to be prepared to give Flynn his freedom. He wanted something from her that she could never give him, and it would be selfish of her to hang on to him on that basis. Selfish and greedy and ultimately destructive, for both of them.

She brooded on the subject on a rainy Wednesday night five weeks after he'd offered her his house key. She was in her car in front of Flynn's place, waiting for him to come home from work. He'd already called so she knew he'd left the office on time, but she'd had a good run on the freeway and arrived earlier than she'd anticipated. She kept the engine running to ward off the chill, staring out her windshield, thinking about Flynn and all the good times they'd shared together.

The more she thought, the glummer she got, until she got to the point where she had to give herself a mental shake.

What's wrong with you? You've got exactly what you wanted—Flynn, on your terms. What on earth is your problem?

She didn't know. All she knew was that she had a pervading sense of doom. The happiness she felt whenever she was with Flynn couldn't possibly last.

Could it?

She frowned, disturbed by her own thoughts. Had she become so used to disharmony and unhappiness in her marriage that she now expected it everywhere? Was the ability to be happy and content something else that Owen had stolen from her, along with her trust and her confidence and her sense of self? Headlights swept into the street and she glanced into her rearview mirror as Flynn turned into his driveway. He flashed his headlights at her and she grabbed her overnight bag and made a run for the door.

"Hope you haven't been waiting long?" Flynn asked as he joined her on the stoop.

"Just got here," she fibbed.

He kissed her briefly before opening the door. Warm air rushed out at them and she made an appreciative noise.

"I put the timer on the central heating," he said. "What do you want for dinner? Pizza? Italian?"

"I thought pizza was Italian," she said as she watched him shed his coat and suit jacket. She loved how rumpled he always looked at the end of the day.

"Smart-ass," he said, reaching for her.

They kissed long and languorously. After a few minutes he drew back to look into her eyes.

"Have I told you lately that you're one hot tamale?" he said.

"I believe you have. But feel free to compare me to other foodstuffs," she said.

He laughed and gave her a pat on the backside before walking away from her.

"Just for that we're having pizza, my choice."

"I was going to say pizza, anyway, so it's my choice, too," she called after him as he disappeared into the kitchen.

"Perfect. Two happy people, one pizza," he called back.

She stared at the doorway, the smile slowly fading from her mouth. *Two happy people.* God, she hoped that was true. She really, really hoped that the tight feeling in her chest was just her being neurotic and anxious out of habit, and that he really was as content with the status quo as he seemed to be. Because if he wasn't, he was going to leave a huge hole in her life. In her heart.

They ate pizza in front of the television while watching a documentary on Edna Walling that Flynn had unearthed. They fooled around on the couch a little afterward and fell asleep in each other's arms. Mel struggled to wakefulness out of a dark, claustrophobic dream to find her face pressed against the back cushion of the couch.

She jerked instinctively, gasping for air, then realized where she was.

She pushed her hair out of her eyes as Flynn's hand landed in the center of her back.

"You okay?"

"Just a bad dream."

"Want to talk about it?" There was no demand in his voice, no insistence. He was offering, openhandedly. The way he did everything.

She started to shake her head. Then she paused. "I can never remember much. Just patches, like flashes."

She told him about her dream in fits and starts, about the memories it stirred up. He listened and rubbed his palm across her back and made a couple of observations and after a few minutes the panicky feeling began to ease from her chest and throat and belly.

"Thanks," she said, laying her head on his chest. "That helped."

"Good," he said simply.

They went upstairs to bed and he curled his body around hers and held her against his chest. She was on the brink of drifting into sleep when he spoke, his voice barely audible.

"I love you, Mel."

She squeezed her eyes tightly closed. If she was a normal woman, she would turn in his arms and tell him that she loved him, too, more than anything. But she wasn't normal. She was scared and she was more than a little broken. So she pretended she was asleep, even though she suspected that they both knew she was awake. And she lay that way for a long time before she finally nodded off.

She was woken by the shrill, urgent ring of the telephone.

She squinted at the bedside clock as Flynn fumbled for the receiver. It was nearly seven-thirty and she realized they'd overslept—Flynn must have forgotten to set the alarm last night when they came up to bed.

"Flynn speaking." He fell back onto his pillow, the receiver pressed to his ear.

She felt his body go tense even as she heard the sound of someone shouting on the phone.

"Dad, calm down. Take a deep breath. I can't understand what you're saying."

He sat up in bed, the covers pooling around his hips as he listened for a few seconds. "How badly is she hurt? Can you put her on? Okay, no, don't do that. I'm calling an ambulance now, all right? Sit tight, I'll be there as soon as I can."

Flynn ended the call and immediately rang emergency services. He requested an ambulance at his parents' address as he flung off the covers and crossed to his closet, passing on the information that they would be dealing with a serious burn.

He tossed the phone on the bed once he'd finished and met her eyes.

"Mom's burned herself. Something to do with the kettle. I can barely get a word of sense out of Dad. He's totally freaking out." His face was grim as he yanked a pair of jeans on.

Mel stood and reached for her underwear. "He couldn't put your mother on the line?" she asked worriedly.

"He was almost incoherent. Panicking," he said as he pulled on a sweatshirt.

Mel tugged up her jeans. "How far away are they?"

"Five minutes."

They finished dressing in silence and she was right behind him when he headed for the stairs.

"Take my car, it's already out in the street," she said when he grabbed his car keys from the kitchen counter.

"Good idea." He pocketed his own keys before getting hers and they exited into a gray, misty morning.

"She'll be okay, Flynn," she said reassuringly as they strode to her car.

"I know. He was just so freaked out.... Before, Dad was always the guy you'd want by your side when the *Titanic* hit the iceberg, you know?"

She didn't bother pointing out that the man his father had once been was a thing of the past. Flynn knew that better than anyone. He slid into the driver's seat and she buckled up beside him.

It was only when he was navigating his way through the quiet, wet streets that it occurred to her that she'd effectively invited herself along on this rescue mission. He hadn't asked and she hadn't offered—it had simply seemed right that she be with him while he was dealing with this crisis. She didn't want him to be alone—to *feel* alone. She wanted to be there for him.

It should have been a disturbing thought, given her constant battle to contain their relationship. But it wasn't. He needed her, and she had his back. It was that simple.

No more than five minutes had passed since Flynn's father's call when they pulled up in front of a gracious Victorian house with a high wrought-iron fence. It was lovely, but it didn't come even close to the grand residence she'd been expecting and it took her a moment to remember that Flynn had mentioned once that his parents had downsized recently. Flynn sorted through the keys on his key ring as they raced up the garden path. He unlocked the door and pushed it open so urgently it slammed into the wall.

"Mom!" he hollered as he entered a wide, high-ceilinged entrance hall.

"Kitchen." It was a woman's voice, faint but audible.

Flynn broke into a run.

Mel followed, passing a number of doorways before she entered a big, bright French Provençal-style kitchen at the end of the hallway. A woman, who looked to be in her mid-fifties, stood at the kitchen sink, her face ashen as she held her left forearm under the running tap. Beside her stood a tall, broad-shouldered man with Flynn's bright blue eyes and bone structure. His hair was mussed, his face creased into lines of abject misery as he hovered with a helpless air at his wife's side.

"I'm okay," Patricia Randall said the moment she saw them. "No one's dying or anything."

"What happened?" Flynn asked.

"So stupid— I was making us coffee and I slipped and the next thing I knew I'd poured it half up my arm...."

Flynn moved closer to inspect his mother's arm. Mel could tell from his carefully blank expression that the burn was grim.

"I've got an ambulance on the way," he said, touching her shoulder. "Hang in there."

The older woman nodded. Mel saw that there were tall stools parked beneath the overhang on the island counter and she grabbed one.

"Here," she said, passing it to Flynn.

He gave her a grateful look before offering it to his mother.

"Thank you," Patricia said as she sank onto the stool. She closed her eyes for a minute. When she opened them again she made eye contact with Mel and offered her an apologetic smile. "I'm so sorry that we're meeting like this, Mel. I promise that we're not usually so hectic."

Perhaps Mel should have been surprised that the other woman knew her name, but she wasn't. In the small hours of the morning, Flynn had told her that he loved her. It stood to reason that he'd mentioned her to his parents.

"The important thing is getting you looked after," Mel said.

Adam made a choking sound and turned away.

"It's okay, Dad," Flynn said reassuringly.

"I'm fine, Adam. Really," Patricia said. "A bit of burn cream and a bandage and I'll be right."

Adam continued to sob. Flynn reached out and grabbed a fistful of tissues from the box on the counter and pressed them to his father. Adam took them without saying a word and Flynn rested his hand on his father's shoulder while he attempted to gather himself.

Patricia's face was both loving and resigned as she watched her husband and son. Mel's chest ached for all of them. So much love here—and so much pain.

A faint siren sound filtered into the house. She glanced over her shoulder toward the door.

"I'll let them in if you like," she offered.

"Thanks, Mel," Flynn said.

The ambulance was pulling into the driveway as she opened the front door. The driver jumped out and made eye contact with her.

"How are we doing?" he called as he helped his partner collect a large medical kit from the rear of the ambulance.

"She's okay. A bit of shock, I think. She's got the burn under cold water."

"Good stuff."

She stood to one side as the crew entered the house, their footsteps very loud in the echoing hallway.

"Straight to the end, the doorway on the right," she instructed. She followed them into the kitchen and stood in the most out-of-the-way corner as they spoke quietly with Patricia and assessed her injury. Flynn stood with his father, one hand on his shoulder still, offering him silent support. Adam watched his wife doggedly, his mouth set.

The crew assessed the burn before applying a thick, foamy-looking pad to the entire area and bandaging it loosely. They gave Patricia an injection for the pain and finally announced she was ready to be transported to the hospital.

"Can't you just do whatever you need to do here?" Patricia asked. "It's really not that bad now that it's settling down."

Flynn opened his mouth to speak but the taller of the two ambulance attendants beat him to it.

"Ma'am, you have a third-degree burn. You need to come with us and get it seen to at the burns unit."

Patricia frowned, her worried gaze flicking to her husband.

"We'll follow the ambulance," Flynn said as the ambulance attendants helped his mother to her feet.

"I'm going with Pat," Adam said. There was a mulish set to his face, as though he was determined not to let her down after his initial panic.

"Is that okay?" Patricia asked.

"That's fine. It's not a long trip—we're going up the road—but your husband is welcome to ride along."

Mel stepped out of the way as they made their slow way out the door. Flynn waited until his parents had left the room before sagging against the sink and scrubbing his face with his hands.

"Are you okay?" she asked.

"It's a pretty bad burn."

"The ambulance guys seemed really calm, though, and I figure that's got to be a good sign. And she did the right thing with the water."

"You're probably right." He pushed away from the counter. "We should get going."

He started for the door, then stopped. "Sorry. Here I am, just assuming— You probably need to head home. I can take Mom's car if you need to go."

"I'm coming with you." The answer was out of her mouth before she could think about it.

He reached out and hooked his arm around her neck, drawing her close and dropping a kiss onto her mouth. "Thank you."

They locked the house and Flynn drove her car to the Epworth Hospital in Richmond. They walked hand-in-hand into the hospital and made their way to the emergency department. An enquiry revealed that his mother was being treated by a doctor and they were advised to take a seat in the waiting room. She sat beside Flynn, talking quietly, doing what she could to reassure and distract him. An hour later the nurse came to tell them that his mother had been moved to a private room and that they were free to visit her. They followed a complicated set of directions until they located her room and found her sitting up in bed with her injured arm carefully resting on a pillow to one side of her body. Her forearm was covered in a thick, many-layered bandage and the tight, pained look was gone from her face. Adam sat beside the bed, his face set in the same dogged, determined expression he'd worn earlier.

"There you are. We were beginning to think you'd gone to the wrong hospital," Patricia said with a weary smile.

"We've been waiting downstairs until the nurse gave us the all clear. How are you doing?" Flynn asked, reaching to take his mother's good hand.

"Better and better. The doctor wants to keep me in overnight so one of the plastic surgeons can take a look at it. Apparently it's a borderline third-degree burn and I might need a skin graft."

"And that's something they'd do straight away?" Flynn asked.

"I have no idea. I forgot to ask them that." Patricia gave him a small apologetic smile. "They'll be back soon—you can ask them yourself."

"But you're comfortable?" Flynn asked.

"Very. A little spacey, but there's no pain."

"Good."

Mel had been hovering in the doorway but Flynn drew her forward now.

"I didn't get a chance to introduce anyone earlier, but Mel, this is my mother, Patricia, and my father, Adam. Mom, Dad, this is Mel," he said.

"Lovely to meet you, Mel. I wish the circumstances were different, but there's not much I can do about that," Patricia said.

"I'm glad to hear you're feeling more comfortable," Mel said.

Flynn's father didn't say anything and Flynn fixed his father with an assessing look. "You doing okay there, Dad?"

His father met his eyes and Mel could see that the older man was working hard to keep a lid on his emotions.

"What's going on, Dad?" Flynn asked gently.

"I'm fine. You're mother is the important one here."

Patricia eyed her husband shrewdly. "You're blaming yourself, aren't you?"

Again, Adam didn't say anything but his answer was in his face as he made eye contact with his wife.

"Don't go all quiet on me. Talk to me," Patricia said quietly. "We said we'd always talk. So talk to me."

There was a moment of silence before Flynn's father responded. "I let you down."

He said it so quietly Mel almost didn't hear him.

"No, you didn't. You called Flynn. That was the exactly right thing to do."

Adam shook his head. "Don't. Don't try to make me feel better. I panicked. I couldn't handle it." The grief and self-disgust in his voice and his face were so real, so deeply felt, that Mel stirred uneasily and dropped her gaze to the floor.

"No," Patricia said. "You got help. You helped me. You waited with me."

"I stood there crying like a baby. I could barely think. I'm useless. Might as well have had a five-year-old in the room."

Patricia surprised everyone by reaching over the edge of the bed to grab a fistful of her husband's sweater. Her expression determined, she gave him a none-too-gentle shake.

"You listen here, Adam Randall. You are not useless. You are not worse than a child. You are an intelligent, articulate man. You make me laugh more than anyone I've ever met. You still beat me at golf, even though I've been taking lessons for fifteen years, trying to beat you. You are kind and you are loving and you are the man I have loved all my life. Those other things you're talking about, that's not you. We both know that. You have a disease. A horrible, shitty, low-down bastard of a disease, and that's the reason you got confused this morning. That wasn't you, and you did not let me down. You have never, ever let me down. Not once in more than forty years of marriage. You are my knight in shining armor. You will always be my knight in shining armor."

There was so much fierce love on the other woman's face, so much determination and vehemence in her voice, that Mel could not look away, even though she knew she was witnessing an intensely personal, private moment.

"I love you so much, Patty."

"I know. Now give me a kiss."

Adam's face was filled with emotion as he stood and stooped over his wife, cupping her head with infinite gentleness as he lowered his head to kiss her lips.

Mel sniffed and finally managed to drag her gaze away, using the sleeve of her sweater to wipe her eyes. She glanced at Flynn to see what he'd made of his parents' touching, humbling display and found that he was looking at her with a fierce, undeniable intensity.

Everything that lay unspoken between them was in his eyes. His love. His commitment. His passion. Everything that he wanted for them, all his hopes and dreams.

Her breath got caught somewhere between her lungs and her throat for long, unblinking seconds.

Then he looked away and the moment was gone.

But she knew she hadn't imagined it. She

knew that what she'd seen had always been there, sitting beneath the easygoing smile Flynn had offered the world—and her—during the past few months. A feeling of dread engulfed her as she pasted a smile on her face and listened to Flynn make small talk with his parents.

Flynn loved her. He wanted to share his life with her in every sense of the word. Five weeks ago she'd thought—she'd hoped—that she'd struck a deal with him, that they could continue on as they had been, spending time together, their friendship deepening, without her having to give up any of her hard-won freedom or security.

But Flynn wanted more. He wanted everything. He wanted love and marriage and babies and growing old together. He wanted everything she had to give, and he wanted to give her everything in return.

She took a step backward, overwhelmed, as always, by the thought of trusting another person in that way again. After years of not protecting herself, she'd learned her lesson too well and she had no idea how to let anyone in. How to let Flynn in.

She realized that Flynn and his parents were talking, that Flynn had asked her something. It took her a moment to play it back in her head and understand that he'd asked if she was hungry. She said yes because it was easier than saying no and listened as he asked his parents if they wanted anything, then she found herself following him out into the corridor.

"Are you okay?" he asked as they approached the elevators.

"Yes," she lied.

They bought muffins and coffee from the cafeteria and returned to his mother's room. After half an hour the doctor appeared to check on her and Flynn peppered him with questions until he was satisfied that he understood the situation. She could see the tension leave his body as he slowly came down from the adrenaline high of the emergency and started to accept that his mother was going to be okay.

By the time noon rolled around, Patricia was sleepy from all the painkillers she'd been given and Flynn decided to leave so she could get some sleep. His father wouldn't hear of leaving her side, so Flynn promised to return later in the afternoon. They walked out of the hospital into a slow, steady rain, Mel's sense of dread growing with every step.

Now that they were alone, now that the crisis had passed, the feeling of impending doom that had dogged her for weeks seemed to swell until it was filling her chest. There was no way she could pretend that she hadn't seen the raw devotion in Flynn's eyes when he looked at her. She'd kidded herself for over a month, but there was no way she could deny the depth of his emotion anymore. He loved her. He'd said it to her last night when he thought she was asleep. He loved her and he wanted to share his life with her.

In her head, a clock was ticking as she waited for him to stake his claim, to demand that his needs be met as well as her own. To destroy the fragile balance they'd somehow achieved—or, perhaps, faked—for the past month.

It seemed impossible to her that he wouldn't say something. She'd seen the look on his face, seen the intensity of his feeling. It was undeniable.

He didn't say anything during the drive home, however, and she grew more and more tense with every passing moment, waiting for the other shoe to drop.

"I might swing by the supermarket and grab some bread for lunch," he said. "The cupboard's pretty much bare at home."

Inside her head, she wanted to scream. She wanted to grab him by the shirt and shake him until he said what needed to be said. She wanted the impasse to be acknowledged, she wanted the disaster to arrive, she wanted to confront it head-on so she could start to deal with the enormous hole he would leave in her life.

She sat stiff and cold beside him as he pulled into a parking spot at the local shops.

"I'll only be a moment. You can wait in the car if you like," he said.

She didn't say anything as he got out. She watched him stride toward the entrance, confident and assured and beautiful, and something inside her snapped. She wrenched herself from the car and went after him.

"Flynn."

He turned toward her, eyebrows raised, waiting for her to catch up. She stopped in front of him, feeling breathless even though she'd only jogged a few steps.

"You should just say it," she told him starkly. "Whatever you need to say. Get it over and done with."

His brow wrinkled into a frown. "Sorry?"

"That moment with your parents... I know what you want from me, Flynn. I know you love me. But nothing's changed. I'm still me." She choked on her final words, strangled by her own misery and brokenness.

His blue eyes looked into hers and she knew, absolutely, that he understood what she was saying. But instead of agreeing and showing his hand and drawing his line in the sand and forcing her to draw hers in turn, he leaned close and kissed the corner of her mouth.

"I was thinking we should grab a quiche instead of making sandwiches, maybe have it with a salad. What do you think?"

He didn't wait for her to respond, simply gave her shoulder a reassuring squeeze before turning and entering the supermarket. She took one, two, three steps after him, following him through the automatic doors before stopping in her tracks.

She watched as he walked into the fresh produce section and started inspecting the lettuces and suddenly she understood not only that he wasn't going to say anything today, but he was also *never going to say anything*.

Ever.

There would be no demand from Flynn. No line in the sand. No ultimatum. He would never force her into a corner or ask more from her than she was able to give. He would never do that to her.

He loved her.

He wanted her to be happy. And he was prepared to sacrifice his own happiness, his own dreams, in order to make that happen.

His love was generous and mature and all-encompassing—but most of all it was selfless, in the truest meaning of the word. He gave, but he didn't demand in return.

The realization rolled over her like a wave, inexorable, undeniable. It was like staring into bright sunlight, painful and purifying at the same time.

This man. This amazing, incredible man...

Tears burned the back of her eyes and slipped down her face as she thought about the way he'd already walked away from his landscape design business for his parents and the long hours he worked to preserve the family legacy and the way he dropped everything when his loved ones needed him. He gave and he gave and he gave. And he never asked.

A wave of heat burned its way up through her belly and into her chest and throat and into her face. It took her a moment to recognize it as pride. Fierce, bone-deep pride in him. Flynn Randall was a man in a million. He was a man who a woman could trust with anything—her heart, her mind, her pride, her passion.

He was a man who deserved a love that was as generous and self-sacrificing and openhanded. A love that wasn't afraid or self-protective or narrow or scared.

He deserved all of her. Everything she had to give.

If she had the courage to give it.

There was only one answer in her heart. There had always been only one answer in her heart. She just hadn't been ready to see it.

Her hands trembling, she reached into her

pocket. Her fingers closed around her car keys. She pulled them out and blinked away tears as she tried to find a particular key on her ring. She slipped her thumbnail into the split and worked the key free. Then she clenched her hand around it and lifted her head.

Flynn was standing by the bananas. She started walking, the key cutting into the soft flesh of her palm. A woman with a stroller looked at her with concern, clearly worried about the tears dripping down Mel's face. Mel flashed her a quick smile to let her know she was okay.

Because she *was* okay. Terrified. Absolutely shit-scared. But for the first time in years, she was really, truly okay.

Flynn looked up as she closed the final feet between them.

"Mel," he said, reaching out a hand to touch her arm, full of concern. "What's going on?"

She caught his hand and turned his palm up. Then she placed her house key in his hand.

"I love you," she said. "More than I know how to say. You have given me so much. Been so patient and loving and generous. I don't want to be afraid anymore, and I know I don't need to be afraid of you. I trust you, Flynn. I'm sorry it's taken me so long to get that, to understand, but I'm here now. I'm ready. I want to do this."

For a moment he was very, very still. Then

he reached out and used his fingertips to wipe away her tears, his gaze warm and tender and full of understanding.

"Good." He pulled her into his arms and kissed her, his arms a bruising band across her shoulders. She didn't mind, she couldn't get close enough to him, either. She clenched her hands into his clothes and pressed her body against his and kissed him with everything she had in her, trying to convey to him the depth of her feelings.

She loved him. God, she loved him.

After long minutes they came up for air and realized they had a small audience—the woman with the stroller, an old lady, a couple of staff members. Mel felt her face heat as Flynn flashed their audience his most charming smile.

"Our apologies. We'll get out of your way." He led Mel outside, where they both stopped and simply stared at each other, eyes searching one another's faces. She reached out to touch his jaw, her thumb scraping over his whiskers, unable to keep her hands to herself now that she'd at last acknowledged her own heart.

"Thank you for waiting for me," she said softly. "Thank you for loving me. Thank you for hanging in there even when I pushed you away. Most of all, thank you for trusting that I'd find my own way."

He caught her hand and turned his head to press a kiss into her palm. "Thank you for being so brave, and for trusting me. I know what that means for you, Mel, and I will never use that trust against you. Ever." His eyes were solemn, and he spoke the words like a vow.

"I know," she said. "I love you."

"I love you, too. A lifetime's worth. Maybe two. Which may become a little wearing for you at times, but I figure you will probably learn to live with it."

Somehow she was in his arms again. It felt absolutely right, their tall bodies a perfect match, their hearts—finally—in accord.

"I can handle it," she said confidently.

She knew she could, too. Because once upon a time she'd been brave and bold, but now she was also wise. She understood that the man in her arms was a remarkable, astounding treasure. A big-hearted, loving, lovely man.

And she was never letting him go.

EPILOGUE

One year later

MEL SHUT THE DOOR on the noise the workmen were making and walked to the front door. Thankfully, this was the last week they would have tradespeople in the house. It had been a long, drawn-out, expensive haul, but, apart from a few minor tweaks, Summerlea had finally been restored to her former glory.

The floors had been repolished, the panelling renewed. New carpets had been laid, the wiring overhauled. No room had gone untouched, but Summerlea was now weather-tight, warm, welcoming and gracious—the last more a testament to Flynn's mother's good taste and perseverance than to Mel's or Flynn's. As Pat had so astutely observed early in the renovation, their hearts were outside in the garden, not in the house. With Mel and Flynn's blessing, Pat had taken over a lot of the decorating choices, offering selections to Mel and Flynn so they could make the final decisions.

It had been the perfect distraction from Adam's health, and Mel knew the older woman had enjoyed it immensely. Mel's only regret was that she and Flynn had not been able to convince Adam and Patricia to consider making their home at Summerlea, too. They'd had the discussion a number of times but Flynn's parents were adamant about not being a burden or cramping her and Flynn's style.

As far as Mel was concerned, the discussion was far from over. When things got more intense with Adam, she wanted Pat to be supported, and she wanted to do her bit, too. She'd grown to admire and love Flynn's parents enormously in the past twelve months, and she was not prepared to give up this battle. Not yet, anyway. There was plenty of room at Summerlea for all of them.

She cocked her head, sure she heard the sound of a car engine. A smile curved her lips and instead of turning into the dining room, she continued straight to the door and pulled it open. The old excitement threaded through her veins as she stepped out onto the porch and looked toward the drive.

Her smile faded. There was no car. Damn. Flynn hadn't managed to sneak away from the office early, after all. Just to make sure, she circled the house to check that he hadn't already driven around to the newly restored garage.

No sign of Gertie there, either. She wrinkled her nose. Well, it had been a long shot that he'd be able to get away early. Flynn had hired a new general manager to share some of the workload, but he was still working punishing hours while the other man got up to speed. Once Steven hit his stride, however, they were both hopeful that Flynn could scale back on his hours, maybe even work from home some of the time.

Then they could start to really realize their plans for the garden. Flynn had come up with an ambitious and inventive update on Edna Walling's original design, and bit by bit, patch by patch, they'd been working together to bring his vision to reality. They were months—years, really—from achieving their ambition to open the gardens to the public again. But they would get there. She had no doubt of that, because her lover—the love of her life—was the most tenacious, patient, creative, loyal, hardworking man she'd ever met. Where he had a will, there would be a way.

Hands tucked into the back pockets of her jeans, she walked slowly around to the front again and gazed out over the garden. Already, they'd achieved so much. The lawns were once again brilliant emerald swathes of well-tended turf. The garden beds had been weeded and re-shaped and replanted, the roses pruned, arbors rebuilt. Last month they'd taken delivery of three new garden benches made from local tea tree and they dotted the landscape, providing strategic vantage points for visitors to sit and contemplate the view.

She took a deep breath, her heart swelling with love and pride and happiness. Once, she'd doubted that she could ever sustain this level of happiness and contentment. She'd been scared of it, hadn't trusted it. Flynn had taught her to hold fast and grin and bear it. He'd taught her that anything was possible.

A distinctive engine noise drifted on the breeze and she turned toward the main gate as the Aston Martin drove into sight. Her heart did a little skip-jump in her chest, as it always did when her man came home. He saw her and braked to a halt beside the house rather than drive around to the garage.

"You made it," she said, walking to join him as he got out of the car.

"I did. I had the world's best incentive—an extra two hours with you."

She smiled and reached out to loosen his tie for him. "How was your day?"

"Busy. What about yours?"

"The tiler is almost finished. We should have the house to ourselves by Friday."

He smiled. "Promises, promises."

She matched his smile and kissed him. As always, desire stirred as he pulled her into his arms, but it was tempered with knowledge and love and certainty that hadn't been there a year ago.

She knew this man, and he knew her. She believed in him. She believed in *them*. She touched his face as they broke their kiss.

"You make me so happy," she said quietly.

It felt like a small miracle that she could say those words so easily, so truthfully.

His eyes were a warm, deep blue. "I love you."

"I know. I love you, too."

More and more every day.

He slid his arms around her shoulder. "Let's go admire our garden," he said.

"Okay."

"And if you're very good, I'll let you take my clothes off and have your way with me beneath the trees in the orchard grove."

"That's very generous of you," she said, not even trying to hide her grin.

"I'm a generous man. Ask anyone."

She wrapped her arm around his waist and they fell into step with one another.

"I don't need to."

She didn't, either. She knew he was generous, just as she knew he was good and a whole other host of wonderful things.

But most of all, she knew he was hers, the same way she was his. It had taken her a while to understand, to get past her fear, to believe. But she'd gotten there in the end. And he'd been waiting for her with open arms.

Laughing and talking, they walked into their garden.

* * * * *

LARGER-PRINT BOOKS!
GET 2 FREE LARGER-PRINT NOVELS PLUS
2 FREE GIFTS!

Harlequin®

Super Romance®

Exciting, emotional, unexpected!

YES! Please send me 2 FREE LARGER-PRINT Harlequin® Superromance® novels and my 2 FREE gifts (gifts are worth about $10). After receiving them, if I don't wish to receive any more books, I can return the shipping statement marked "cancel." If I don't cancel, I will receive 6 brand-new novels every month and be billed just $5.44 per book in the U.S. or $5.99 per book in Canada. That's a saving of at least 16% off the cover price! It's quite a bargain! Shipping and handling is just 50¢ per book in the U.S. or 75¢ per book in Canada.* I understand that accepting the 2 free books and gifts places me under no obligation to buy anything. I can always return a shipment and cancel at any time. Even if I never buy another book, the two free books and gifts are mine to keep forever.

139/339 HDN FEFF

Name	(PLEASE PRINT)
Address	Apt. #
City	State/Prov.	Zip/Postal Code

Signature (if under 18, a parent or guardian must sign)

Mail to the **Reader Service:**
IN U.S.A.: P.O. Box 1867, Buffalo, NY 14240-1867
IN CANADA: P.O. Box 609, Fort Erie, Ontario L2A 5X3

Not valid for current subscribers to Harlequin Superromance Larger-Print books.

Are you a current subscriber to Harlequin Superromance books and want to receive the larger-print edition?
Call 1-800-873-8635 today or visit www.ReaderService.com.

* Terms and prices subject to change without notice. Prices do not include applicable taxes. Sales tax applicable in N.Y. Canadian residents will be charged applicable taxes. Offer not valid in Quebec. This offer is limited to one order per household. All orders subject to credit approval. Credit or debit balances in a customer's account(s) may be offset by any other outstanding balance owed by or to the customer. Please allow 4 to 6 weeks for delivery. Offer available while quantities last.

Your Privacy—The Reader Service is committed to protecting your privacy. Our Privacy Policy is available online at www.ReaderService.com or upon request from the Reader Service.

We make a portion of our mailing list available to reputable third parties that offer products we believe may interest you. If you prefer that we not exchange your name with third parties, or if you wish to clarify or modify your communication preferences, please visit us at www.ReaderService.com/consumerschoice or write to us at Reader Service Preference Service, P.O. Box 9062, Buffalo, NY 14269. Include your complete name and address.

The series you love are now available in

LARGER PRINT!

The books are complete and unabridged—
printed in a larger type size to make it
easier on your eyes.

◆ Harlequin® *Romance*

From the Heart, For the Heart

◆ Harlequin® INTRIGUE®
BREATHTAKING ROMANTIC SUSPENSE

◆ Harlequin® *Presents®*

Seduction and Passion Guaranteed!

◆ Harlequin® *Super Romance®*

Exciting, emotional, unexpected!

Try **LARGER PRINT** today!

Visit: www.ReaderService.com
Call: 1-800-873-8635

◆ Harlequin®

A *Romance* FOR EVERY MOOD™